FOR
ELEVEN MILLION
REASONS

Crime, thriller, mystery story.

By

M.L. Weatherington

ISBN: 978-1-942622-05-5
ISBN-10: 1-942622-05-8

This book edition is published by:
Pynhavyn Press
First Edition: April 2016
http://www.pynhavyn.com

ACKNOWLEDGEMENTS

In 2004, my husband, Warren, parked our ATV and announced that there was a man I should meet. He took the tea towel from me, gave me the keys to the ATV and shoved me out the door. That was the most momentous meeting; it changed my life and allowed me to finish a project I had only dreamed of: Writing the details of a break-in that occurred at our home. **Jon Clem** was the man I met that afternoon. Jon was Lieutenant, Detective Bureau (or Division), Palm Springs Police Department, Retired 1994. He also served: Coachella, CA P.D.; Lieutenant; Vacaville, CA PD Sergeant; B.A. Criminal Justice, University of Redlands; A.A. Police Science, Solano College. After retiring, he worked for a time at Cabazon Indian Police Department then moved from California to Idaho where he spends time fishing and enjoying the outdoor life.

Over the months to follow, he read my work and directed me in police procedure so my story would have the sound of reason. I want to thank Jon for the many e-mails and the visits to my home. On behalf of seeing this project rise out of the many pages, into files, and finally into book form.

I want to thank my family **Robert Doyle, Daniel James and Amanda Burton** for your guidance. **Lessie Bond** and **Suzanne Bruns,** my photographers. **Marie Jewitt, Mike Jewitt, Linda Wiggins, Edie Ward, Caroline Neeley, Kathy Ennis,** and **Jon Clem** for listening as I read *For Eleven Million Reasons* aloud. I valued their comments and criticisms. Special thanks to **Ray Karker,** he and his wife, **Bert.** The character Sam Nelson was patterned after Ray. A special thanks to my editor **M. Garrett** and my proofreaders, **Rene Averett** and **James Neal,** my beta and edit readers, I could not have completed this task without their help. A special thanks to **Jan Neal** for Slipper's name. Finally, to **Rochelle McGrath, Shamrock Designs** for my fantastic cover. While my husband and I were vacationing in Mexico, two people broke into our home ransacked it and took items of value for their benefit; they were caught in the act. We came back from Mexico to identify our belongings and catalog missing items. We spent many days at this task, much time with the Insurance Company, and sitting in the courtroom listening to the facts of our case. Out of all that pain came these twisted facts entitled FOR ELEVEN MILLION REASONS.

To my readers, enjoy.

Reviews

Lillian I. Wolfe, author of "Funeral Singer: A Song for Marielle."

If you think winning the lottery is a dream come true, think again. In *For Eleven Million Reasons*, mystery author M.L. Weatherington takes you on a suspenseful journey of murder and intrigue as Lt. Arthur Franklin pursues a vengeful killer through a thrill ride of a novel showcasing the dark side of publicized sudden wealth.

James Neal, avid reader and lover of books.

Mary Weatherington hit the ball out of the park with her first at bat. For Eleven Million Reasons grabs you on the first page and takes you on a journey full of twists and turns until you reach the thrilling conclusion.

Simple man believes anything,

but a prudent man

gives thought to his steps.

Proverbs 14:15

The Township of Lodi nestles in San Joaquin County, California's northern portion of the Central Valley. It has some of the best farmlands in the state. Crops of every variety, including grapes, grow here. The Mokelumne River runs through the land and the residents enjoy many river sports. Warm days bring laughing children and happy families to fill the Lodi Lake area.

It was on a balmy June afternoon, in this charming municipality of 62,134 residents, that our story takes place.

Chapter One

3:45 P.M. June 28, 1995

As Art sweated over his backyard grill coaxing two thick steaks to perfection; a tickling sensation had his free hand moving. Art grabbed the pager off his belt to read the displayed numbers, and his shoulders slumped. A homicide.

His fifteen-year-old daughter, Melissa was standing in the doorway talking on the phone with her friend; she waved at him as he turned to her. He gave her a conspiratorial smile. As a result, he chuckled at the thought; we can't have one peaceful dinner at home. Art waved his pager high in the air indicating he needed the phone. She nodded and said goodbye to Sandy and held the phone out to him as he hurried across the lawn carrying his solid one-hundred-eighty pounds with ease.

In passing, Art took the phone and handed her the fork gesturing toward the barbecue pit. "Watch them." A sparkle flashed in his hazel eyes as he entered the kitchen and plunked himself down on the bar stool. The long phone cord snaked over the floor, coiling at his sandaled feet.

"You paged me?" Art said when dispatch answered.

"We know you didn't want a call out, Art. We've got a homicide; your team is up. The call came in a few minutes ago."

1

Art's auburn and blond mustache twitched as he listened to the dispatcher. He spun the bar stool around to look at his daughter. Smoke curled around her lean body, wafting out over the Mokelumne River while fingers of it carried the aroma of searing steaks into the house. *Another disappointment for her.*

"What do we know?"

"We're rolling. First perimeter's set, FET's been called. Beyond that, not much."

"Okay, I'm on my way." He looked at his watch; it read 3:55 p.m. Art brushed his hand over his wavy, copper hair and rubbed at his military style sideburns, all in the name of stealing time. He walked back to stand by Melissa's side. "Honey, I'm going out. The Field Evidence Technicians have been called out. I'll be gone about five or six hours, so go ahead and eat."

Art bent over close to the steaks. "They smell good." He pulled the fork from her, pressed the tines onto the sizzling meat, and with a knowing grin, announced. "Just right. Take 'em off now." Leaning, he kissed her forehead. "I'm sorry sweetheart I wanted to celebrate our early Fourth of July, just the two of us." He looked deeply into her eyes sending all the love he held. After a pause, he left for his room calling over his shoulder, "I've got to change."

Slipping out of his shorts and into his gray slacks, he grabbed a clean shirt off the hanger, nabbed a tie, and pulled on socks and his black wingtips. After he had buttoned his shirt, he slipped his tie over his head and pulled it tight. He surveyed his mirrored appearance leaning close to his reflection, looking for new lines. His scrubbed, ruddy face looked younger than his forty-five years. Art positioned his tiny comb, looking to the left then the right, narrowing his focus on aligning the hairs just under his nose. Satisfied with the look of his mustache he ran a hand through his hair. He straightened to his full,

2

commanding six-foot height and grinned at Arthur Franklin, Detective Lieutenant, Lodi PD.

Jogging down the stairs, Art ducked into his home office and flipped the switch turning off the police scanner. He stopped in the doorway, pulled the handle and locked the door. He grabbed his car keys and hurried out of the house.

Art drove to an older neighborhood with single-story ranch style homes that spread across their lots, resting among superior plantings shaded by mature trees. On the lookout now for the address, he slowed and set his lips tight when he sighted, in the middle of the block, yellow tape fluttering. The front of his vehicle came to a stop behind a black and white. Art acknowledged two officers as they nodded to him. Ducking under the tape, he sauntered up the driveway allowing his mind to take in the scene.

A dark blue Suburban sat in the middle of a driveway that curved to the side-load garage. Art noticed the driver's door still open and the body on the ground. *As though he'd stepped out of the vehicle and dropped to the pavement,* Art thought. Some kind officer had placed a brown tweed sports coat over the upper torso and head of the corpse as it lay alongside the car. Art nodded agreement with that respectful act. *Probably the vic's coat* Art thought. He leaned over and lifted the collar of the jacket to look into the face. The man was in his thirties. A hard worker, Art decided, by the calluses on his hands. He looked his whole body over and noticed the worn soles of the man's shoes. He came back to the two holes in the shirt and the blood. Art stood and turned, carefully looking into the front seat of the vehicle. Clipboard, some papers, coffee from the truck stop Flag City. He placed the back of his fingers on the exterior surface of the Styrofoam mug and found the container cold. Backing out of the vehicle's interior, Art straightened and looked around.

Art stepped toward a lush planting of medium sized maple trees rising from a bed of feathery ferns and bordered by vivacious colored, fragrant petunias. The direction he chose led Art over a flagstone path to the front door where Sergeant White and another officer were talking.

"Sergeant White," Art said as he approached the officer in charge. A born pessimist, White wore a scowl across his face like a banner.

"Lieutenant Franklin," Sergeant White replied as he shifted his attention. "Looks like the wife did him in. Two right to his heart." The sergeant tapped his chest and gave Art a knowing glance. "The wife's got blood all over her shoes and dress. We like her for it. She's not talking." White's face transformed into an ugly scowl.

Art nodded and said, "Get a female officer to go into her closet and pick out some clothing. I want what she's wearing bagged and tagged." Art looked into the front room through the opened front door. Officers were going in and out. "How many possible witnesses do we have?"

"Not many. The neighbors on both side and the one across the street. I have someone going through the neighborhood asking if they saw or heard anything."

"No other family here?" Art asked.

"None," Sergeant White answered.

"She in the house?"

Sergeant White nodded as he said, "I got a ride coming now to take her in. We'll talk to her there."

"Good. Did you look at the wife's hands? If she's our shooter, she should have residue all over them. Make sure you test her for G.S.R." Art looked at Sergeant White, "Any weapons found in the house or vehicles?"

"Just as soon as the Techs get here. We've got her isolated on the couch, cuffed so she can't touch anything or clean any residue off her hands." Sergeant White flipped his notepad, "Yeah, we got a 12 gauge shotgun, a 38 revolver, and a 22 rifle. None of them were fired recently, and the weapon that was used is still missing."

A pink and white tricycle with steamers and a wagon filled the grassy area of the front yard, waiting for children, "Where are the kids?" Art asked.

Sergeant White twisted his neck to followed Art's gaze, and the two stood looking at the empty toys. "The neighbor took the two little girls. Subsequently, an aunt came and got them before we arrived. I've got someone over at the Aunt's house now. It seems the missus wanted them out of here. Uh-huh, she knows the score."

Art sliced his eyes sidewise to catch Sergeant White's expression. "Don't get sloppy on this," he warned. "Check everything including the kitchen sink, the phone, the keys, letters, the computer; you get the idea. Maybe there's something that will tell us what happened here today." Art gestured with his hands as he spoke, "Make sure you include all the vehicles and any other buildings on the property." Art slipped a mint into his mouth, hungry now for his steak.

The technicians arrived and began spreading out to search the grounds for evidence. They would be at it for hours, he knew from long years of experience.

The breeze picked up, and Art noticed the neighbors lining the other side of the street. Knowing how they'd enjoy the drama of the coroner's wagon entering their community, he asked, "Painless coming?"

Sergeant White nodded, "Yeah, I called the Sheriff's Department, got the coroner's office soon after I arrived. He's on his way."

Art nodded, looking around. He let his eyes fall to the ground, "They'll do the autopsy in the morning so send Oliver to attend the Post."

Chapter Two

4:00 P.M. June 28, Across Town

Lodi's Sam Nelson Wins Latest Lottery Jackpot shouted the headline on the two-day-old edition of the Lodi Gazette. Raymond Michael McNamare sat in his car re-reading the headlines just to feel the adrenalin rush. He smirked at the picture of an old man holding up a giant check made out to him for eleven million.

A smile spread across his handsome face. *I've found a solid pigeon.* His strong chin, covered with stubble rose, as though he had a score to settle. The gold and green glints in his eyes mirrored a cunning mind.

Through the windshield, Ray watched the old neighborhood. Oh, how he hated it, hated the people living there.

The money's God sent. What old man needs that much?

Excitement coursed through his body. Ray was plain sick of hearing how, at twenty-five, he should be "gainfully employed." In his mind, he could hear his Grandmother's whiney voice as he thought about those words. His skin crawled. This score had to work today; he clamped his lips tight as the fear crept in reminding him of past failures.

The paper rustled as he folded it and placed it on the car seat. He looked into the rearview mirror, raised his right hand to adjust the blond wig making sure his dark hair didn't show. Ray took hold of the metal car door handle. Ready, he thought. He squeezed down and opened the door, at that point stepping from the car. Ray walked to the trunk, slipped his key into the lock, and stiffened at the 'pop' as the lid opened.

He shrugged into the camouflage hunting jacket he took from the interior. It settled on his shoulders over his beige T-shirt. Today promised to be hot and make him miserable. Too bad. This jacket was an essential part of Ray's work clothes.

The Italian sunglasses he placed on his prominent nose complimented his olive skin tone and boosted his ego. His faded blue jeans gave him the fresh look of a college youth. Satisfied, Ray pulled down on the trunk-lid until it was closed, and he heard the clunk. He checked the time, 4:12 p.m.

It was four blocks, so he began with just a hint of a swagger, passing lush lawns around simple homes. Built during the Second World War, they looked box-like with only their color to distinguish them. Empty trash cans waited at the curb. Ray knew he'd hit these homes now if he didn't already have a target.

The Nelson property seemed well-tended with neat shrubs hugging a white-trimmed, gray-sided house. While walking along the west side of the yard up to the house, Ray picked some of the purple berries growing abundantly over the hedge and tasted them. He spat the sour crap out of his mouth and wiped his lips on the back of his sleeve. Some of the hairs on the wig caught on the hedge as he rotated his neck to look around. He pulled the hairs free, thereupon he turned. Ray jerked his hand away as he grazed the painted wood siding and became aware of the sun's radiating heat. He moved from the side of the house toward the back yard. Ray bent forward as he wrapped his fingers around the corner of the house and peeked around the edge. The yard held a large lawn and fruit trees casting appealing shade over the ground. He saw a

7

driveway on the other side of the house that ran back to the garage.

Slipping his right hand into a white cotton glove his fingers squirmed into place. Ray shook the left glove out and wiggled down to the tips. He peeked again. *The back door's about thirty feet away*, he figured. He stepped out and sneaked along until he arrived at the cracked cement porch. Ray surveyed the backyard as he probed behind him for the door. It opened as his fingers wrapped around and turned the knob. At just that moment, he spotted an old man working in the garden behind the garage, his back bowed and partly hidden by a large cherry tree.

Ray entered a mud room, a place crowded with tools and gardening pots. He stepped through the next doorway and the aroma of simmering beef stew filled the pleasant country kitchen. He took a moment to look around. High-shine, cream-colored enamel paint covered the walls and ceiling. White lacy curtains hung at the windows accented by the black and white kitchen appliances on the counters. Red salt and paper shakers and a napkin holder sat on a tea cart. He'd circled the room bringing his attention back to the wooden table with today's newspaper folded on top next to a chair that was still scooted out.

Ray told himself, *Remember why you're here. Eleven million would be great, but don't expect to find a large amount of money. I want account numbers and the man's signature that I can turn into money over time.*

The rest of the house looked old, the decorating outdated. Most rooms were dim from the draped window coverings. The well-worn carpet showed a traffic pattern going from the kitchen straight down the hall. In the first bedroom, he found a large square closet filled with women's clothing. *That's a good hiding place,* he thought.

Ray walked through the house learning its layout. Other than that one closet, there didn't seem to be any other place to hide. An attic opening was just outside the bathroom and the second bedroom in a narrow hall. With a crouch and spring, he jumped, his fingers pushing the thin plywood cover out of its place. He jumped again and grabbed the rough two by four framing. With resolve he hauled himself up until his head poked a few inches into the attic. A bit of light trickled through a vent casting sunshine stripes that danced with millions of particles. He let himself down.

Not great, it's going to be hard to get up there. He teased the cover back into place. Satisfied that it looked undisturbed, he went back to the first bedroom. Ray opened the dresser drawers and went through them. His hand sifted through soft fabrics, all women's undergarments.

Ray ran his hands between the box spring and mattress. He studied the pictures in heavy frames. They looked odd to him. Wires were strung from the picture frame to a nail up by the crown molding and back down to the frame. One of them caught on the fastener, and he jerked it free. The nail sailed, clattering over the floor until it came to a stop. He took each of the pictures down looking for anything taped to their backs. Finding nothing, he left the pictures on the floor, leaning against the wall. He checked the bathroom, lifted the tank lid, and opened the medicine cabinet. Ray swung the cabinet door closed too hard, banging it. His heart pounded. The house remained still. Only a ticking clock resonated everywhere. Cold fear grabbed him as he thought of the old man out back. At any moment, he was bound to come inside.

In the second bedroom, it surprised him to see the dresser cleaned off. He expected to find a wallet, comb, cigarettes, anything that said this guy lives here. There was nothing but a small tray with a nut and bolt, two screws, and a toothpick. *This house doesn't seem right. There's always a few dollars left out or change, at least. It's too clean as though it's been sanitized. That doesn't seem right either because there's plenty of dust on everything.*

Ray targeted the closet. He shoved the man's clothing aside and scanned the floor for a safe, or box where the old man might keep important papers. On his knees, he ran his fingers over the planks, hunting for a false floor. Step by step, he moved across the room. He ran his hand between the mattress and box spring, got down onto his knees, and looked under the bed. Just dust bunnies. Disgusted, he stood, walked to the framed pictures, and took them off the wall; they were clean.

He returned to the dresser, opened the top drawer, and rummaged around. His finger caught a ring sitting on top of a gentleman's jewel box. He pulled his glove off and slipped the ring onto his middle finger admiring the flash of the deep green stone as it caught the light. It went into his jacket pocket. Ray fit the glove back in place, picked up a tie pin and tossed it when he realized it was junk. He looked in the jewelry box he found the green ring on and picked up a fine piece.

A diamond pin. Nice. I should get something for this.

He probed in the third drawer, feeling under the clothing, and his hand bumped something hard. The chill of a leather holster surprised him. His fingers roamed over the shape of the firearm inside. His lips spread into a proud smile, and he bit down on his lower lip.

A gun!

Chapter Three

4:20 P.M. Behind the Garage

S am Nelson's bony hand held his short-handled hoe as he knelt in the dirt. Slender for his eighty-one years, he moved his body as though he were thirty years younger. His steel-gray, flyaway hair grew sparse over a balding, sunburned crown. Sam's face held few lines and those that reigned supreme were laugh lines surrounding his sparkling blue eyes. Tired and thirsty, he rose and leaned the hoe against his leg. Sweat dripped from his forehead and bushy brow, staining his denim blue work shirt. He spied his stainless steel water jug near the cement bench, the one he and Cora put in just after they married and bought this house.

Sam sniffed the air and turned his head to look at the back door. *Closed, that's why I can't smell Cora's stew.*

He walked to the ornate cement bench. Tiny cherubs covered the legs, and the scalloped edge where he always sat was worn. Surveying the garden and admiring the thick growth and dark green leaves, he grabbed the water jug, uncapped it, turned it up, and gulped allowing some of the water to run down his chin. He wiped his jaw, shook the jug, realizing it would need refilling. It could wait. He wanted to have a talk with Cora in the quiet of their little garden world.

11

"Sweetheart," Sam began as tears filled his eyes. "I miss you so much." He choked on the words and paused to take a deep breath. "What am I going to do with all the zucchini?" He waited for her answer. It would come to him with a feeling of her presence.

All their fifty years together he could always go to Cora. No matter what was on his mind, she made him feel like it was the most important thing in the world. He choked up as the pain of loss built; his cheeks flushed red, and the tears fell. Filled with emotion, he poured out his frustrations, "God I miss you." He fought the hurt, and it always won. He set the water jug down and turned toward the garden and said in a sobbing voice, "Cora, I don't know what to do with the money. Oh, I've made the provisions we always talked about, but the money I've kept, it's all so meaningless without you." Tears poured down his cheeks; his mouth hung open in silent anguish, and his heart ached.

Sam's legs weakened as he dropped down heavily and felt his bones settle on the cement bench. He didn't have enough padding anymore. He let his legs separate and placed his elbows on his knees, cradling his head in his hands. As the sadness settled in Sam shook his head in despair. He cried out to the zucchini as a breeze ruffled their leaves, "I hate being the one left."

"Meow."

Sam felt Slippers rub against his right leg and before he could pet the old girl she jumped up on the bench beside him and leaned hard against his right arm purring. "You miss Cora, don't you?" He brought his hand up and stroked Slippers. She moved away as though she didn't want his affections. "You've always been that way, haven't you? You're a ladies cat and always will be, huh?"

It irritated Sam when he realized he was drowning in sorrow. His gaze followed Slippers as she moved into a sunspot and stretched out. He stood, untied his scarf, dried his face, licked his lips, took some deep breaths, and fought for control.

He wiped his glasses, made a mental note to water and feed the fruit trees, took one last appraising look around the garden, and thought, *in a few weeks, I'll need to turn it all under and let it rest.* His left hand tucked the scarf into his back pocket then he cradled the jug under his arm. Picking up the short-handled hoe and the shovel, he carried them to the back door where he tapped the dirt off his soles. Stepping inside Sam slipped out of his shoes and left them by the door. He leaned his tools against the wall by the kitchen door. At that point, Sam walked to the sink and rinsed the dirt off his hands. Fragrant stew caught his attention as he grabbed the black and white cow terrycloth towel and dried his hands. "Cora, you'd skin me alive if you saw what I was doing." His hand shook as he smoothed the damp cloth over the oven handle.

Steam singed Sam's face as he lifted the lid from the stew pot. The room filled with fragrant spices, beef, onions, peppers and fresh tomatoes from the garden this morning. He picked up a large spoon, "God, that smells so good." He filled the spoon with some of the broth, blew on it, then tasted it for seasoning. He reached for the bread and dished up his dinner. The chair scraped the floor as he sat down and pushed the newspaper off to the side. He looked at the clock, 5:35 p.m., Bridge at seven. He'd have to hurry.

Sam switched the Crockpot to low and put his dishes in the sink. Suddenly, he headed down the hall. He rechecked his fresh clothing that he'd placed in the bathroom this morning. Soon after, he stripped, got into the shower, closed the door with a click, and turned on the water. The spray soothed him as it struck his face. He turned and let the water run over his shoulders and back.

He stepped out onto the bath rug, dried off and, grabbed the shirt off the hanger, talking to himself as he

13

shoved his arms into the sleeves. The fabric hung loosely over his lean body. He frowned at his image; thereupon he tucked the plaid shirt tails in and zipped his pants. He buckled his belt and put on his dress shoes before he headed for his ring. It wasn't on the jewelry box. *It should be right here like always. What did I do with it?*

He checked the carpet in case it dropped there. His eyes slid across the floor to the leaning pictures and tracked up to the empty wall. "What the hell...?"

Fear stabbed him and raced through his body as he realized someone had been through his things. His ring was missing. Cora had given it to him. His fingers poked at the screw and nut sitting on the bureau top. *It's not here. Another piece of Cora's gone.* Tears rimmed his reddened eyes and his stomach hurt. He gripped the bureau wanting to shake it until the ring showed up.

Someone's been here!

Sam walked to the first bedroom and flipped on the light. The pictures were down, too! He turned to the closet and raised his eyebrows, setting an expression of wonder. Wasn't the door left ajar for ventilation?

The door swung open as he grabbed the knob. Cora's pink robe filled the space; clutching the terrycloth belt, he let the familiar weight of it settle in his hand. A smile played on his face as he remembered pulling that sash free and the welcoming sparkle in her eyes. *No one's in the damn closet,* he assured himself. Sam let the fabric drop away. His stomach fluttered as he walked out of the bedroom and to the phone. Spooked or angry, which? He couldn't decide as he placed the call. An officer would be there shortly, the dispatcher told him.

His hand lingered on the phone a moment after hanging up. It was 5:45 p.m. He should call George to tell him he might be late for cards, but first, he wanted to check the living room.

The closed drapes made the room dim. He crossed to the lamp. With the click of a switch, defused light played over the floral, overstuffed sofa and love seat. Cora had done the room in muted pastels with pink and gray the predominate colors. Needlepoint pictures that both Sam and Cora had made hung on the walls. Crochet doilies, fashioned by Sam's mother, protected polished tables and hosted delicate figurines, items Sam and Cora had collected over the years. It was her room, and he left it just the way it was with one exception. His easy chair, a dark leather Lazyboy recliner, was now pulled into the center of the room with a side table to hold the remote. The focus of the room was now on the television. *Everything looks okay. Nothing's been disturbed in here.*

Sam heard an automobile pull up, so he walked outside.

The officer stepped out of the police car and surveyed the residence. He squared his shoulders, settled his duty belt, walked around the front of the vehicle up onto the Parkway, and up the walk. He extended his hand to meet Sam's, and they shook, "I'm Officer Murphy."

Sam looked the officer in the eye, "I'm Sam Nelson." He swung his hand, in a welcoming gesture, toward the house. "Thank you for coming."

As they walked into the house and to the bedrooms, Sam said, "I'd just showered and went in for my ring. That's when I realized it was missing, at that point I saw the pictures taken from the walls in both rooms."

The officer directed his flashlight beam into the closets, looking over the floor area, "There's no one here now. This intruder's probably left already."

They moved throughout the house together to make certain it was clear. Officer Murphy checked the latch on each window to make sure all were locked.

They walked back into the hall, standing under the attic opening. The clock announced six p.m. with a melody

15

of bells playing "Ava Maria." A long moment passed as the last bell rang out the long ee—ah. Sam studied the officer as the young man looked around. He figured the dark haired fellow was somewhere in his twenties, clearly a bright guy. "You new on the force?"

"Yes," Officer Murphy answered, "I've been on for almost a year now."

"Do you like the work?" Sam asked.

His smile broadened, and he chuckled, "It's never dull, and I get to meet nice people like you." His expression grew serious as he said, "I advise you to keep your doors and windows locked at all times." They began a slow stroll back to the living room and outside. The officer stopped on the front porch and made out an incident report and gave Sam the form to fill out showing what was missing. "Just list the items and where they were located in the house. The insurance company will want some proof of value. Just so you don't duplicate your work, what you give the insurance company will work for us, too."

He stepped off the porch and said, "Call if you need further assistance." He smiled as he slipped one of his business cards out of the case and extended it to Sam. He took the card, placed it into his pocket and waved to the officer as he drove off.

Muttering, "I'm in too much of a rush these days." Sam headed straight to the bathroom mirror, picked up his brush, and pulled the flyaway hair straight back over his head. His left hand snagged his jacket; Sam hurried down the hall as his right hand chose the deadbolt key. Outside, he locked the back door, and jiggled the knob to be sure the lock caught. Before long, he made his way across the grass to the garage.

When the lock clicked, Ray dropped from the attic to the floor, dashed to the bathroom window, and using just two fingers, he moved the curtain. As the car backed out, he scurried to the living room window and watched the rear bumper of the vehicle disappear. The neighborhood looked quiet. He let the window coverings drift back into place. Turning with confidence, he thought. *There's all the time in the world now.*

Ray jerked the cushions off the couch and the overstuffed chair. He pushed his hands down the couch lining feeling for anything. He found dust, wadded paper wrappers, a rubber band, and some change. Nothing that he wanted. He worked his way through the living room inch by inch. A half hour passed. He couldn't find any important papers or banking information.

It was a home filled with rubbish, sentimental junk. Seizing a Chinese vase, he roared and with great velocity, he flung it against the wall shattering it into a million pieces. His eyes glazed over as he righted himself, hauling a knife out of his pocket, his finger pressing down on the button, snapping the blade open.

Chapter Four

6:33 P.M. The Senior Center

A wisp of cool air ruffled Sam's sparse hair as he stepped into the Senior Center. He looked around the large rectangular room as the sliding doors closed behind him. He faced a fireplace, unlit on this summer evening. Windows along the same wall showcased the clouds arrayed in purples, oranges, reds, and stunning gold heralding the night to follow. Several card tables and folding chairs sat vacant waiting for tonight's tournament.

Echoing voices caught Sam's attention, and he turned, recognizing the two women speaking. One's bright coppery hair piled high on her head, the rest of her sparkled with gold jewelry hanging around her neck, on each arm, and all her fingers. The other, a shorter woman, with graying hair, wore silver studded flip-flops showing off her bright-green toenails and matching fingernails. Her eyebrows, permanently painted on, so Cora had told him, arched boldly in black. These women were characters and well-known in the community for their volunteer work. He smiled at them and nodded when they saw him.

Sam looked up at the beige-colored ceiling. The same color covered the walls. He surveyed to the south end of the room where it connected to a kitchen area: those doors were closed now as serving hot meals to seniors was done for the day. The hall just to the east of the kitchen led to the bathrooms.

He spotted his friend just as he heard his voice. "Over here, Sam," George Helms, his bridge partner and old friend, called from the coffee service table, his cup held high as a signal. A retired military man, he still held the stance even in his eighties, giving him an aura of command.

Sam turned to his right and joined George, poured a decaf, and took a couple of oatmeal cookies. Both men stood by the service table as they greeted each other.

"How's it going?" George asked.

Sam nodded a quiet affirmation and sipped the coffee, looking into George's face he drew in a breath, dropped his eyes to his empty finger, and said, "Someone broke into my place. Cora's ring..." His voice cracked. "Gone."

"Oh God," George said, as he placed his hand on Sam's shoulder. "I'm sorry."

Tears filled his eyes and glistened as he related, "Pictures were down off the walls. Might be other stuff gone, too, but I'm not sure yet. I called the police; they sent an officer around. Now I've got to fill out a lousy property report. It never rains but what it pours."

Sam cast a weak smile at George and gathered himself. He took a deep breath. "I've spent this past week going through every box, drawer, and shelf. Any place Cora and I stashed our papers. You know what I mean. I took all that mess to my CPA this morning. I've had to close out all my old accounts and open new ones. Remember what we used to talk about, George? You, me, and the girls? What we're going to do if we ever got rich?" His eyebrows lifted as though he would wait for an answer, but leaning in towards George he whispered. "I've kept $10,000 cash for me. It's in the safe."

"I don't plan on looking at it for a long time. Going to sit on it and spend it carefully." A sad expression covered his face. "Bum part is, Cora's not here to enjoy it with me. God, George, there's enough to do it all. Just like the four of us talked about, but the work I've gone through to find all my personal papers, well, I'm pooped. Now I guess I'm going to start hunting to find what was stolen and determining its worth. I don't think I care a gnat's ass about anything but that ring."

George nodded and reached for a packet of sugar, tearing the paper, and letting the grains pour into his cup of coffee. He stirred while stared hard at Sam.

"Yeah?" Sam said as he bit his cookie, aware from the look on George's face that he was about to make a point.

"What if kooks were in your home?" George's bushy eyebrows raised, his forehead wrinkled.

Sam's eyebrows lowered over his eyes hooding them, with a curious expression and he asked, "Kooks?"

"Someone wants to do you some harm." George tapped his spoon on the side of the cup, studied it a moment before setting it down.

Sam bit down too hard on the cookie, and it broke into bits and morsels. He brought his fingers up to his lips to control the loose crumbs. He grabbed a napkin and wiped his mouth. Through his mouthful, he managed a garbled, "Why?"

"Oh," George replied with flair, "There are maybe eleven million reasons?"

"After today there's nothing lying around," Sam said.

"I know, Sam." George selected a cookie. "Do *they* know that? You've got to admit it was a dumb, stupid move on your part."

"What?" Sam replied as his cheeks reddened.

"Right there for the entire world to see. Front page. Sam Nelson, residing in livable, lovable, Lodi has a pot full of money. Come on over and get some."

This day has been too much already; now George is acting like this. Sam drew in a deep breath. "Oh, God, George, I did that because they asked me to do it. They wanted the advertisement." He shook his head. "And, who's going to remember what was on today's front page next week? Huh?"

They worked their way through a maze of card tables to their assigned table. When they arrived, George said, "Get your head out of your ass, Sam. It's a whole lot more than that. How many people can you point to with your kind of money?"

Sam stiffened. "What's the matter, George? There are people in this town who can buy and sell me twice over, and you darn well know it." The cup clattered as Sam set it brusquely down. He'd had just about enough crap off George when the Senior Center doors slid open and in walked Pete and Louie.

Sam's face lit up in a bright smile directed at their opponents as they made their way to the table. He hoped their arrival would shut George up.

At that same moment, George leaned over touching Sam's shoulder and whispered, "I'm worried about you, Sam. I'm beginning to wonder who's tying your shoes."

Sam glared at him.

Chapter Five

6:35 P.M. Back at the Nelson House

Loud air exchanges accompanied the rage that powered the blade through the back of the couch in long gashes. Rip.... Ray jammed his hand inside and pulled the filler out; he slammed his hand into the metal springs and wooden slats; again he found nothing. He sliced open the pillows, tossing them aside.

His respiration increased, his nostrils flared as his eyes darted wildly. The fury building inside him took on a life of its own. In his shaking hand lay seventy-three cents, coins he'd found on the couch between the cushions. He hurled them against the wall and lumbered into the kitchen where he systematically turned every drawer upside down, dumping the contents onto the countertops. His arm swept over the tile with all his strength, and all manner of items went sailing. He didn't care. Never mind the clock on the wall. Never mind the rule get-in-and-get-out. *Where's the checkbook, the bank statements? Where's this guy's signature?*

Sweat dripped off his forehead as he threw down the last drawer. Nothing taped anywhere. The sharp pain, when his ankle twisted, didn't stop him as he stumbled over the drawer. The clutter, now in his way as he headed for the refrigerator, made him madder. There he jerked the freezer door open and filled with emotion, roared out

22

his frustration. He pulled the wrapped packages from their resting place, letting most of them to drop on the linoleum. Trembling fingers tore at the wrapper uncovering a hard ball of hamburger! His temples pounded, he needed time to think. He stood in the middle of the mess. *Unbelievable, friggin' unbelievable!* He grabbed the hoe as he rushed through the mudroom and out the back door. In ten minutes, he'd torn through the lush garden.

No buried treasure!

Ray brushed at the mud stuck to his pants as headlights flashed in the driveway. He ran to the porch. *Did he see me?* His heart pounded as he slipped behind the mudroom door, his hand wrapped around the handle of Sam's hoe. The deadbolt slammed into place with a resolute thwack! His eyes went wide; *I'm trapped.*

Sam walked from the garage to the porch glancing at his watch as it showed 8:45 p.m. *I'm so angry at George. Maybe I'll sit outside for a while and cool off.* Sam looked up into the heavens and spotted the Big Dipper. He smiled, remembering how he and Cora would sit out on warm nights in their lawn recliners, holding hands and looking into the studded vastness to watch for shooting stars, satellites, and airplanes. *We'd imagine the people on board and their adventurous destinations.* He pouted his lips together and realized how many things reminded him of her.

He slipped the key into the deadbolt and turned the key with a smooth movement. Sam stepped right over the fresh dirt on the porch and mudroom floor and on into the kitchen; he saw the chaos. "Son of a bitch!" he roared.

Anger flared as he reached into his pocket for the officer's card, took a careful step through the debris toward the phone, and as he did, the hair rose on the back of his neck. He froze!

Something's wrong.

A thump behind him.

He turned.

Yellow hair, whipping from side to side, framing a face filled with rage, and eyes blazing pure hate filled Sam's vision.

Petrified, Sam's heart pounded in his ears making him deaf to the fanatical scream accompanying the assault. His eyes grew even wider as his breath caught in his chest.

That contorted face! Sam's eyes slid from face to hoe as it elevated even higher above him, terror rooted him to the floor as the hoe came swinging downward. The first blow cut his neck and shoulder, sprayed his blood and rocked him. On the second blow, Sam's knees buckled and he fell. Blow after blow, over and over, assaulted his body.

Ray chopped at the body until he shook. His hands slipped from the bloody handle.

"Where's the money?"

His grip on the hoe loosened. Exhausted, he sobbed. Through his tears, he managed to ask, "Where?" His knees gave out; the hoe fell to the floor, and he dropped down next to the old man, his breaths coming in gasps. He rolled the old man over and seized his wallet. Ray stood and fumbled with the worn tri-fold, pulling the bills out, fanning them. There were three one-dollar bills. He stared in disbelief at the money. He threw them at the body and watched the bills float down like dry leaves settling gently on Sam's back. One bill slid slowly down Sam's side and came to rest on the floor next to Sam's right hand. Ray looked at the driver's license; the name appeared blurred through the yellowed plastic window on the wallet. It didn't matter. He put the wallet in his pants pocket.

He shuddered, cried out his fury, "You selfish old geezer!" Ray looked about the room, stood and backed up into the mudroom, leaned down, and picked up his jacket that he had dropped when the old man walked into the kitchen. His hands shook as he pulled the stained cotton gloves off, shoving them into the jacket pocket before digging in his pants pocket for his car keys.

Chapter Six

9:00 P.M. The Franklin Property

Melissa ran towards his car as the garage door opened. Art pulled into the garage, got out of the car and embraced her as she collided into him sobbing uncontrollably. He pulled away from her, leaned, and looked in her face and asked, "What's wrong?"

She told him again and again, but he still didn't understand. Her long red hair whipped around as she blubbered.

"Calm down; I don't know what you're saying." He stroked her head with his hand, "Take a breath and tell me so I can understand you. Okay?" He softened his eyes and let a smile play across his face.

Tears dropped from her eyes as she nodded and they looked so sad as she steadied her voice, "Nevar's dead. Nicole just called. He just dropped dead!" Tears flooded again, and Art gathered her to him. His eyes focused on a spot on the garage wall as his jaw dropped. He stared without seeing as the enormity sank into acceptance. His arms tightened around his daughter drawing her in for protection.

He shook his head in disbelief. *Nevar's one of my best detectives. He would be my go-to-guy if Walt weren't available. Melissa just loved the guy. I loved that guy.*

"Come on, honey, let's go inside." He took her hand and led her around the side of the car and through the door into the laundry room. He hit the garage door control and heard the chain grinding. They walked into the kitchen, and he sat her at the counter. "Water?" he offered.

She shook her head.

"I'm going to call Nicole now; you sit there quietly, okay? So I can hear her. I'll put it on speaker."

She nodded.

Art pulled the tissue box closer to Melissa soon after he reached for the phone. He dialed knowing the number by heart and Nicole picked up on the first ring.

"I saw your number on the caller ID," she said, her voice shaking.

"You're on speaker so Melissa can hear," Art said as he sat on the bar stool listening to her, questions racing through his mind.

She told him that Nevar went to the store and two hours later the coroner's office sent two officers to tell her that he was dead. "They just knocked on my door like everything was normal." she told him. She blew her nose.

"I let them in. They told me I should sit down. They walked me to the couch before they told me. Art, they said Nevar just dropped on the store floor." Her voice sounded thin with a high-pitched, pleading whine. She sobbed a few minutes. Before long, she calmed. "He was gone when the paramedics arrived," she said, her voice rising in pitch.

Art heard her pull another tissue just as Melissa did the same.

Her breath caught, and she gasped. "I kept asking them to tell me again what happened. I must have asked five times. I just couldn't believe what they were saying. They didn't know anything. An autopsy has to be done before we are going to find out what happened to him. Oh, Art, he was only thirty-five. What am I going to do?" She cried hard. "How am I going to be Mom and Dad for our kids?"

Art didn't know what to answer. "Nicole, Melissa and I can come over right now if you like?"

She sniffed, "Thanks, Art. No, my folks are on the way. They'll stay for a few days to help with the kids. God, Art, I had to go with one of the officers to take possession of Nevar's car." She cried and blew her nose. "I don't know how to do this."

She dissolved into a flood of tears. As did Melissa.

Art didn't know what to say as he listened to Nicole and looked at Melissa. He needed something for his nerves. Two females bawling at the same time was too much. He reached for the cupboard and took the bottle of whiskey down and poured a half glass. He looked with longing at the freezer and imagined opening the drawer and taking some ice cubes. He held the phone, letting the new widow talk it out. He lifted the glass to his lips and allowed the warmth to drift over his tongue and burn down his throat.

Art heard her doorbell ringing; she said goodbye, and Art hung up. He walked to the freezer, pulled the door open, wrapped his fingers around three cubes and dropped them into his glass. He smiled at Melissa, "Did you understand any of that?" He asked as he sat at the table.

She nodded, "I could hear her. Why'd he die? I can't believe it," she said. Melissa got quiet as tears glistened in her eyes. She came to him, and he made room for her on his lap, her long red hair draping over his back as she buried her face in his neck and cried. "What's going to happen to Nicole and the kids?" she said. She jerked up and looked into Art's face.

"I don't know," Art answered.

"This is bogus, Dad," she said as she wound some hair around her finger.

"I know, honey. It'll be a couple of days at least before we'll know anything solid," he said with a soft voice.

The girl stood, moved around to a chair and plunked herself down deep in thought. After a long moment, in which the silence in their kitchen magnified, Melissa said, "Dad?"

"Yes." Art answered as he began to clear the table. His steak waited in the refrigerator. The condiments and Melissa's plate sat on the table with her glass and utensils.

Melissa leaned over and opened the dishwasher, "What if something was to happen to you, and I could never, ever, talk to you again?" she said as she sat back up.

"That's not going to happen," Art said as he rinsed the dishes. He was doing his best to sound comforting as he loaded the dishwasher.

"It could! Look what happened to Nevar. One minute he's here and the next, he's gone. It's so forever," her voice trailed off.

Art pressed the start button and listened for the cycle to begin. "Let's call it a night. It's best not to borrow trouble." She stood up, and he gave her a hug and flipped off the light switch, feeling all the frustrations from the day settle on his shoulders, stiffening them. Together they started up the stairs to their rooms.

Chapter Seven

9:15 P.M. Lodi Lake

Darkness draped over the wilderness area of Lodi Lake, cooling the still humid air. The ducks had bedded down, and the only noise besides Ray's passage came from the bugs that set up a steady hum. Ray worked his way through the brush, pushing branches out of his way, and protecting two black plastic bags. He stepped out of the rough growth onto a small bit of ground and a makeshift dock he'd constructed many years ago.

This place was his haven from the world. As far as he knew, no one knew about this hideout. It snuggled along the Mokelumne River, just one of a hundred eddies where no boats ever came, protected by a jungle of growth. He fumed at himself for what happened tonight because it might cause him problems.

He jerked the wig off his head and placed it on a piling. Ray pulled the bloody clothing off. Blackberry brambles stung like bees as they snagged his exposed skin. Ray opened one of the black bags and stuffed the bloody clothes inside. The jewelry pieces and the gun, he placed in the other plastic bag. He hated giving up the hunting jacket. He'd used it for years for burglaries. *It's got to be bloody.* He pushed the jacket in with the other clothes; thereupon Ray shoved the blood-spattered shoes on top of the jacket. His fingers shook with nerves as he gathered the plastic bags together, and tied them off.

Standing in his shorts in the small clearing, he listened to the night sounds, letting the air cool his fevered body and mind. No one else was on the river. The animal sounds told him that, it settled him enough to consider one of the bottles of wine he'd secreted. *No, not now.*

Instead, he pulled out a metal suitcase hidden under the dock. He rubbed the dirt off the surface. Inside was a blue tarp, a clean T-shirt, jeans, socks, and shoes.

The normal sounds around him ceased. At first, he figured it was just his movements as he dressed, but then the steady, rhythmic, hammering of the air grew in volume. *It sounds like a helicopter.* His eyes sought the sky, through the canopy of oaks and vines. The sound increased. Were the police after him already? Agitation rushed his moves as he dipped into the river, it's cold water cleansing as it ran over his skin. He washed up his arms past his elbows and noticed the watch-face seemed odd.

He grabbed the wig and placed it carelessly back on his head. Gathering the two black bags, Ray started out of the hideaway heading for a pathway that wandered under large redwood trees, past a parking area, and came out by the lake. As he reached the clearing, he looked again at his watch and saw the dial covered with blood. Disgusted, he pulled it off his wrist, walked to the edge of the lake, and with one swift movement, sailed the timepiece out over the moon bright surface.

As he snapped his wrist in the final motion of throwing, a beam of light swept the ground. *Shit.* Fear flowed through him. It was about 9:00 p.m. when he'd left the old man. TV's were playing, nothing unusual. He passed one car on Turner Road and came straight here. *What the hell is the chopper doing?*

He rushed back to his car and placed the two plastic bags filled with evidence in the trunk. He looked all around for the security guard. Every forty minutes he makes his rounds except at midnight when he checks the bathrooms and the food stand. *I need to be off the lake property by then.*

As he reached for the car door handle, a human form stepped from the shadows.

"Raymond?"

Oh, shit! He swung around. "Allison? How'd you know it was me?"

"Duh, your car," she said as she pointed at the old blue Ford. Allison's dark brown hair was tucked up under a black baseball cap, and the rest of her trim body covered tightly in black. She stood five-foot-six with a sweet expression and smiling eyes.

"You scared the crap out of me. When did you get back?" Ray asked.

"I've got to get away from here now," she said. Allison walked around the front of the car talking as she went. "Get me to the Crazy Lobo; I'll buy the gas."

"Where's Roland?" Ray asked, his eyes following her movement.

"He'll meet us there," Allison answered.

Ray studied her. *I can't go home. Shit, if I do my Grandmother will question the hell out me. I don't want to buddy up with anyone either.* His muscles tightened as he vacillated between going home and going with her. *If I go with her, it could work out as an alibi.*

Ray switched personalities. He'd take Allison to the Crazy Lobo and get some beers. He smiled, opened his door, and said, "Get in. Hey, what's with the helicopter?"

"No clue," She said. Through a stifled smile, she asked, "What's up with that wig?"

Ray reached up and grabbed the hairpiece, pushing it under the driver's seat. "I like it."

"You're sure uptight. What's up?" she asked as she gathered up food wrappers from the front and dumped the papers onto the backseat.

Ray adjusted himself behind the wheel, started the engine, and moved along the levee road, passing gnarled trees on the left and the lake to the right. He watched his rear view mirror for the guard. "I told you, I like it here. I didn't have anything else to do, so I came to see if anyone was hanging out."

"Oh, do you think that some of the old gang still comes here?" Allison asked.

"Remember the bonfires and us kids drunk and splashing around in the lake?"

Allison looked at him and said, "That was a long time ago, ten years at least."

Ray focused on her, a figure shrouded in darkness with a baseball cap pulled down over her head. His curiosity increased. *If I question her, she'll have fair game to me.*

He wasn't ready to talk about tonight. He switched the headlights on, and they drove in silence to the Crazy Lobo.

Allison stepped out of his car. "You coming?" she asked bending down and looking at Ray through the open door.

"Yeah." Ray parked, hopped out of the car and pushed through the doorway as he entered the busy bar. His hand guided Allison as the two squeezed past a group of bikers crowding the pool table. They spotted Roland in a booth on the back wall.

Roland seemed relaxed as he smiled at Ray and Allison. He was twenty-five, five-feet-eleven, husky with dark curly, brown hair of medium length. "It's hard to talk in here," Roland yelled over the loud music.

"Yeah, I see that," Ray yelled back.

Ray watched both of them as Roland asked Allison if everything was okay and she patted the lump under her jacket, Roland nodded, and they turned their attention to Ray.

"You'll never guess where I met up with this guy," Allison said as she pointed at Ray. "Lodi Lake." Allison focused on Ray. "Hey, Ray, what'd you toss into the water?"

She saw. This night just keeps getting better. Ray forced his voice to be calm and managed a controlled, "Nothing."

"Huh," Allison said as she pulled the pretzels closer and thoughtfully selected one.

"You guys in trouble?" Ray asked as he first looked at Roland then swung his attention to Allison.

"Naw," Roland answered. "Allison and I just got back; we're low on dough. We heard there was this huge stash. Shit, man. Guys were flying out of this place on Garnet. Cars were coming and going, people all over. We go in the back of the place," Roland paused making a gesture with his hand, as though to go behind. "We're in there one, two minutes max, we see it... the money, sitting on the table. And, get this, the window's open. I boosted Al inside. She grabs some dough, and we're getting out of there, man."

Roland shoved some pretzels into his mouth and raised his hand. The bartender came over and brought beer. "We managed to get a little of what they had. One thing for sure, we're not going back there. If we weren't so broke, we'd a never done 'em, man, and that's the God's truth." Roland raised his glass. "Here's to their never finding out," he said.

Ray emptied his brew and set the bottle down. Roland told him they did okay with the small stuff, not great and that they needed one big strike, one big con. Roland took in a breath at that point, and he told him that they had a scam. He gave the floor to Allison, and she explained how the scam worked. Ray looked at Allison.

As Allison talked, Ray could see how Sam's millions might play a part. Maybe he could still get his hands on

34

that money after all. The beer relaxed him. "How big is big?" he asked.

"The bigger, the better," Roland said as the breaking the balls at the pool table brought cheers that drowned out their conversation.

"Eleven million big enough?" Ray mouthed.

Roland's eyes lit up as he asked, "How do you know about that much money?"

Ray sat straighter and leaned toward Roland. "There's this old geezer; he won the lottery. Thing of it is," Ray darted his eyes around the room then at Roland and finally Allison, "The guy's dead."

Willy Nelson strummed a guitar medley from the scratchy jukebox as Roland's brows knit together, and he asked, "For real?"

"Yeah," Ray said almost under his breath.

Roland shoveled more pretzels into his mouth while listening to Willy sing. After several minutes, Roland said, "It could work."

They talked through four more beers, and somewhere during the discussion, they decided it was time to take off for Tahoe. Ray was mellow enough not to care. When they walked out into the night air, Ray tossed his car keys to Roland. They piled into the car, and he stretched out on the back seat.

Chapter Eight

4:30 A.M. Heading for Tahoe

Through a gentle night and with a few other vehicles, they swept up into the chill of the high mountains on Highway 88 East. Ray lay on his side listening as Roland talked about turning on the car heater.

"It's warm enough for me."

Ray squeezed his eyes tighter as Allison twisted around on the car seat to look at him. She pulled her legs up and stretched toward Ray poking his arm. He watched her through the tiniest of slits.

"Is he sleeping?" Roland whispered.

"He seems to be."

"Too many beers."

"He did down them pretty fast," she said as she sat back in her seat.

"I'm not sure it's a good idea teaming up with him again. Boy, this is one heck of a winding road. He's a wild ass."

"Do you think he's acting strangely?" she asked.

Roland chuckled and said, "What do you mean, Allison, stranger than usual?"

Ray watched as they talked, his body bouncing against the seat lulling him.

"Well, yeah." He saw Allison lift her baseball cap off her head and let her hair loose, running her fingers through to the ends before scratching her scalp.

"There's something off about him," she said with a sigh.

"If I were in his skin, I'd be tense, too," Roland said.

"What do you think about this old man of his?" she asked.

"We could get the name from him and go alone," Roland said.

"Yeah, we could. We don't want Ray pissed at us. He goes off when he's mad." She leaned forward and set the baseball cap on the dashboard.

"Not good?" Roland said as he glanced at her.

"Definitely. What'll we do?"

"Shit, Allison, I don't know. Give me a cig and light it for me. I don't like these tight turns."

Ray listened as she dug in her bag, pulled the pack out, and lit one. The cigarette went between Roland's parted lips, and he took a long drag. "But I do know one thing." The lit ash flashed as Roland spoke. "He knows where we can get our hands on serious dollars." Roland let the smoke out in one long stream and took another drag. "I'm thinking we run the scam, and as soon as we've got the money, we're gone. Agreed?"

She took another look at Ray, and as she turned back to Roland, she asked, "You mean to cut him out?"

Ray was all ears now, he stiffened.

"Uh, no, too dangerous. Ray gets his share, but at some point, we cut ties. Okay?" he answered. "We'll find out if this guy did win the money. And, Allison, make certain no one else can lay claim to it. After that, we'll decide what to do next."

"How do we do that?"

"Get a copy of the newspaper for starters," he answered.

They were quiet for a while. Ray tuned into the sounds around him. The car, the tiny bit of air squealing in around the window. The seams in the road as the car hopped over them as the tires hummed. It lulled him. What kept him awake was the fact that he didn't trust them either. He would have to watch both carefully. *Right now, I need to be low profile, so I'll go along for as long as it takes.*

It startled him when she spoke.

"Roland?" she paused. "Does it scare you?"

"Does what scare me?" He answered her as though he had a dozen other things on his mind.

She said, "You know. Getting married? I think we've done just fine without it."

Allison moved in the seat, and Ray tried to see what she was doing.

Roland grabbed the cigarette from his mouth. Ray watched the glow circling as Roland waved his hand. The car rocked when Roland looked her direction. Ray thought for a second that he was going to roll off the seat and hit the floorboards.

Roland blew smoke and said, "Al, we've been over this a thousand times. It's the smart thing to do."

"But, Roland, you know I've always dreamed of my wedding. It's got to have flowers and the church and dress."

The ashtray clicked open as Roland pulled it down. He snubbed the burning tip out. "You're a dreamer, Al. Do you really think you'll ever have a so-called normal life?"

Ray smiled. *You tell her.*

"Do you think you'll find an up and up guy to marry?"

Yeah, Ray thought, *do you?*

Roland rolled down the driver's side window and let the smoke escape, then rolled it back up. "And where's this so-called family coming from? You ain't got one, girl. Come on, get real. It's not in the cards."

The cold air blasted Ray. He fought the temptation to pull his legs up and wrap his arms around his chest. He couldn't move. Not now, he wanted to hear more. Ray bit his lip and fought the shivers.

"You don't need to remind me my life sucks. So does yours." Allison chopped the words out. They rode in silence a few minutes when she said, "Well if we're going to do this marriage thing, I want the dress, a pretty one. I want flowers- daisies and roses. You can do that much. And, Roland, fix yourself up, too."

Ray's eyes popped open. Would Roland blow up?

A long moment passed. "Already being the boss, huh?" he asked with a soft voice. There was movement between them and Roland said, "What?"

Ray wanted to sit up and look, too.

Allison moved like she was going to the floorboards on the driver's side and Ray wondered what she was doing.

"There's something coming out from under your seat." She sat up and laughed. "This wig. Ray was wearing this when I met up with him at the lake. Why would he want people to think he was a blond?"

"Something's dried on it," Roland said.

"Oh, look!" Allison pointed. "Lake Tahoe."

The car swept over the road closing the distance. Finally there, Roland yawned out, "Good, I'm tired."

The lights on the motel blinked a welcome and Roland pulled up to the motel's office, turned the car off, and pulled the keys.

Stepping out of the car, Allison said, "Let's get a room and just sleep."

"Sounds like a plan." Roland stood by the car door as another yawn escaped. Finally, he opened the car door "Hey, Ray, we're here."

1:00 P.M. Tahoe.

Ray spent the time watching birds and eating tacos from a stand around the corner from the motel. Didn't seem to matter how hard he tried to forget about the evidence in the black bags, it just haunted him. He had to get rid of it and soon. Now he had a new job; it was keeping an eye on the happy couple. They went off together about noon to get their license and the other stuff they wanted. *Until they get back, I'm on my own.*

At three fifteen Ray wandered back to the motel room and was about to switch on the TV when Roland waltzed through the door, plastic garment bag in hand.

"Here, Ray." I've got to get a shower and cleaned up. Roland handed him a bag with a tux in it and said, "You put this on and take Allison to this address at 5:30 p.m. tonight. She wants romance. She's going to get romance. Now, one last thing..." Roland made eye contact. "Here's the ring, give it to me at the right time." He left Ray holding the bagged tux, the ring box, and the brochure as he moved into the bathroom.

Ray's eyes narrowed. He spun around calling after Roland, "Hey, how will I know?"

Roland yelled through a closed door. "Someone will tell you. Hell, dick-head, this is the first time for me too."

Ray set the bagged tux and the brochure down and opened the little box. Inside nestled a wedding set. It had a wide gold band and a diamond centered on top. Ray appraised the stone. It looked as big as a large kernel of corn, its color clear with flashes of blue. He blew across the stone's surface. *It's real.* Ray figured Roland got a little five-finger discount somewhere in town.

Roland yelled through the closed door, "She doesn't want me to see her until we're getting hitched. You stay with her today and take her to the dock. You got that?"

"Sure," Ray called back. "Where are you going?"

"Don't know. Just have to find a place to stay until I meet you two."

As soon as Roland left, Ray looked at the brochure and his eyes widened. *So, we are getting married on the*

M.S.Dixie, a paddle boat on Lake Tahoe. That's pretty grand. Yeah, Allison will think that's romantic.

Excited now, he showered and dressed in his tux, curious to see what else might come with a night out in such high-toned threads. Ray positioned his body before the mirror and rubbed his hand over the shiny cloth, admiring his image. *These are nice clothes; they are so different from my jeans and T-shirt. My face even looks handsome.* His shoulders shifted back lengthening the spine giving him a taller stance. His puffed his chest out. *These clothes are something.* He clamped the lapel between his thumb and fingers running his hand up and down to feel the textile. *Sharp! Pants are too long.*

He took the good clothes off and lazed around in his jeans and t-shirt waiting for Allison.

Later, on the boat, Allison cracked the door to the ladies room slightly and took the daisies and white roses Ray handed her.

"They're ready," Ray whispered as he leaned close to the door. He wondered if he should warn her that Roland had cleaned his wig and was wearing it right now.

Her hand shook as she smoothed her dress. She swallowed hard, raised her chin high, took Ray's hand, and walked into the dining room. The peach-colored dress floated. With each step she took, her smile, at first tentative, grew bolder. She smiled at Ray and he back at her as he gave her hand to Roland.

The ceremony was over quickly, and the newlyweds walked hand in hand to the bandstand for their wedding photos.

"Stand over here, please, and I'll get one of the two of you. After that we can include your witness," the photographer said. At the proper moment, Ray stepped beside Allison.

Ray couldn't contain his smile at how silly Roland looked wearing that blond wig. Now it was captured forever in an 8 x 10 matte finish photo, and he could hardly wait to see the picture.

In the first few minutes after they started married life, the boat slipped from the dock. They sat at a petite table covered with white linen, a tiny bowl of white roses, and a candle that flickered. The waiter approached and filled their fluted stemmed crystal glasses with pale, amber Champagne. They giggled as the bubbles tickled their noses. Roast beef, browned potatoes, and a crisp green salad made up their menu. All through their first meal, Roland and Allison stared into each other's eyes. Ray didn't mind. He enjoyed the fine meal.

They weren't even aware when the waiter cleared their plates. They looked at him for the first time as the man poured steaming, fragrant coffee into their cups. Everything was wonderful, and they sipped the coffee smiling at each other. Only then did they realize that Ray had shared their meal with them.

Afterward, they all walked outside and wandered around the railing, watching the sunset and the lights coming on in the houses along the shoreline. They aligned themselves along the railing at the stern, watching the paddle wheel whip the water into silver trailing that raced away from them.

Eventually, the evening gave way to darkness, and Ray found it hard to put his feelings into words. This dressing up was wonderful. As his grandmother kept harping, find your niche. Ray believed he'd found it. Roland and Allison's scam was the smart way to go. Go big. He was done chasing small stuff. He had a taste now for Champagne and dinners like the one they had tonight. A new beginning for me, Ray enjoyed the thrill as it raced through his body.

Chapter Nine

7:30 A.M. June 29, 1995

Sitting at the table in the Franklin kitchen, Walt spoke in hushed tones, "... a small handgun." Melissa entered the room and looked at the two men. Walt, a man in his late fifties, overweight and balding, had gray-brown hair ringing his head just above his ears. His dark, olive-toned skin showcased his Italian background, and his hand gestures accentuated his heritage. He had deep brown eyes, and short, stubby fingers. His old-world accent was warm and inviting.

He took a breath, "Hey, Kid," he said to Melissa. Dropped his eyes and returned to his report. "Two shots perfectly placed, both entering the heart. He died immediately." Walt patted his chest to show the wound entry as he spoke. "Sergeant White got the warrant from the Judge and the team was over on Nebbiolo Avenue until five this morning. We went through everything with a fine-toothed comb. "Still no weapon."

Art asked, "Did the wife meet with anyone before the police got there?"

"I have no idea. It's possible."

"Do we have a motive?"

"We're still working on that." The detectives were talking with the wife and had been through the night.

"She's not been helpful, and it ended this morning when she asked for her attorney."

Pouring another cup of coffee for Walt, Art finished with a warm smile for Melissa. He stepped around her to put the pot back. "Mornin'."

"What are you talking about?" she asked.

"The homicide over on Nebbiolo last evening," Art answered. "Want some breakfast?" He looked at her for an answer.

"I'll have cold cereal. I'm not very hungry." She moved to the cupboard and took a bowl, gathered everything else and sat at the table listening as the two men talked about the homicide and the missing gun.

Finishing her breakfast, she downed the last of the orange juice and, she set her dishes in the sink.

She kissed her Dad and Walt on their foreheads. Art stood and gave her a hug. She ran out the back door and Art moved to see what she was doing. *She's taking her bike, probably going to see a friend.*

Art made another pot of coffee. He sat back down at the table, and he and Walt continued their discussion about the homicide on Nebbiolo Avenue listening for the final dispensing of the fresh coffee into the carafe. Art stood, brought the coffee pot to the table, and poured both mugs full. They talked at length throwing out ideas to each other and not coming up with anything new. The clock ticked an hour away as they drained the last of the pot.

Breathlessly, Melissa raced through the back door excitement in her voice as she said, "Dad, look what I found." With a flare, she laid a firearm on the table. She rocked from one foot to the other, waiting for them to react.

They just sat there staring at the plastic lunch bag with what appeared to be a small handgun.

Hungry for the first time today, she pulled the cupboard door open and got the bag of chips. It rustled as she jammed her hand inside. "Can you believe this? Isn't it great?"

Both men knew what was in the sack by the sound it made as it met the Formica. Art reached and gently coaxed the wrapper. His hand went to his breast pocket, and he took his pen, using it to open the bag and position it for better viewing. Walt's eyes met Art's at that exact moment, and a silent message passed between them. *Aw, shit.*

Art exploded and jerked up from the table looming over Melissa. Startling her so that some of the chips fell to the floor. "Good God, is this," he pointed, "what I think it is? Have you been over at the Nebbiolo Avenue scene?" He paced toward the sink and turned. "I can't believe you would do such a stupid thing. For God's sake, you should know better."

"You're a cop's kid and not just any cop's kid." Art patted his chest just under his chin, the sound hollow, and drumming. "My kid. Haven't I taught you anything? Haven't you been listening? What in hell were you thinking? Were you thinking at all?" Art's body twisted left, then right, looking for something to wreck, anything.

"You've compromised me as chief investigator." His shoulders dropped, along with his vocal volume. "We may lose jurisdiction." He turned to her, brought his fingers to his chest, his eyes boring into hers. "I have to remain totally neutral and disinterested. Or the whole matter might just get itself turned over to the Department of Justice. Is that what you want? Are you trying to discredit me?"

Melissa's pilot ignited, and she growled out, "I was careful. What'd you want me to do, just leave it there?"

"That certainly was the option you should have taken." Art held up his hand as Melissa stepped forward

45

and opened her mouth to speak. "I'm not finished." He gave her a searing look. "Please tell me you didn't touch the gun." He smacked his forehead. "Well, stupid of me to even think of that. Of course, you did. Otherwise, how in hell did you manage to bring it here? I suppose you want a stroke on the head along with a nice job, Melissa? Well, young lady, you're not getting it. Have you any idea what trouble you've caused? No, you haven't."

"But— "

He whirled around. "Just shut your mouth and keep it zipped. What's happened to you? You used to be such an obedient child."

Her confident smile faded. Tears welled in her eyes.

"Let me get this straight. You think you have to help the Department in this investigation? You're not trained. It takes years of training to handle evidence. You may have ruined the case. Do you realize that? Do you get it? I can't believe you would interfere, Melissa." He raised his hands to God. "I'm at a loss for words." He moved around the kitchen like a caged animal. Art grabbed the dish towel off the rack and tossed it into the sink.

Melissa stepped toward him. "God, Dad, I know more about handling evidence than a lot of so-called cops. I didn't go anywhere near the property. I found the gun," she said, stepping closer. He moved away. She stopped moving forward and rocked back on her heels.

"Not the least bit impressed." He looked at her as though smoke would come out of his nostrils at any minute. "You sure as heck didn't show it by picking up the weapon and handling it."

Melissa, her hands on her hips, said, "I used a stick, Dad. I stuck it into the barrel. I'm not stupid," she yelled back at him. "I dropped it into the baggie, one I had in my pocket. I never touched that gun."

Art's face flushed red, obscuring his freckles." You just don't get it; YOU DON'T KNOW A DAMN THING!" He paced away.

"Art, maybe it won't be so bad if she handled the evidence as she says," Walt said.

Art turned on Walt. "Cut the good cop, bad cop crap. Melissa is my daughter, not some perp we're working." Art saw Walt look at his knuckles. Walt's face took on an expression that said he'd like to drop through the floor about now. Seeing his friend react in that way made Art even madder, mostly at himself.

Melissa took the moment, she planted her feet squarely and said, "Why are you so lame? What is it? Are you jealous that I found the gun and your *ladies* didn't? That's it, isn't it?"

His eyes narrowed, his face screwed up, scarlet and steaming, "That'll be enough."

Art was beside himself. He knew he was messing up. He had a sense that he had somehow joined a herd of terrified buffalo rushing headlong toward the edge of a cliff. Caught up in the frenzy of hoof beats, frantic bellowing, and blinding dust. Unable to stop, he plowed on, "Let me see if I've got this straight. You, a fifteen-year-old citizen. No, make that smart-ass girl, go over to a crime scene and dig up the weapon in a homicide investigation. You get fingerprints all over the suspect weapon." He turned to Walt. "Now we have to fingerprint her for elimination."

Walt nodded.

"You're part of the chain of evidence now. Do you know what that means? You don't. Do you? Well, Melissa, you may find yourself in court explaining just what you did this morning. How would you like that? I know one thing for a certainty; you're going to have a nice little chat with the Chief." Art shook his head and looked at his shoes, his voice almost inaudible. "Oh, he's surely gonna want a talk with you. He's going to be so pleased to have a do-gooder on his side. If he doesn't chew my ass out on this one, I'll be damn lucky." His hands moved to his head, holding the temples and forehead in his palms. "This could discredit me and put a black mark in my file," he said.

"I don't even want to talk to you right now. Get yourself upstairs and write down everything you did, how you came up with the gun, everything. Make a copy for my records. You write a letter to the Chief and the D.A., stating what you did and tell them that this kind of action on your part will never happen again. Got it?"

Melissa glared at him. She turned on her heels heading for her room as he called after her.

"We're not done with this, Melissa. Now get upstairs and do what I told you." Art couldn't sit still; he moved like a cat prowling the kitchen totally forgetting Walt sitting there, privileged to the drama unfolding. "How could she do this? Why would she do this incredible, this stupid thing? What on earth possessed her to go over there in the first place?" Art finally sat back in his chair, looking into Walt's eyes and shaking his head he asked, "Do you see any good side to this?"

Walt shook his head at the same moment Melissa stomped up the stairs sobbing. She swung the door to her room, slamming it for emphasis and a muffled, "I hate you," drifted downstairs.

Chapter Ten

11: 00 A.M. The Chief's Office

A rt sat directly behind Melissa on a cold metal folding chair, at the moment focusing on the ceiling. His embarrassment appeared to amuse Chief Miller, whose lips twitched as they fought a smile, Art noticed the tell-tale twinkle of humor in his eyes.

A tall, slender man, in his early fifties, Chief Robert Doyle Miller wore his blond hair short. He brought his glasses down from his light brown eyes, wiped the lenses, and slipped them into his shirt pocket. He clasped his hands behind his back, lowered his gaze on Melissa, and now stood before her like a wall.

My girl's hell bent on showing both of us she has the right stuff, Art thought.

Melissa, dressed in a white blouse, navy blue skirt, white bobby sox, and black shoes, held her chin high. A slight smile pulled at the corners of her mouth. Her voice grew strong. "I rode my bike over to the scene on Nebbiolo Avenue and by accident, I stumbled over a box filled with grass clippings. I found the gun hidden at the bottom of the box. The container was two feet from the boundary line. I mean the yellow tape. I honored the crime scene tape." Her hand shot up, her red hair swished. "I swear. As soon as I knew where the gun was, I figured how to keep it safe and take it to my Dad." She turned slightly toward him then back to attention. "I used a stick and a plastic bag, dropped the gun inside the bag. I never touched it at all. He told me to write this report." She lifted an envelope she held in her left hand bringing it into view. Her hand slipped into the envelope, removed the report, and handed it to the Chief. She remained at attention. Chin high.

Art brought his eyes down and locked them with the Chief's when Miller looked his way. The Chief brought his gaze back to Melissa, staring for a long moment to make her uneasy. "Well, Melissa, you carefully handled the gun. I understand why you did what you did. I'm glad you found it and that we have it. However, you need to know you may find yourself in a court of law being grilled by the District Attorney. The way you handled this piece of evidence may have precluded our being able to use it in our case. Your actions may have lost the case before it ever gets started." He paused. "In the future, I want you to allow the department to do its job. I'm sure that if you had given it some thought, you would have left the gun right where it was untouched by you. Don't you agree?"

She looked down for a second, but answered, "Yes Sir."

"Good. Well, I think it's time to get on with it, don't you, Art?"

The door swung open after a gentle rap. Walt stepped through, nodded to the chief, and handed Art two reports.

Art straightened up, took the papers, and scanned one. He looked up at Walt. "When did this come in?" he asked waving the medical report.

Caught leaving the room, Walt with his body half in the doorway and half out, leaned back into the room. "We just got it."

Art stood, twisted his neck, and heard the bones crack. He handed the report to the Chief as Melissa looked from one to the next.

"Nevar died from an aneurysm. He was dead before he hit the ground. A ticking time bomb," Art said to her. As Art handed the other report to Chief Miller, he approached Melissa. "I need you to go home now. Come on. I'll walk you out."

Melissa grabbed her dad's arm. "Aw, Dad."

His free hand spun her around, pushed her forward toward the main entrance. Art whispered into her ear, "You need to get out of here. The press knows you found the gun. They'll be all over you."

"What?" she said as his hand propelled her across the polished floor and down the hall to the front of the station. She was shocked at all the people just outside on the entrance walkway.

Cameras were thrust into their faces as Art pressed his hand against the large glass door of the police station and shoved. "Later," he said. They faced milling, yelling reporters, who crowded closer.

Melissa turned to him. "But, Dad?" Melissa broke off as she bumped into someone.

"It'll keep." Art said as he pushed her forward into the crowd.

"Are you the girl who found the gun?" a blonde woman asked and thrust a microphone toward Melissa.

"Lieutenant Franklin, over here. Tell us about your daughter finding the murder weapon," a man in a light blue shirt yelled.

Melissa held her palm up to shield her face and the anger that grew at being cut out. Art gripped her elbow tightly wanting to protect her and feeling the human pressure all around.

"Turn off the cameras. There will be a release by our Press Liaison later today," Art said as he stepped in front of some pushy women using his body to shield Melissa. Her head brushed his chest.

51

"Lieutenant Franklin, one question. Can you tell us about the murdered man? Was he one of your detectives?" a woman in a sage green suit asked.

"No," he answered while looking straight at her. With command, Art moved Melissa through the crowd and down the front walk.

"Is it true one of your detectives is dead?" a reporter asked.

He waved to Officer Murphy. "Take her home for me," he said. At the last moment, he grabbed Melissa's upper arm. "The report you typed for me, do you have it with you?" he asked.

"No, why?" she said.

Art's mustache twitched. She moved closer, and he whispered into her ear, "To put in my file, I'll get it tonight." He leaned to kiss her but thought better of it with the cameras so close.

Art helped Melissa get into the front seat. He leaned down, looked through the window past Melissa, and said to Murphy, "Drive safely, stay at the house with her if these people are there too." Murphy nodded. He said, "Melissa, don't answer the door or the phone. I'll be home as soon as I can." He straightened up, lingered at the curb, watching as the unit with Murphy and Melissa cleared the crowd. At that moment Art pushed his way back inside the station.

"What's that all about?" Millie, Chief Miller's secretary, on her way to the court office, asked.

"The media knows Melissa found the gun, and they know she's my kid."

"They love cops in trouble." Her words trailed over her shoulder as her heels clicked on the glossy tile.

His secretary, Tracy stepped alongside Art and kept pace. "The snoops have been calling for over an hour wanting an interview," she said.

"They're already here. Turn Bradley on them. PR is his job, not mine," Art said.

Walt looked up at Art and yawned just as Art walked into his office.

Art saw the gaping mouth, rubbed his hand through his hair, and yawned too. A mumbled, "The media are on about Melissa finding the gun. They smell blood; they get one whiff, and they're on it like dogs on a bone. I told Tracy to get Bradley on it." He moved to his chair and sat heavily down.

"Bradley's a good idea," Walt said. He let his head drop forward, moved his neck to loosen the tension building up. They both heard the popping sound as Walt cracked his neck.

Art cleared his desk of papers. He placed his pen into the holder, surveyed the top of his desk. What else could he do?

Art turned toward his secretary, who was on the phone with her back to him. "I've got the damnedest headache." He stepped to the doorway and drummed his fingers on the doorjamb.

Rubbing his neck area and looking at the floor caused Walt to ask, "Got aspirin?"

Art's back was to Walt as he looked toward the detective's area. "In my drawer," Art said over his shoulder.

"They doing you any good there?" Walt inquired.

Art turned and stared. "Walt, you're mothering me again. Ya got anything I can put into my mouth? Gum?"

Walt stood, "Got a box of raisins," Walt slid his hand into his pocket and extracted the small box.

Art took the raisins, popped the top open, and shook the box. Nothing fell into his palm. Looking into the box Art asked, "How old are these?"

"I don't know. I don't eat the raisins every day."

Art fished in his pockets for his mints but came up with an empty wrapper. He balled up the torn paper and tossed it toward the wastebasket. It fell just short. Anger flashed across his face setting a throbbing in his temples as he reached again for it and missed. He got it, jerked up, and flung it into the trashcan. "I tell you, Walt, I'm just about ready to go back to smoking."

"Your bet still on with Melissa?" Walt asked, his expression mocking Art.

Art had heard from just about everyone that it was a dumb move betting Melissa that he could stop smoking. "Yeah, I don't smoke, Melissa doesn't marry until she's twenty-five."

Walt pushed, "How's it working?" His smile broadened as he saw he'd hit the bulls-eye.

"Well, she's still not married if that's what you mean," Art said, as though he'd listened to just about enough from Walt on this particular subject.

"No, that's not what I mean. Mel's only fifteen, and you need to smoke. You've got ten years ahead of you." Walt sat with his eyes trained upward, "I sure hope you didn't bet anything too expensive."

Art gave him a stern look. "Probably be easier if I smoked and kept a loaded gun just for the guy who thinks he's good enough for her."

Walt gave a half-hearted chuckle and shot back, "You do carry a loaded gun, two, in fact."

"Yeah, well, I meant a special one," Art said smiling at his friend.

"Ah huh, I see, an untraceable piece," Walt said rubbing his hands together.

Art turned to Walt. "You know, Walt, I was so proud of her. She conducted herself like a pro with the chief." He looked away. "I should have told Melissa that before I sent her home."

"Well, I've more good news for you, we got a confession from the Mrs. this afternoon. Her lawyer was with her, and so we can proceed. Nebbiolo Avenue is now a closed case," Walt smiled as Art looked him in the eye.

"When did that happen?" Art asked.

"An hour ago. The wife was talking with her attorney and called us in and gave us a signed statement."

"Motive?"

"Same old one. The husband had something going on the side one time too many, and the little woman ended the affair."

Chapter Eleven

10:35 A.M. July 2

"Mrs. Concord?"

Feisty, ninety-five years young, Wilma Concord rose when she heard her name. Setting her deck of cards aside and grabbing her walker she pulled her frail body up.

"Yes, can I help you?" she answered, working her way to the screen door. Her fingers, twisted with arthritis, circled the metal bar.

A tall, thin gentleman stood silhouetted by sunlight and framed by her wooden screen door. Holding a hat that was at the moment rotating at a snail's pace, he said. "I'm George Helms, Sam's friend." He leaned down and closer to the screen so she could see him better.

He's ill at ease. "Ah, yes," she said. Her round face beamed. "I remember you now." She moved her walker closer and unlatched the old wooden screen door. It had been painted a forest green some years before. It now showed wear and tear as her hand pushed against it near the hook.

He stepped into a room filled with crocheted doilies, antiques, and this tiny woman dressed in blue calico. Wilma's blue-white hair, caught in a bun on top of her head, and sparkling blue eyes welcomed him. "How's the hip? You had just fallen when I last saw you."

She frowned, "It's slow, but I'm coming along. I'm getting used to this dang contraption." Wilma jerked the walker to move it out of the way. She smacked the top of George's right hand as he attempted to help move the walker. "I don't need this damn thing anymore, but the crotchety, old witch doctor insists I use the dang thing."

George rubbed his hand. "I was wondering," he hesitated, looked around the feminine room then back to her, "have you seen Sam lately?"

Wilma paused, rolled her eyes, pouted her lips in thought and said, "Well, the last time I saw him was Wednesday. I think. Come to think of it, the last time I saw him, he was driving away to play cards with you." She looked at him to catch his expression.

"Yes, and that was the last I saw of him. I can't get him on the phone. I just knocked and rang the bell at his house, but he doesn't answer. I wanted to ask him to a barbecue on the Fourth at my place, thought we'd go to the lake and see the fireworks after."

George was tall. Wilma felt like it about broke her neck to look into his face. "That would be nice. Well, when I see him, I'll tell him you were here and to give you a call. You know, since he won all that money, he's been busy. He told me he was seeing his bookkeeper," Wilma said.

George nodded. "But would he be on the Fourth of July weekend? Today's Sunday, I doubt it. It's just strange," he said, smiling at her as he stepped out onto the porch. "It would be odd for him to do that today." Wilma followed him out of the house. George thanked her for her time and said goodbye, then walked to his car. Before he drove, he gazed over the top of his car to look once more at Sam's.

Now curious, Wilma sat in her wicker chair and followed George's gaze toward Sam's place. The heavy weight of the cat's body wound her furry self around Wilma's leg. Slippers mewed. Wilma's crippled fingers found the cat's arched back and slowly rubbed her fur. She knew Sam pretty well, enough that if he were going away, he would tell her. She sat forward, narrowing her eyes. *So, deary, it's strange. Why wouldn't George know where Sam was? It's a mystery.*

Using her walker, Wilma, worked her way across the street. Her finger pressed Sam's doorbell. She listened to the ding-dong sound and thought of Avon Calling. She pushed it again. He wasn't answering. She jiggled the door handle. Locked. Wilma couldn't think what to do, so she made her way back home.

She fixed lunch and placed it on her tray, added a napkin, some iced tea, and two oatmeal cookies she'd made last night. Her kitchen still smelled of cinnamon and raisins all melted together in friendship. Sam liked her cookies and usually came over in the afternoon when she'd serve him something to drink and the cookies. They'd sit out on the porch and catch up on each other's worlds. He hadn't come lately. She thought it was because of the money and all the extra work he was doing.

Looking the tray over for anything missing and deciding the tray was ready she carried it through the dining room and living room, to the front door and her porch. It wasn't a heavy tray but one she'd used her whole married life. For Wilma using this tray was like meeting an old friend, at a determined time, each day. Wilma liked eating among her ferns and geraniums, shaded by birch, elm, and one pine tree growing in the front yard. The birds sang to her while the breeze fanned her and she let the past be the past and the present her whole world.

A sick, heavy scent lingered on the air, fouling her tuna sandwich. The odor came and went, making her unsure if she smelled it at all. She put the half-eaten sandwich down, made a face at it in disgust, and drank her iced tea. "That tastes much better," she said to the empty chair.

A dog howled a long, sorrowful call.

Gayle, her neighbor, drove into her driveway next door, got out of the car, and walked to Wilma's porch railing. She had a scowl on her face. "I just bought out the store. Now I've got to get it all out of the car and into the house." She adjusted her handbag strap over her shoulder and placed her hands on Wilma's porch railing. "Boy, I think I hate shopping."

Wilma nodded. "Gayle, have you seen Sam lately? George, his friend, was just here and said he hadn't heard from him since Wednesday last."

Gayle swung a look at Sam's place, "No, I haven't seen him myself. He's probably busy with his new-found wealth." Gayle sniffed the air. "What's that God awful smell?" Her nose wrinkled. "Some animal must have crawled up and died. I think if it gets any stronger I'll call animal control."

"I smelled that, too," Wilma said then she picked up her sandwich and sniffed, she took a small bite. "It's alright," she said.

"Gosh, just look at the time," Gayle said as she waved and backed away. "See you later. I've got to get dinner going. The kids are coming over this evening."

As she walked away, Wilma turned back to look at Sam's place. She stood and walked back over to his house. Slippers stayed close by Wilma's side as she made her way across the street, this time working her way to the garage where Sam's car waited. Wilma looked slowly from the garage toward the back door. Everything looked right. She walked alongside the back of the house, stepped up on the porch, and turned the knob. The smell hung heavy here.

"Sam, you home?" The walker banged against the doorjamb as she went inside. "Sam, it's me. Whew." She noticed the pots were lying all over the mudroom, not stacked neatly as Sam kept them. Her stomach turned as

59

she saw the mess strewn over the floor. Her heart stopped when she made out Sam's body lying in all the debris, his grotesque form spotlighted by a shaft of sunlight.

Flies circled frantically, buzzing around the body, some crawling over Sam's face and into his gaping mouth. She sucked in her breath, and her jaw dropped open as she looked at the blood spattered over the walls and the ceiling. Her eyes came back and stared at the dark pool where Sam's body rested.

Wilma's hands gripped her walker. There's nothing she could do to help poor Sam. Wilma backed out of the house. "Call the police. Sam's dead!" she yelled.

Gayle came out of her house just as Wilma came around the side of Sam's house carrying her walker and shuffling one white nurse's shoe before the other. "Call the police, Gayle. Sam's dead on the kitchen floor," Wilma waved her hand to hurry.

Gayle rushed back inside and returned to Wilma's side. "I've called the police. He's dead?" she asked.

Wilma nodded, and Slippers meowed frantically. "Gayle, it's horrible. There's blood everywhere. Slippers, stop that. She's been after me all day long." Wilma's eyes went wide, and she looked down at the cat. "Oh, good God, Gayle, she's hungry. Bet she's not been fed since last Wednesday." Sadness engulfed her, and tears flowed down her wrinkled cheeks. "Poor cat," she said as she dabbed tears with her lacy hanky and watched Sam's house. "She's been trying to tell me about Sam all this time."

"Lodi-55, copy traffic, see the woman, reporting party called advising possible 1144." Murphy listened carefully to the address, then remembered the call about five days ago. He knew this was the same place. As he stopped his car in front of the two women, he keyed his transmitter and acknowledged his arrival on the scene. He stepped out of the car and approached the two females.

Murphy judged one to be in her nineties and the other in her sixties.

"Ladies, did you call in the discovery?"

"I did." Gayle pointed toward Wilma. "She's the one who found him." She placed her arms protectively around Wilma's shoulders.

"He's in the house, on the kitchen floor." Wilma's voice trailed off.

"I'm going to ask you ladies to wait here for me." His hands settled on his heavy, black leather duty belt." I'll check it out. Then I'll have some questions for the report." He noticed they watched mutely as he carefully checked the front door and windows. They kept their eyes glued to him as he opened the swinging doors to the garage.

He turned his attention to the interior of the garage. It held a car and various boxed items and some tools. No one was there. He looked back and saw the two women holding each other. John lost sight of them as he moved along the back side of the house. He looked the yard over and saw the garden, just behind the garage, torn and broken. He moved under the cherry tree, walking the same path Sam had taken for almost fifty years to the cement porch. John noticed mud caked on its surface. He placed his foot down judiciously and opened the door and stepped inside. The smell made his bile rise.

John noted the planting pots scattered on their sides. He moved past them, his hand over his mouth to help keep the contents of his stomach from coming up any further. As he placed his foot down it crunched something, and he cringed, knowing he mustn't contaminate the scene. His eyes adjusted and as they did his blood chilled as he looked at that gentle old man. Murphy was fully aware he had spoken with him only days ago. Frozen for the moment, his eyes fixed. Although trained and knowing what to do, he panicked. Swallowing hard, his shaky legs moved closer, fully carrying him into the kitchen. There was no point going over to the body; the man was dead. Tears glossed and ran down his cheeks. Flies buzzed fitfully crawling into the old man's mouth and made John's skin crawl. He had to get out of there now.

John rushed back outside, grabbed the corner post, stepped off the porch, and retched. It came up again. He breathed heavily, then wiped his mouth with the back of his cuff. Robotically he took two deep breaths. His hand shook as he keyed his microphone. In a shaky voice, he said, "Lodi-55, I have a confirmed 1144. Notify the supervisor and detectives. Send two additional units." He swallowed hard, but his stomach emptied again. His knees felt like jelly, green, stinking jelly. How embarrassing. How unprofessional, he chided himself. Deep breaths wouldn't clear his nose. The stench lingered in his nostrils, sharp and sour.

The police academy had seen to it that John viewed his share of pictures displaying violence upon the human body. It was meant to desensitize, but nothing prepared him for the real thing. His view of Sam Nelson's body would forever remain tucked away in his young mind. A dark, nightmarish memory that would come to visit at all the wrong times.

He made himself go back out front, pulling on every hardcore fiber of his being just to get there. *There must have been something I missed that night.* The realization dogged him as he wrapped the roll of crime scene tape around a tree trunk. He pulled the tape from the tree to a hedge and then to a tree in the parkway. He was just walking from that tree to the next when Homicide Detective Walt Culpepper slid his car to a stop. The two extra units Murphy had ordered arrived and the neighbors were beginning to come outside. John handed the tape off to the officer who reached him first and pointed out Wilma and Gayle to his partner. Afterward, he joined Walt to fill him in as they walked.

The older detective bowed forward as he moved. John found himself bending to meet the man as he explained how he had visited here last Wednesday afternoon, around five-thirty and taken a report. "I met Mr. Nelson and walked through the house with him. Everything was satisfactory when I left him."

Walt stopped short, staring at the fresh pile of puke by the porch. His mouth stretched into a grim knowing smile. His hand found the young man's neck and pulled him slightly toward his body. "You did all the right things, kid. You can stay out here and make sure no one else walks through my crime scene."

With that, the detective entered the house, leaving Officer Murphy outside and eternally grateful.

Chapter Twelve

7:45 A.M. July 3, At The Franklin Residence

Balled fist ready to pound, Art hesitated as the radio blared. Melissa would never hear him knock. The message was clear, Drop-dead Dad. *I'd have to hammer the hinges off to get her attention. I'm not going to engage in war with her, not at this level, and not on her turf.* Art relaxed his hand.

The Gruen pinged a warning. Stepping back and seeing the time, he had to leave for his meet with Walt at the new crime scene.

Pausing on his way out the front door, he looked up the landing at her door, tuning in the sounds from her room one last time. He rolled his shoulder blades up, rotating them backward, then took three deep breaths. *Too much coffee this morning. We'll have our talk this evening, young lady, you can bet on that. I'll bring a three-cheese pizza, your favorite. That should smooth the way.* He kept his eyes on her door until the front door blocked his view. Then he tried the door handle to make sure it was locked.

Art pulled his keys from his pocket and drove to the address Walt gave him.

He spotted Walt's car and slipped his unit in behind. "Morning," Art said as he reached Walt. The lawn in the parkway needed mowing Art noticed as he stepped on the grass, and the tips of his shoes almost disappeared. He scanned the neighborhood seeing neat older homes, some Craftsman built. Many trees grew in the front yards hiding a few fences along a block that bent like a fish hook. This home, where he and Walt stood, sat on the straight end of the hook. *Most the houses have wood siding*, he noticed. *They look like homes that have seen their share of games played in the street. They've come full circle to retirement age where the trees matured, the birds are unbothered, and life goes quietly on day by day.*

"Same to you," Walt replied as he unbuttoned his suit jacket. "How are you?"

"I've seen better," Art said, his eyes cast on the pavement. He looked up. "Bad one, huh?" He jerked his head toward the house.

Walt nodded, taking the time to look around the neighborhood before saying, "The worst." He extended his hand offering a roll of mints.

"Thanks," Art said, pulling the mint free of the wrapper. He knew why Walt gave him the mint. The smell of death is often so sickening that sucking on a mint can help keep the stomach down. He could make out the dense, sweet smell already and expected that where they were going it would be dreadful. The breeze built. Art noticed the yellow crime scene tape pick up like a pennant. He slipped the mint into his mouth. "Any leads?" he asked.

Walt looked down the street and said, "Not yet, too soon. My impression, though, might interest you."

"Shoot," Art said as he rolled the mint wrapper closed and handed the candy roll back. They turned toward the house and walked up the driveway.

"One person. He's extremely immature. Possibly the guy's in his mid-twenties." Walt stopped and placed his hand on Art's arm, his eyes narrowed. "This chap, I don't know Art, he's someone full of rage. This guy's scary."

65

"Hmm. I don't like the sound of that. It's a man?" Art asked.

Walt nodded, "You're not going to like anything else about this case. Come. Let's go around back. You know John Boy? John Murphy?" He waited for Art to acknowledge that he knew him. "He caught this one. First time for him, and he lost his cookies."

"Oh, yeah?" Smile lines deepened around Art's eyes and he grinned, "There's always a first time. Nice looking property, for an older home I mean."

Walking up the driveway side of the house almost to the garage, Walt said, "Shit, he barfed up the Rockies by the back door." They were nearing the garage, Walt leaned over and grabbed the garage door handle and pulled. "It's clean." The door swung easily, and they stood looking at the car parked inside.

Art asked, "Walt, you didn't answer me earlier when I asked how you were?"

"I'm not going to make it." Walt stood a long moment then continued. "At least, that's the way it sounds to me."

"You're going for treatment?" Art asked as he looked at a neatly coiled hose and tools hung in a line.

"I doubt it. Just let it run its course," Walt said, as he studied a ladder hanging in the rafters. "Will you look at that old ladder? My grandfather had one like it. It's got to be a hundred years old if it's a day.

"Walt, I don't want another partner. You're my man." Art noticed and appreciated the round rungs each step of the ladder had.

Walt's voice saddened. "This isn't anything I want either, but it is what it is. They want to do tests because of the pain."

"Doesn't sound good."

Walt shut the heavy garage door securing the latch. "We have some good prints in the garden, behind the garage, and in the house." Walt started for the walkway to the garden as Art followed. "For some reason, he trashed the vegetable garden. Looks like a war zone."

"Appears he was looking for something buried," Art said looking at the broken zucchini stalks. He shook his head in disbelief.

"The vic just won the lottery." Walt turned to peer into Art's face waiting for his reaction.

Art's eyebrows shot up. "Bingo."

They turned toward the back door, and Walt nodded as they continued walking, "We didn't find any evidence of a break-in. This perp must have entered the house by the back door."

"Someone Nelson knew?" Art asked.

"Distinct possibility," Walt said. They walked under the cherry tree. "This is an old tree." Both their eyes followed the trunk up into the branches, "Look at the size of this thing."

The two stopped within ten feet of the porch. "Nelson took good care of his property," Art said then observed. "There's a lot of work for an old man. Could be he hired some help, and they decided to give themselves a raise."

"We have one witness. Wilma Concord, the woman who lives across the street. She saw something on the afternoon of the 28th of June. But she's not sure what. She also found the body." Walt paused a moment for Art to catch up for the next bit of information. "She's ninety-five," he said.

Art brought his bottom lip over the top one, pulling down the hairs growing there and said, "Hmm, We have an interview with her?"

"Working on it," Walt told him.

"Okay, let's go inside."

"Murphy found the back door was open. Mrs. Concord said it was open when she entered. We got the call yesterday about 3:30 p.m. while you were in Sacramento, so I took the lead." Walt yawned as he pulled his notepad out and thumbed through the pages. "Murphy was rolling, arriving 3:35 p.m. He spoke with Mrs. Wilma Concord and her neighbor, Mrs. Gayle Crenshaw. Both women knew the vic and had lived in this neighborhood several years. Mrs. Crenshaw said she didn't see anything."

Walt pointed. "Notice the dried mud? Mud's all over the cement porch, and inside the mudroom." Walt used his notepad, pushing the door open so Art could see better. "There's a pretty good footprint just behind the door. It looks like someone stood there a while. It doesn't match any of Mr. Nelson's footwear, but it's exactly like several in the disturbed garden soil. So we can place the perp in the garden and inside the house. We got one real interesting print on the wall across from the bathroom. I think the son-of-a-bitch hauled his ass up there and was in the attic crawl space when Murphy went through the house with the vic. I bet you anything he was there when Murphy came in answer to Mr. Nelson's request concerning a burglary on the 28th of June."

"Handprint?" Art asked looking into Walt's eyes.

"Nope, foot. It's weak, but it matches the molds we made from the mud room and the garden."

"Make of shoe?" Art asked as they arrived at the back door.

"A running shoe," Walt answered then pulled his latex gloves from his pocket.

Art followed suit and the snap from Art's gloves followed Walt's in seconds.

"Yep, lab's working on the manufacturer now," Walt said. "Okay, you ready?"

Art grabbed Walt's pants at the belt by his spine. "Yep, let's do it." The men moved into the house with Art placing his feet exactly where Walt just stepped.

Walt said, "After applying woulda, coulda, shoulda I've some sense of what happened."

"Whew, he was ripe," Art said moving the mint around in his mouth. "Nobody boiled coffee?"

"Uh huh," Walt said pointing toward the floor about two feet from the stove. "The body was there. You can see the rage in this guy from this mess. We couldn't use the Vic's coffee; it was all over the floor."

Art swung his gaze taking in the drawers thrown down on the linoleum. Kitchen items were strewn everywhere, frozen food melting. The only clean space was where Sam had been. "Someone's going to have to boil a lot of coffee to get the stench out of here."

"Yeah. It was the vic's hoe. Looks like, from the blood spatters, that the perp came at him from the mud room. When you and I come back through this way, you'll see the guy we're looking for is around five-foot-ten and on the skinny side. He left a clear blood spatter, outlining his body, on the wall," Walt said.

Art nodded his head as Walt explained the directions the investigation had taken and his early conclusions.

"I think it went down like this. This guy shows up with no good on his mind. He can't find what he wants; it makes him crazy. Nelson comes in, sees the mess. Maybe scaring him, maybe getting mad at the mess in the kitchen, and maybe he confronted the perp, which forced him to act. It's not a planned homicide. I believe it's a crime of passion." Walt said as he stopped to catch his breath. "Just look at the damage to this place. He would have had to be in the house for a long time."

Art shook his head and said, "It's senseless."

"I've got the time of death at about 9:30 p.m. to midnight, I don't have it solid yet from the coroner, but it's coming."

They were through the kitchen and almost to the hallway to the bedrooms and the bath. The room to the left was the living room. Walt and Art stopped in the doorway.

"Perp leave anything behind?"

"We're not sure yet. We're going to be sifting for a long time," Walt answered.

"Do we know Nelson's whereabouts during his last twenty-four hours?" Art asked as he saw old knick-knacks resting on their sides clearly out of place.

"Ah, we have his whole day documented. The last activity we know of was on Wednesday, the 28th. He went to the Senior Center. Mrs. Concord saw him drive away from home about 8:45 P.M. Careful there," Walt pointed out some broken glass. "He came home, putting him here at about 9:30 p.m."

"Yeah, that's what I think," Art said. "Who was last to see or talk to him?" Art glanced around at the cushion material draped over the recliner. The springs in the couch caught the glare of the overhead light. Curios lay smashed where they landed against the far wall, their remains in bits and pieces.

"We're working on that," Walt said.

"Let's see the bedrooms," Art said.

Walt stopped for a moment by the footprint on the hall wall to let Art view the smudge. "We're working on identifying the maker of the cotton gloves. It's a long shot, though, they're sold nationally. We've ruled out Nelson owning that type of cotton gloves."

"Good, and keep the info on the three ones quiet. We'll withhold that piece of information," Art said making a note of the mess in the bedrooms.

They circled back. "You have photos for me?" Art asked.

"Being processed. You'll have them today," Walt answered.

They stood staring a long moment at the kitchen wall with the door to the mud room, and the blood spatters that outlined the perp. "You're right. A skinny, five-foot-ten did all this." Art looked at Walt's tired expression. "You need sleep. Why don't you take off? I'll sign you out." Art patted Walt on the shoulder.

"Thanks," Walt said nodding his head, "I'm tired."

Chapter Thirteen

10:30 A.M., July 3, Back in Lodi

Ray watched as Allison jumped out of Ray's Ford and unlocked the roll up door on their storage unit. As Roland gathered their things from the back seat, he told Ray to be back here in a week. Or they would be going without him.

"I'll be back, man," Ray said with assurance.

Roland told him they were going to get some extra dough tomorrow at the lake. Then they'd start collecting names and addresses for the scam. He asked Ray if he was sure about Nelson being the name.

"Uh-huh," Ray answered. He reached for the folded newspaper and handed it to Roland. "There's a picture of the old geezer holding the check."

Roland clutched the paper. He said he hoped they'd be done by the time Ray got back. If not they would call his Grandmother and leave a message. Otherwise, Roland said, they'd wait for him by the tables at Lodi Lake about 9:00 p.m. He backed away from the car waving the newspaper at Ray.

"Sounds good," Ray said tapping the accelerator, revving the Ford's engine.

"You're going home now? What are you going to tell your grandmother?" Roland yelled.

"I'll tell her that I drove you up to Tahoe, and we stayed until this morning. She'll believe me. It's cool. I don't give a damn what she thinks," Ray yelled back.

"Yeah, sure," Roland said as he turned away.

Ray could tell his grandma pretty much the truth. *The little matter of my whereabouts on the night of the 28th can stay a mystery forever, as though it never happened. That's the way it's going to be as soon as I can dump the stuff in the black bag.*

At the same time in Lieutenant Franklin's office.

Lieutenant Art Franklin's voice cut sharply, "Tracy?"

Twenty-nine, stylish, wearing a burgundy dress with silver accessories Tracy swung her body around to face him. Hoop earrings, dangled inches from a necklace to match, twisted freely. Her makeup flawless and her lips the color of her dress made her look as though she'd just stepped out of makeup at some fancy store. "Yeah?" she answered, returning his mood in kind and every bit one of the guys.

"Where's my aspirin?" he demanded staring at her as though she had done something with them.

Her shoulders dropped, she pushed back from her keyboard and swung her rolling chair. She had great legs, and her black patent leather pumps showed off well-turned ankles. Even though they were several feet apart, they were, for that moment, eye to eye. She spoke low and controlled, "For the umpteenth time, top drawer, like always."

"Yeah, yeah," he said sounding annoyed. He jerked the drawer handle as though to prove her wrong and saw the aspirin right up front and in plain sight. He picked up the bottle and shook two out feeling Tracy's presence almost as soon as her fragrance reached his side.

Tracy handed him a glass of water. She said, "Take that aspirin before your headache gets any worse."

Art looked into her face and smiled a weak thank you. He considered the narrow shape of his secretary's head, which seemed like it might have been molded while in a vise. It reminded him of a bird's head, the nose so like a beak. He wasn't making fun of her. He enjoyed finding likenesses of people and animals. A part-time hobby, he used to relax. The bird-like sense of her ended with the appearance. She was a tigress guarding his office. He'd had occasion to appreciate her talent in that area more than once since she'd come to work for him.

"Melissa called," Tracy said, "Quote, 'Tell Dad.'" She reached into her pocket for a folded piece of paper. Her fingers sparkled with silver rings. One rested above the knuckle on her left thumb. "'I'm going over to Sandy's tonight. Her mother has gone out of town, and she doesn't want to be alone.' I'll leave this on your desk. It's got her phone number. Don't lose it." She set it down and pressed her forefinger on the notepaper.

Art brought his brows together. *Damn. Face it. The kid's ducking me royally. Well, so much for a father and daughter talk over pizza tonight.*

"Thanks, Tracy," he said in acknowledgment. Then made an effort to raise his spirits. "Get your pad, Gal."

Tracy returned with pad and pen, looking at Art as she sat down.

"This is for Bradley in public relations. On July 2nd, a body, you can get the address from records, was discovered in a Lodi residence. You can get the full name of the victim and spelling too," Art said.

Tracy nodded as she wrote.

"The homicide appears to have occurred in late June." Art looked at Tracy and said, "Now we need to get info out to the agencies in the five western states asking for any similar cases. Tell them that this killer used a hoe and chopped at the body several times, leaving a bloody scene. We believe the murder happened after the vic's property was trashed, every single room in the house and the vic's garden."

A pencil tucked above her ear waited. She turned a page and looked over her glasses for reassurance that she had heard him correctly.

"Yep, tore the garden to pieces. This perp's a real ass. There's one piece of evidence that we're withholding, so let them know we have something in the hole on this one." He saw her nod as she wrote. "I guess that'll cover it for now. Except, it looks like this all went down while we were at the Nebbiolo Avenue scene the other night." Art looked at the clock. "Tell Oliver to step in here, will you?"

Tracy found the detective and told him to see Art.

Art caught Oliver's approach out of the corner of his eye. "You seem well rested from your two weeks off. Did your family have a nice time?" Art asked.

"We sure did. We went to Disneyland. I think I rode every ride twice. For a little while I was a kid again," Oliver said.

"Great. It's good to get away. I remember taking Melissa there when she was five or six. Her face lit up, and she loved that mouse. In fact, she still has her mouse ears." The room quieted as Art took a long pause. "Well, Dennis, are you ready to get back into the harness?"

"You bet. What's popping?" Oliver said sitting down across from Art.

"We've got a new homicide. I want you to head up the team, two or three guys, to canvas the neighborhoods four blocks deep around the victim's house. Someone saw something. I want you to find him," Art said.

As Oliver stood to leave, Art handed him the Nelson report and said, "You'll need this."

"Tracy, any pictures yet?" he yelled.

"Got them right here," Tracy answered.

Art watched her pick up the envelope from her desk and walk it to him.

He opened the envelope, and both the color and black and white photos slid out, landing across his blotter. Art read the report accompanying the pictures carefully. They were dry, fact-filled lists of items with their locations and positions as well as the condition when found. *Somewhere in here is a thread that will lead me to the scumbag.*

Tracy just sat at her desk when he called out, "Williams... I want to see him now."

Art looked at Tracy as she pushed her wheeled secretarial chair backward and gave a thumbs-up point toward Art's office.

The slap of Williams' feet on the tiled surface announced his approach a few seconds before he draped his long, lanky body against Art's doorjamb.

"Good. Head out and attend the Nelson Post," Art said to him. Art watched Bill's nose wrinkle. Bill hated this detail, certain he'd pulled it more than most. He'd told Art that some time ago. *Maybe, Bucko, that's why you're going again,* Art suppressed a smile and said, "It's scheduled to begin at noon. Make sure you tape the commentary as the coroner works. Don't miss a thing, Bill. In fact, take notes, just in case your recorder takes a dive again."

"Gotcha," Bill said. He disconnected himself from the doorjamb and sauntered away.

The aspirin was beginning to dull the throb in Art's temples. He read the reports once more. He doubted the killer would strike again, which was good, on the one hand, bad on the other. If he drops off the face of the earth, the case is never solved. It goes cold. Finally, he put the reports down and looked at the pictures, spreading them out to make a story of the facts. It was the first time he'd seen Sam's body in the surrounding clutter.

Tell me your story, Sam.

"Tracy?"

"Yes?"

"Tell everyone who worked last night I'm calling a briefing in half an hour and to get their butts here, all but Walt. Is there a chance you could get me a sandwich and Coke? I'm starved. Then let the chief know I'll be ready to see him at 11:45. I need the crime lab on the line now."

At Ray's Grandparents Home.

It was eleven a.m. when Ray entered the kitchen. The house remained quiet, so he walked toward his room and gathered some clean clothes. His dirty clothes fell in small piles leading toward the bathroom. He drug his feet into the shower and let the warm water rain over him, washing away the bad feelings, leaving only exhaustion. He lathered up until suds ran down his back. Ray's shoulder muscles were taut, and he cracked his neck. *Where shall I dump the crap? I can't go too far, I don't have the money, and I've got to hook up with Allison and Roland by Friday.*

He turned and let the water strike his face and ears. Ray finished his shower and stepped out onto the rug, allowing the water to sheet off. *I'll get a map book and find a lake on the western side of the US of A. Most everything I need is in the garage.*

Ray dressed, then laid on his bed. *I promised to go to the lake for the fireworks with Gram tomorrow. Grandpa will be fishing all day, so I'll have to take the old lady. I can't get out of it.* He yawned and drifted off to sleep.

Clattering in the kitchen roused him, he yawned, stretched. *I might as well get this over.*

Chapter Fourteen

1:35 P.M. Monday, July 3

Ray staggered to the kitchen doorway and leaned against the doorjamb. He could see by his grandmother's stance that the fight was about to begin. He just knew it, knew her.

She spoke first, saying that she wondered when he was going to get up. Asking what he'd been doing. Emily busied herself at the sink, wiping the countertop off. She turned toward Ray when he didn't answer.

He yawned and scratched his mussed hair. "I was with Allison and Roland. We went to Tahoe," Ray said.

He heard the sneer in her voice when she said, "Those two."

Ray took an insolent stance and sized his Grandmother up. She was dumpy, short, and silly looking in that housedress. Her run down white socks that rolled down by the ankles to her running shoes. She had Kleenex coming out of her apron pocket for her allergies. Her hair would have been white if she didn't color it dark brown. He tried to ward off his feelings about her, so he changed the subject. "You're not going to believe this, but they got married, and I was their best man."

Emily stopped cleaning and turned to him. "You're kidding?" Her voice sounded as though she didn't believe it at all.

He brightened, and said. "Get this. I wore a tux."

She said something about liking to see that for herself, then with an incredulous expression, she asked, "Any pictures?"

It was all over her face, her doubt in what he was saying. He could read her mind. Now her mouth was working with that old line about him finding his niche in life.

She pointed, "Hand me that bowl. That's the road to true happiness, that and a darn good job."

He handed her the yellow mixing bowl, then drew a glass of water.

They were exchanging words in an older kitchen. The cabinets were wood painted yellow with fern green trim and pulls. The sink top was narrow and long and covered with a dark brown streaked patterned linoleum. An old stainless steel sink, with a bright green plastic scrubber, sitting in a strainer by the old faucet, sat in the middle of the counter space. The floor, a checked pattern linoleum of beige and browns, had a bright shine. Her table sat in the middle of the kitchen. Even though the space was outdated, it was clean and serviceable and, most of all, homey.

Emily set the bowl in the cupboard and shook out her tea towel. Her tone was authoritarian as she continued. "You rarely pursue employment, and when you do find a job, something always goes wrong." She turned towards him, "You want something to eat?"

"No," he said.

"I don't get it, Ray. No young woman worth her salt is going to be interested in a man with no future." Her eyes strayed to the window. She put her hands on her hips. "Ray, your Grandfather and I are not going to be around forever. Mark my words, you hang around with those two, and you're heading for trouble."

Here it comes. He changed the subject. "Yeah, I don't have any, but they do," he said.

She lifted the damp dishrag and wiped the faucet then turned back to him and asked, "What?"

"Pictures of me in a tux," he said innocently.

"Oh. See if you can get a copy. I'll put it in our album." Emily opened the refrigerator. She paused, then grasped the container of milk. She walked back to the table and poured a glass. Setting it before him, she said, "Drink that, Ray. You look like you need it. You didn't go boozing, did you?" she asked.

"Milk, ick. I had champagne," Ray said.

She opened the refrigerator door and replaced the milk. "Don't make a habit of it. You must know your parents wouldn't be happy."

Ray's eyes shot up to the ceiling. *My parents died in a car accident when I was eight months old. I have no faces in my memory bank. I can't believe she still thinks of them like they mattered.* He didn't say any of it. Instead, he dreaded what would come next. She always brought this up just before the big speech. *Oh God, not again.* "Gram, I'm over twenty-one. You can't tell me what to do anymore."

Emily's eyes widened, her face inched closer to his, and she said, "Hello, bucko, news flash, you're still under our roof. I can damn well tell you to jump off that roof, and you'd better do it."

Ray slammed down the glass of milk, stood, grabbed the chair back, lifting the chair off the floor, then roughly shoved it into the table. The loud sound of wooden legs, as they met the floor, came with his next word. "Bullshit. I don't want no fucking job that pays minimum wage. Why don't you get that?" he yelled.

Emily jumped. Her voice raised, and resentment dripped off each syllable. "You know, Ray, Allison and Roland have always meant trouble, and if you hang around with them, you may be caught up in something unspeakable."

"I thought the subject was me working. I told you, we weren't in any trouble. Gram stop thinking like that." He was looking straight at her and softened the look in his eyes and calmed his voice. "They got married," he said with his most pleasing smile.

"Yes, I know. Still, I have a hard time thinking anything nice about those two. How'd you come to meet up with them this time?" she asked.

Tired of this inquisition, his temples pounded, Ray's voice registered low and adamant. "I went to the lake, and Allison was there. We met up with Roland. Then we went to Nevada." He congratulated himself; it was true. He stared at her.

Emily said, "Well, just the same, I don't want you running with them."

Ray moved toward her, flashing that winning smile that always melted her heart. "You worry too much." He leaned down and kissed her cheek.

She looked into his eyes, smiled, rubbed his jaw with the back of her hand, and told him to sit down.

I've got to sweet talk her until I can figure out how I'm going to get out of here. It's the only way to shut her up.

She poured herself a coffee and came to sit across from him, stirring sugar into her cup. She brought her eyes up looking him over. "Ray, you're a hard worker when you work. I don't understand why you don't have a job."

His fingers rubbed the temples, "Gram, not again," he said.

"Yes, again. It's important. You have skills and talent. I don't understand why you don't get it that everyone works."

He took his fingers away and looked at her, "Gram, let it go. Not everyone works for peanuts all their lives.

82

That's the way you and Gramps did it. That doesn't mean it's right for me."

"As long as it's honest money, Ray." Her face brightened as she said, "Oh, we're due at the lake for a picnic with the Williams and the Applegates at noon."

Ray cringed.

"Now don't start that."

Ray looked down, knowing there was no way to get out of spending the day with a bunch of old people. "Why can't Gramps go with you?"

"You know why." She finished her coffee, stood with her mug and walked around the table toward the sink, and leaving the mug on the counter, she turned and rumpled his hair. "He goes fishing every year at this time. You've always been my fellow for the Fourth of July," she said smiling at him.

July Fourth, 9:00 P.M.

Emily reached for Ray's hand, bent her knee and allowed her body to sink onto the blanket she'd spread. The lake area, now full of people, hummed with their voices. Some unhappy baby let everyone know how badly he or she needed care. Others laughed, and the warm evening lingered as the clock ticked closer to the appointed time of illumination.

Emily, dressed in a cotton print she'd ironed this morning, pulled at the neckline. "Thank you, honey, this is nice. Now, Ray, I just need you for a few days. You be a nice boy and help your Gram. You know it's almost hot enough for a fan." Emily reached up and pulled at her collar again then smiled at her friends.

Ray glared at her. He leaned over enough to touch her shoulder. Then he whispered, "I said I had to go, Grams. Why can't you leave it at that?"

She shot a look at her friends and saw they were looking away, "Ray, all I'm asking for is two more days," she whispered through clenched jaws and set lips.

Everyone turned westward, waiting for the night to darken. A breeze brought warm air to circulate then leave, allowing the summer heat to linger.

The crowd hushed momentarily as the first boom sounded. Burnt powder scent filled the air as the sky lit up to collective oohs and ahs. Ray watched the brilliance color the dark sky. *She has no control over me.* A slight smile played at his lips with the thought.

Chapter Fifteen

8:00 A.M. July 5, At The McNamara Home.

Early Wednesday morning, Emily rushed into the kitchen holding the newspaper out to Ray, "Oh, my God, look at this!"

Man Murdered in His Lodi Home

As Ray read the headline, his fork dropped from his hand. The story was about the old man. He turned away from his grandmother, her voice cutting through as his heart pounded. *I should have packed the car last night.*

Ray jerked up from the table leaving his half-eaten pancakes and rushed down the hall. As he went through the entryway to his room, he swung the door shut. It missed closing by a fraction of an inch. Trembling all over and not knowing what to do next, he sat on the side of his bed. *Everything's closing in on me.*

Emily pushed the door partly open reading loud enough for him to hear.

Exactly eight months after Lodi's first double homicide, a man, was found murdered in his home July 3rd. Police officials soon ruled out suicide and they classified the death of Sam Nelson, 81, as a

> homicide, said spokeswoman,
> Gayle Fairspin.

"Are you listening to me?" She pushed the door fully open and continued reading as she walked to the foot of his bed.

> It appears that there was a struggle
> inside the home, Fairspin said.
> Describing it as a very bloody
> scene, no motive has yet been
> determined. Officials have no suspects
> as of the night of July third, though they
> are following leads."

"Can you believe this?" Emily pushed the paper toward Ray.

> Neighbors suspected foul play when
> they had not seen Sam Nelson for
> about a week and they smelt an
> unpleasant odor emanating from the
> residence.

"I'll just bet they did, at this time of the year. It wouldn't take too long for him to ripen up, that's for sure. Hey, what's wrong with you? Why are you just sitting there like that? Don't you care that someone's going around killing old people and leaving them to rot in their homes?"

Hate radiated from his eyes.

She turned her attention to an article about the homicide on Nebbiolo Avenue. Pictures of Melissa and Art Franklin, Lieutenant of Homicide, Lodi Police Department, took the center of the paper.

"Oh my goodness. There're two murders! Ray, do you know what that means? You can't go now, not with

Grandpa out fishing. He won't be home, and you can't leave me here alone."

He rushed past her, into the kitchen grabbed the cookie jar, flipped off the cap, and took a handful of bills. He pushed out the back door while jamming them into his front pocket.

Emily was right behind him as he headed toward the garage. "Ray, what are you doing? You can't take money from the cookie jar. That's our emergency fund."

Ray felt her hand grab at the back of his shirt. "Leave me alone," he roared.

She ran to keep up with him, "What's going on?" she asked.

"Stay out of it."

Emily was right on his heels as they crossed the yard together. Her eyebrows knitted as she watched him gathering camping gear. He dropped the equipment near the back of his car and went back to get the lantern and inflatable boat.

"What's wrong with you?" she asked again as he came back and shoved the items into the back seat.

His smoldering eyes riveted hers, "Just go inside and leave me alone. Get out of my way, old woman."

She took a step back staring at him.

Shaking, he opened the car trunk and tried to jam the camping apparatus in alongside the black garbage bags. Nothing wanted to fit, so he shoved the bags to make room, it didn't help.

"What's all that?" She said pointing to the trash bags.

"Nothing, just trash."

"Well, you sure don't need to haul it around. You'll have more room if we take it out of there." She said as she grabbed the bag holding the bloody clothing.

Ray's fingers wrapped around her wrist squeezing.

"Let go, Ray. That hurts, let go. I'll toss this in the trash."

"No." He placed his hand on her shoulder and shoved, forcing her away from his body.

Emily dug her heels in and pulled away from him. "Why are you acting this way? Just what the hell is going on here, Ray? What do you have in this bag? You tell me now!"

The contents were bound to be on the ground soon, and Ray couldn't let that happen. He jerked the bag.

Her nails ripped into the plastic as she tightened her grip. "Ray, stop this, let go of this bag. I want to see what you have here," she said.

"No," he said.

"Now you listen to me, young man. Let go of my wrist."

He held on, increasing the pressure as she winced in pain.

"Why are you doing this? What's your big rush to go camping?"

Ray bent her fingers backward.

"Ouch." She said and finally let go.

Ray propelled the plastic bag back into the car's trunk and bringing the lid down, he locked the trunk. As things quieted between them, they turned toward the house. The phone was ringing.

Emily, angry to the bone, turned her back on him and marched toward the back door, her head high, her skirt flipping up with each step. "You be right there when I get back."

Ray sat in the car watching her back as she hurried, "Like hell, I will." His foot slammed the accelerator and for a second the tires spun then smoked. Peeling off the lot, he headed for the gas station.

After he had fueled up, he bought a copy of today's paper. As the clerk dropped the change in his hand, he studied the young girl in the picture. He found her name, and he made a note to himself that she was a cop's kid. *That's not good.*

Ray laid everything on the seat opposite him, then reached for the map book. He flipped it to the general page showing all the states and chose Oregon.

Chapter Sixteen

8:52 A.M. July 5

A rt's footfall added cadence as he jogged among tall trees, some spreading liquid amber, medium elms, and mauve crape myrtles. He moved easily over a quiet, restful street in the heart of town lined with homes left by the earliest settlers. Several built of brick, many of boards, some with columns while others had grand porches. Each with their story.

He favored this street and this time to exercise under the welcomed shade these trees offered. Sweat stained his dark blue T-shirt under his arms and down the center of his back and his chest. He snatched the white towel from around his neck and wiped his head and face.

With peripheral vision, he realized a car paced him. He twisted his neck to see. It was Walt in his unmarked, white unit. He had something; Art knew, and he was feeling crowded like he wanted Walt to fade away and let him have this small amount of time alone.

Where I can think is all I want, a few minutes to run, to clear my head, to organize my day, to stay sane. To stay sane, nice trick. Shit, in half an hour I will be at my desk. Can't that business just wait fifteen more measly minutes?

Right now, the subject was Melissa. Every time he thought he had her figured out, he realized he was wrong.

Truth be known, she was driving him nuts. A fifteen-year-old had the best of him.

She was a good girl. Art knew that. It was just when something like this gun divides us... Art stopped the thought. I lost it the other day, plain and simple.

He was the adult, what he says should go, period. There's the rub. She's not a little girl anymore. She's stepping out into her world, and I'm not going to be able to protect her from what comes. *I won't be able to protect her anymore!*

Walt leaned across the front seat and yelled, "Hey, Art."

Art kept on going.

When he could, Walt brought his car back alongside. "What the hell, Art?"

"Yeah?" Art stopped abruptly and walked up to the car window. "What?" he snapped.

Seeing the look of exasperation on Art's face, Walt changed, "You going to stop anytime soon?"

Art looked around at the manicured lawns, the rose trees lining walkways. The only sound at the moment was Walt's car. He checked the time and answered. "About ten minutes."

The steering wheel squeezed Walt's stomach. He huffed as he said, "You said you wanted the information as soon as it came in."

"Concerning?" Art said grabbing the ends of the towel and wiping his forehead and cheeks.

"The pictures from the bird Gilbert had up the night of the 28th," Walt said.

Art nodded, he understood, "And?"

"There're no unknowns parked in a three-block radius around the Nelson property on or about the afternoon or evening of the 28th," Walt said.

"I'd hoped that the helicopter that was up that night might have captured this perp's vehicle." Art said as he sobered and took a long look at his old partner's face. "You're breathing like you were the one running. Why are you still working? Aren't you a couple of hours over on the clock?" Art asked.

"Yeah, but this was coming up," Walt said tapping the report.

Art looked at Walt's perspiring upper lip. The bags under his eyes hung low, every line in his face contrasted. "You okay?" Art said, then he smiled at Walt. "Did you figure how you were going in for the test?"

"Naw, I checked on a taxi, but the hospital told me they wouldn't release me to use a taxi. Dumb rule," Walt said.

Art placed both hands on the top of the car as he leaned into the opened window, "So?"

"So, get off my back," Walt said, his cheeks flushed.

Art looked up the street, then back at Walt. "I'll be your driver. Just let me know when."

"Maybe I don't want to know," Walt said as he rubbed the steering wheel.

"Yeah, I know. We've lost enough good men around here lately. Don't add to my personnel problems," Art said.

Walt placed the file on the car seat, "It's my gut, and somehow this is now about you?"

Art rose, smacked the car's roof for emphasis. "You know it seems we've been together too long, we fight like we're married," he said then took off jogging.

He left Walt watching him jog away while he pondered his remark. Art was a car length ahead when Walt realized he hadn't told him everything. He hit the accelerator. "Hey," he yelled.

"Now what?" Art said and kept his head high as though to ignore the voice.

"All the first neighborhood reports are in." Walt did his best to see Art's face, but it bounced just beyond his view. "Hey, if you're going to ignore me, I'll go home.

Leaning over like this is killing my back, I'll see you later," Walt yelled.

"Wait." Art said and stopped. He took the towel from his neck and wiped his face. He stood on the street for just a moment. At that point, he got into the car. "Okay, you can tell me everything while you drive me home. You get some rest and make that appointment. There's an outside chance you have nothing to worry about, and we could know that."

"Okay, Art. There's no point in arguing with you. Boy, I'll be glad when we get the Delta breeze back, this is one sticky morning." He wiped his face with his handkerchief.

"Glad we agree." Art settled himself in the seat and plopped the damp towel on his lap. "Shoot."

Walt started the car for Art's place, saying, "Samuel Torrance Nelson, 81. No arrests, no warrants, a widower, owned his home, free and clear. Had lived in the neighborhood for fifty years, an upstanding citizen. Had no money problems."

Art turned, "Except one. Nelson won eleven million in the lottery."

"Big one." Walt agreed, "He had friends and no enemies. We've canvassed the neighborhood for two blocks around his house. Not one word came up that would lead us to believe he had problems in his community. This guy retired from the post office, spent twenty years as Lodi's postmaster. It appears that no one was hired to do odd jobs around the property." Walt's eyes met Art's. "There's just nothing about this man that sticks out, except that eleven million dollars."

"Big Money problem."

Chapter Seventeen

12:00 P.M. July 5

T he Hot Tamale, a small Mexican restaurant with its architecture right out of old San Antonio and the Alamo, was Art's favorite spot. A shaded tunnel dripping with magenta bougainvillea covered the entryway. Only a few cars were parked in the lot today as Art pulled in next to Lieutenant Gilbert's city unit. *I'll say hi to Gil then sit alone.*

There were times lately when Art seriously doubted his ability to parent. Now he was wondering, worrying, and second-guessing the decision he'd made fifteen years ago to raise Melissa as a single parent. He was so damn sure of himself then. When he took the baby from Evie's arms and walked out of that hospital, he was on top of the world. He believed that his offspring would have the world at her feet. His youngster would grow up knowing he loved her. His child would be perfect. He wouldn't make all the dumb moves that mess a kid up.

What a difference fifteen years can make. Back then he was naive. He knew that now. He understood a lot of things now. Then he'd had the guts to be a father, where were those guts now when he needed them?

Was he wrong, was Evelyn right? No. Emphatically no! He couldn't imagine life without Melissa in it and couldn't fathom how Evelyn could go on without having Melissa close. Evelyn never wanted children, said so up front. When she found she was pregnant, she insisted on abortion. Nothing was going to change her mind. She wanted her life unaffected by children.

My God, how Melissa has enriched my life, he thought. He remembered pleading for the baby's life. He promised Evelyn wouldn't need to do anything, ever. She was free. He'd kept his word, but lately, he wished there was another parent in the mix.

"I hate you," drifted down the hallways of his mind as he thought back on the day Melissa brought the weapon home. Slowly, he shook his head. A deep sadness enveloped him as he stared at the cobblestone walk and the welcome mat at the front entry of the Hot Tamale. *If I make a botch of rearing Melissa, I'll never forgive myself.*

Art pulled the heavy glass door and stepped inside the dimly lit restaurant. A tinny-sounding horn blaring staccato notes filled the air. It made him smile as he glanced around the room. Glazed pottery filled with flowers decorated every nook and contrasted with framed black and white photos, figures out of Mexico's revolutionary history. The Hot Tamale was his favorite place in town, and as close to the coziness of a bar Art allowed himself. After all, he had his good name to protect. His booze would wait for him in his private bar at home. His mood lifted.

"Hola, *Senor*, what can I getcha?" Carlos, a youth with a Bronx accent asked.

"My usual," Art answered, pulling bills from his wallet.

"I'll bring it to your table. You gonna sit with the other cop?" Carlos asked.

Art nodded.

Carlos made change and handed it to Art, as he took the money he heard fat hit the grill and begin to sizzle. His lunch was only a few minutes away. Art walked over to the drink machine, chose a diet coke, put the lid on the container. He drew a straw out of the holder then walked to Gil's table.

"Hey, how's it going?" Art asked as he slid into the booth. His counterpart had a pained expression, and Art decided to stay a little longer with this man.

Gilbert looked up at Art and said. "You haven't heard yet." He held a napkin over his mouth. "Raven's been missing for over a week."

Art counted the days back, around the 28th of June. *Shit.* "What was he doing?"

"Same stuff, undercover. He went under about ten months ago." Gil wiped his mouth as he answered.

"Yeah, I remember." Art said, slipping the cover off his straw.

"He's been working the same four druggies almost six months. They were paying off real good. I thought we had everyone sewn up and called the raid. The OP date set. Somehow, the word got out. It must have been someone Raven was running." Gilbert said.

Gil carried a worn expression. Art knew how hard it was to be responsible for others' lives. He felt his pain.

"When we rushed the place, it was empty, not a soul in the place. We must have spooked them. The only problem is, we don't have a clue where they went or where Raven is." Gil said as he pushed his plate aside, wadded the napkin, and took a deep breath.

"You should have seen the cash they left behind, piled on a table in the back bedroom. We counted over 500 K. They left the windows open. Anyone could have gone in there and taken whatever they wanted." He put his elbows on the table and let his hands cover his mouth, speaking through his fingers. "Raven was to be on the scene when we arrived. We were going to arrest him, too." He hung his head and shook it slowly. "I don't know. I don't like it. It just feels wrong. He would have made contact by now, nothing," he said. Lieutenant Gilbert hung his head.

Art didn't know what to say. "Any contact with his girlfriend?" he asked.

"She's haunting us. The woman's been on the phone and in my office constantly. She knows shit."

"This is the place on Garnet?"

"Yeah," Gil answered.

"The raid was set to go down on June 28th?" Art asked.

"Yeah, we were going in around 5:15." The two sat in silence. Then Gil moved, "Well, I guess I'd better get back." He wiped his mouth and dropped the napkin onto the table. "See you back at the ranch," he said as he pulled two one-dollar bills and left them on the table.

"Later." Art said and watched the man as he walked away, then smiled up at Carlos as his steaming lunch came to rest before him.

Carlos' right hand grabbed the ones, and he smiled at Art. "Careful, that plate's hot."

Art picked up the knife and sliced through the middle of the burrito, exposing the sour cream and shredded beef, a steaming mixture. Then he poured fresh salsa over the whole plate and savored the colors and smells just a moment before he put the first forkful into his mouth. "Ah." Art sat back and looked up at the ceiling letting all the flavors come alive.

A trumpet blared a crescendo as Art's mind added Gil's troubles to his own. How might Raven's disappearance fit with the Nelson case? Is there a connection? Now his mind was even more crowded; Melissa, Raven, and George Helms.

Tracy can set up an appointment with Helms this afternoon. She can gather all the info on Raven. Yes, that's two good places to start. Helms will know more than he thinks. Art nodded. He had eaten half the burrito before he took a drink. *God. A chilled beer sounds good right now.* A belch came from down deep, and Art rocked to release the gas. Oh, how he loved this kind of food while his gut hated it. His gastric system preferred plain oatmeal, which Art felt should be fed only to babies. He searched his pocket for his Tums and popped two into his mouth, then stood, dropped a tip on the table and waved goodbye and said, "Next time, Carlos."

The sun felt good on his shoulders. What's the point of life if he had to give up everything he enjoyed? He started the car and drove back to the station parking lot.

Art pulled his jacket on as he walked toward his office and saw Tracy at her desk. "Hey, Kiddo, good lunch?"

"Yeah, great, and yours?" Tracy asked in return.

"Mexican," Art stated.

She swung her chair around and glared at him. "Art, why do you eat that stuff? You know how it affects you."

"I like it," he said as he straightened his tie.

She shook her head, "That's just nuts. You're certifiable. You know that, don't you?"

"Okay, enough about my digestive system. Make an appointment with George Helms as soon as possible, today if you can." Art said.

"You got it," she said as she pulled her pencil down from over her ear.

"And. . ." He leaned close to her ear." I want everything on Steven Bird, AKA, Raven. He's one of us, a narc," he whispered.

She swung around and said. "I know Stevie."

"Oh." Art's eyes locked onto hers. "Tell," he said.

"Nothing. I don't *know* Steven. His girlfriend is my girlfriend. That's all."

Art was backing away from her as she said that. He stopped in his tracks. "I want you to tell me everything you can about those two," Art said.

"I don't know anything, really," she said as she stood with her hands out from her sides, pleadingly.

"You know more than you think you know. You and I need to have coffee this afternoon. Around four, my office, if I'm back."

She turned away.

He strolled toward the detectives' area, chatting with the fellows. Oliver sat back in his chair smoking a cigarette as Art approached.

Detective Oliver shook the package, urging three cigarettes to slide forward, then he extended the pack toward Art.

Art's hand rose, he wanted to take one. "No," Art said.

Oliver smiled, and said, "I'll never give up smoking or anything else I like to do. Shit, my plan is to pay the guy to get her off my hands, she and her friends eat like a hockey team."

"You don't mean that." Art said.

The phone rang. "Don't I?" Oliver said as he stubbed the cigarette out and grabbed the phone. "Oliver here," he said.

Chapter Eighteen

2:35 P.M. Art's Office

A rt looked up. "Hey, what's up?" A smile crossed his face at the sight of Walt. "You look like you caught some winks."

Walt eased his body into the seat, his right hand pulling to loosen his tie. "I went home after I dropped you off this morning. My head hit the pillow, and I was out. I don't want it to get upstairs, but all-nighters are tough." Walt, leveling his eyes on Art, raising his left eyebrow for emphasis said, "I'm talking to my friend, not my boss."

"Got it, it'll stay right here." Art stood and moved to the coffee pot. "Have a cup?"

"Sure," Walt said as he crossed his legs, relaxing further he asked, "How'd your fourth go? How are things with the kid?"

Art took a little time before answering, busying himself with the mugs and the Columbian. Art poured, watching the fragrant stream settle in Walt's mug, then his. "Can you have sugar or the fake stuff?" he asked.

"Sugar," Walt answered.

Art handed the mug to Walt, set his on the desk, and seated himself. Sighing he said, "I guess I messed up pretty good, Walt." He brought the mug to his lips and sipped. Shook his head. "Hot." Looking through the steam from his coffee mug into Walt's eyes, he said. "She's staying as far from me as she can. Right now, she's over at Sandy's. I hope Meredith can talk some sense into her. He shook two Tums out of the bottle and slipped them in his mouth."

"She will," Walt said as he sat forward. "The weapon Mel found. . . Walt stopped speaking and then he asked, "Art, what's wrong with you? Melissa's growing up. She just wanted to help you. When she brought the gun to us that morning, she was so pleased. Remember how she bounced all over the kitchen when she first came back? It wasn't a little girl act. She thought she was helping us. You always talk about her becoming a cop and the first time she does something toward that, you jump on her." Walt eased his body back into the chair and lifted his mug. He caught Art's eye, "Ever think maybe you don't want her in the field? Maybe it scares you to think about her facing the scumbags out there, and that's why you got so mad?" Walt rubbed his hands together and glanced around the office then said, "I just think you could explain to Melissa how handling the evidence is harmful in an even tone, and she would get it."

Art nodded, he hated to agree with Walt, but it did make sense." I don't know, Walt. I do know I want things back to normal between us. I don't know how to make that happen, and I'm scared it won't ever be that way again." He looked up into his best friend's eyes and let the vulnerability show.

Walt smiled and said. "Well, you're going to have to eat humble pie. Hope it's the kind you like."

Art laughed his infectious, pleasing chuckle, let his eyes come around to Walt's. They sparkled, then he said, "I hate humble pie."

"Don't we all." Walt stood, his body resuming the bend, "God, I'm stiff. Well, much as I'd like to hang here and jaw, I've got to crank out a report. See you later," he said. He headed for the door, stopped and turned. Walt picked up his coffee and said, "Oh, you'll get your mug back later, this is good."

July continued to be hot. The temps were hovering around 100 degrees with a touch of humidity. The air was thick enough with moisture to make your skin feel sticky. Art's office fan was wearing itself out whipping the warm air and lifting the papers on his desk. Sunlight filtered in through the window screen pooling on his desk right by the phone. He wanted to take a moment to call Melissa before he left his desk, but just as he was about to pick up the phone, he heard Nicole and Tracy embrace. He looked up as Nicole turned from Tracy and came walking toward him on shaky legs.

"Hi," she said.

Her voice seemed much too bright, full of forced joviality. The eyes glistened with tears. She wore jeans and a gray sleeveless top. Her feet were in copper colored sandals, and her toenails painted burgundy red. She managed some makeup, the cheeks too pink, the lipstick in place but not quite perfect.

He wondered if she could see or if her world seemed blurred through that covering of tears. "Hi to you, too," he said. He had a pretty good idea how she was feeling, but he asked. "How are you?" Art gathered her to himself and felt how stiff her body felt. She trembled as she rested against him.

She sniffed her nose, then backed away, keeping a smile plastered on her face. "I've been better," she said. She turned and moved to the personnel chair, running her hand along the back. She bit her lip and said. "Oh God, Art. They've been getting all the paperwork started for me. They say it'll take a few weeks to work out, but when finished, the kids and I should be okay." She looked at him

102

with an expression that asked how anything could ever be okay.

Art felt lost for words.

"I have to set a date for the funeral. That's why I'm here." She let go of the back of the chair, moved around, and sat down.

He moved back to his seat and studied her face giving her room to talk.

Slender hands worked together in her lap, moving the wedding rings around and around, a nervous, grinding movement. "I think I'd rather have a quiet family service. Not the elaborate affair the department says I can have. Does that sound strange or selfish?" Her doe-like eyes looked straight into his as her face drained of color. "I talked with the chief this morning, and he said it would be okay."

Art answered, "I do know that there are many here who would want to attend. Whatever you decide on, you won't cut them out, will you?" he asked as he looked down then up, steadying on her eyes. "We're a family, too, Nicole." He wanted to tell her how much she was loved and how much Nevar was loved and missed, but he didn't.

"You're a boys' club with girls," she said. "No, no I don't mean that." She grabbed a tissue from her purse and wiped her eyes then blew her nose. "I thought instead of the big service and the long march to the resting place, we'd just meet at the cemetery and hold a small service there," she said.

He saw her tissue was unable to keep up with the flow, so he handed her his handkerchief and watched her wipe her eyes and blow her nose yet again.

She wadded up her tissue and tossed it into the wastebasket Art held up for her. She said, "I figured we could all go back to our place, I mean the house when it's over. My friends say they'll bring food, and I won't have to do anything." Nicole looked down at her hands moving Art's handkerchief through her fingers.

"But, Nicole, what would you think of this? How about we have a small service here at the department? Where everyone can attend? A short memorial." Art paused his voice lowered to a whisper, "Nevar needs his last call." She managed to say, "I guess we could do that."

"Good, of course, Nicole, I understand. Is there anything I can do to help you now?" he said with a warm smile.

"Well, there is," she said. "Mom and Dad had to go back home. Dad's got a medical problem and an appointment he's got to keep." Her head sank, hiding her face, and he looked at the crown covered by soft curls piled together and held with a clip. He waited. Nicole's husky voice portrayed her fear. "Art, I can't stand being home alone. It's dead quiet. I keep listening for Nevar's breathing in the house. Can you imagine not hearing him in the house ever again? It feels so still. Sometimes I think I see him sitting there watching a ball game." She looked up, and her eyes misted. "Could Melissa come? Can she stay with the kids for a little while, just until I get all the arrangements finished? Would you mind? I've got an extra bed, and she's out of school right now. I sure could use the help with keeping them fed and on a regular schedule. Things have been all messed up for all of us since...." Her voice trailed off as she wept. "The whole family's a mess. Oh, God." She dissolved into sobs, rocking back and forth.

Art rubbed his forehead as a sense of bewilderment filled him. He honestly didn't know what to do or say to this obviously exhausted widow. He thought it wouldn't hurt for Melissa to go over there. She is good with the kids, and it could be just what the doctor ordered, giving us time to work out the mess we're in right now.

"You know, Nicole, that's such a great idea. I'm sorry I didn't think of it myself. Of course, we'll have to ask her. She might have plans. She's all of fifteen now and getting a life of her own it seems." He looked away. "Let me give her a call and I'll ask her. You have a couple of minutes for me to do that?"

Nicole nodded and sat back, relieved.

Art looked up Sandy's number and punched it in, smiling at Nicole as he waited for an answer. When Meredith answered, he asked, "How are things?"

"Art. Things are great," she answered.

He knew she had talked with Melissa and was hopeful that everything was headed in the right direction between them now. "Thanks," he said to Meredith.

"No problem," she said.

"I need to talk to Melissa, is she there?" he asked.

Melissa came to the phone and said, "Hi, Dad," as though nothing had happened between them. Art's shoulders dropped, and he smiled.

"Hi, Honey. Listen, Nicole is here with me, and she's asking for some help."

"How is she?" Melissa asked, her voice floating with warmth.

"Fine. She wants to know if you could come to stay with the kids for a few days." He caught Nicole's eyes searching for confirmation, and she nodded. "You know, helping her with the kids' meals and bed and nap times," he said and paused, waiting for Melissa's response.

"Now?" she asked.

"Melissa wants to know when?"

"As soon as she can come," Nicole answered.

"She said..."

Melissa cut him off. "I heard. Tell her I'll be there in a couple of hours. I'm going home to take a shower and get some clothes together. Then I'll be over."

Art said, "Okay, thanks, Pumpkin. I'll talk to you later. Take care."

"Melissa will be over at your place in a couple of hours," Art told Nicole as he hung up. "Will you be okay? I hate to push you out, but I need to get going. I have an interview at three, and I'm going to be late."

"Oh no, I'll be just fine. Thanks, Art," she said, smiling as she stood.

Chapter Nineteen

3:10 P.M. The Helms Home

A delicate Japanese maple grew close to the front porch of the Helms home. It's red foliage shaded the entryway and made a place for birds to sing. There were two rocking chairs on the porch and a small table separating them. A cement cocker spaniel guarded the premises as George Helms held the screen door open.

Art stepped through into the living room. "I'm sorry for being late." Art noticed the clock on the wall.

"No problem. Your secretary called and told me you were held up and would be here soon. It's hot out. How about a glass of iced tea?" Helms asked.

"Yes, thank you." Art sized the man up as he turned and walked into the kitchen. Helm's was in his eighties, six feet tall and without an ounce of fat on his frame. His hair had traces of blond mixed in with the gray and a bald spot right on top. The man's eyes are sincere and engaging.

A man I would like as a friend, Art thought. He scanned the room, taking in the comfort of the overstuffed furniture. *Clearly there's been a woman's touch.* Two paint-by-number oils hung over the couch complimenting the heaviness of the maple end tables and wagon wheel lamps. Creams, rusts, and oranges with splashes of yellow and green filled the room, making it feel friendly and peaceful to Art. Heavy drapes hung beside tall, slender windows with sheer curtains covering the glass, softening the dated room.

Just as ice cubes clinked into tumblers, George hollered, "Please sit down. My mind has been on Sam so much. I'm just not thinking."

"Thanks," Art said and chose a plaid upholstered chair in earth tones.

Mr. Helms carried the two tumblers to the table at the end of the couch. He placed them so that Art could reach his easily, then smiled warmly and sat on the Chesterfield next to the armrest and crossed his long legs. George lifted his glass, tipped it toward Art, then sipped.

Art took the tea from his lips and said, "Good, thanks. You've lived here in Lodi a long time?"

"Since Sam and I got out of the Navy. We came here and settled down. Never went any place else. I figure we'd seen enough of the world." George said as he studied the ice cubes swirling around in his glass.

Art nodded, pulled out his notepad and pen, and said. "I'm hoping for a clearer picture of Sam Nelson. I understand you two were friends going way back to the Second World War."

"Yes." George set his glass down and looked off into the distance. "We were. I can't believe what happened to Sam. It's the last thing I would ever expect to occur, especially to Sam. We went through boot camp together and spent all our time on one vessel after another in the Pacific campaign. Boy, could we tell you some hair-raising stories. Sam and I got in the brig a couple of times. Oh, nothing bad, mostly bar fights." His eyes sparkled as he jabbed his fists into the empty air. George looked down for a second, then gazed at Art and said, "You had to be there." He smiled and asked. "How can I help?"

"Tell me what you know of Sam's last five days." Art said and sipped again.

George looked at his hands, spreading the fingers. "I think he spent most of the time with a lawyer and his CPA. We talked a little about that at the Senior Center on the 28th. He said he gathered all his papers and took them to the bookkeeper that morning. Said something about having to close all his accounts and open new ones." George looked off toward the television. "I remember he told me that he kept ten thousand for himself. It's in the safe." George looked back at Art. "We talked about the house being ransacked; I've told all this already," he said.

"How did you part the night of the 28th?" Art asked.

"Oh, well, as I said to the detectives, I made Sam angry by telling him he had his head up his ass, or something along those lines. I think this guy came back to Sam's, and Sam came home and caught him in the act. Bet you anything it was all about the lottery money. That was it, you see, why he got mad at me." George picked up his glass, narrowed his eyes, and said, "I told him, in no uncertain terms, that the picture in the newspaper was a dumb, stupid move. I knew he was mad at me when we left that night. But Sam's been mad at me before. He's always gotten over it. He just needed a few days. I figured I could smooth things over between us by having him over for a barbecue. So when I didn't hear from him, I began calling. I finally went to Mrs. Concord's house, across the street from Sam's. She found the body, you know." George shook his head. "Poor soul. That's pretty much all I know. I have no idea who he might have talked to that day, other than the people at the Senior Center and his bookkeeper."

Art noted the new information about the ten grand. "You mentioned that Sam had kept ten thousand dollars of the lottery winnings for himself. That's all? Out of eleven million?"

George nodded.

"Do you know where he put that money?" Art asked.

"Yeah, in a safe in the living room," George answered.

"Of his home?"

"Yep," George said.

I don't remember a safe mentioned in the report. Art put the glass down and sat back. "Where is this safe located?"

George smiled. "It's in the living room right by the recliner. I helped Sam and Cora put it in. It's hidden by making it look like an outlet for the heat and air duct. That damn oak planking. I'll bet Sam, and I broke ten or more blades cutting that blankety-blank hole in that oak floor. Sam welded a box to fit the opening, then dropped it down into the crawl space under the house. All you have to do is unscrew the two screws holding the cover in place, reach down, catch the box by the handle, and haul the sucker up. Everything that Sam wanted safe went into that box, everything except Sam's ring. You know about the ring?" George asked.

"The emerald ring?" Art asked.

"Uh-huh. That ring was special to him, he rarely took it off, just when he worked in the garden." George said as he smoothed his hair back.

Wouldn't that just frost your cake if the perp missed that kind of money and anything else of value in the safe? Art stood, extended his hand to George. "I want to thank you, Mr. Helms. You've been a help. I'd like to be able to come back if necessary at another time." Art said as he gathered his notes and placed them in his pocket.

"Anytime," George said. They walked outside together and parted by the curb. When Art reached the corner, he placed the call asking Walt to meet him at the Nelson property. The drive over took five minutes, and he was pleased to see Walt standing outside his unit as he pulled the keys from his ignition.

"What you got?" Walt asked as his hands rested on Art's car door.

As he lifted his frame out of the car, smiling at Walt, Art replied. "Maybe ten thousand dollars your guys missed."

"You're shitting me. No way. Every inch of the premises was covered."

"George Helms claims that Nelson put ten thousand in a safe located in the floor of the living room." Art said.

"Oh, yeah?" Walt's eyebrows arched.

Art watched the old bird dog. He pulled on latex gloves, snapping them into place even before Art had his out of the pocket.

"This I gotta see," Walt said.

"Let's go have a look-see, shall we?" They walked around to the back door. "Get hold and let's do it."

Art grabbed Walt's belt at the center seam of his pants, and the two moved slowly forward.

The house held a dead silence. The clutter had been neatly bagged, tagged and taken to a warehouse downtown where it was undergoing intense scrutiny. Blood-stained linoleum marked where Sam's body had lain.

Walt moved them into the living room. The room stood in an eerie silence.

"It's next to the recliner." Art said as they looked at the old leather chair. "I don't see anything by the recliner, do you?" Art looked around and noticed that the recliner had sat along the wall, and the carpet showed where the chair had been. Their eyes located the heat and air duct. "Got a Philips?" Art asked.

"In my bag," Walt said as he dug the tool out and began removing the screws. His hand grabbed the vent cover and pulled it free, then he leaned over and looked down into the darkness.

"See a handle?" Art asked.

"Well, hang on. I'm going to see if I can feel the handle. Got it." Walt announced as he pulled the metal box up and out. "Now we need a key."

"Pretty sharp idea," Art said.

"Yeah, hey, wait a minute. What's this?" Walt felt the side of the metal safe running his hand over a catch built into the side. "Maybe this thing's not locked," Walt said.

"You've got to be kidding me. It's not locked?" Art said.

"Not sure yet. Let's go outside and look at it." When they had the sunlight to aid them, they saw the catch was a combination lock needing four digits to open. "Okay, Houdini, do your magic." Walt handed the project over to Art.

Art used every combination he could recall from the reports on Sam Nelson, then tried the date Sam won the lottery, 6,9,95, and they heard the click as the lock opened. Slowly, Art lifted the lid, and right on top held together by a rubber band, lay the ten thousand dollars.

There were other papers in envelopes that the department would have to go through and catalog, but that bundle of money meant the world to Art as he smiled at Walt and said. "Son-of-a-bitch. Sam Nelson lost his life, but he won the battle. That asshole didn't get a dime."

Chapter Twenty

4:55 P.M. July 5, The Detectives Area.

Oliver waved Art and Walt over to his desk. They walked into the homicide detectives' area and to his space as Oliver said, "We've got a lead in the Nelson case. It seems there's a guy they pulled in late last night. He fits the Nelson perp's profile, and it looks like he can't provide an alibi for his time. He's being arraigned and held for grand theft auto."

Oliver pushed back in his chair with his hands cradling his head, interweaving his fingers. He put his feet up on the desk and looked relaxed. Then he said, "We just put two and two together about half an hour ago. He looked at his watch, "It's 4:55 p.m. now, I was just about on my way down to interview him. Want to come along Walt?" he asked.

Both Art and Walt stood silently at the edge of Oliver's desk smiling like a pair of cats who had the heads-up on where the mouse was hiding.

"What?" Oliver said as he looked from one to the other.

"You want to tell him?" Art asked, looking straight at Walt, a big smile plastered across his face.

"I thought you might want the honors," Walt answered, bowing slightly and placing his hands out to give the floor to Art.

"It's all yours, my friend." Art said.

Oliver took his feet off the desk and sat forward keenly interested, "Come on you two, drop the act. or take it on the road."

Walt stopped smiling, changed to a shrewd look, and said, "The Nelson perp missed ten grand." Walt's expression shifted to a serious one as he dropped the bomb on Oliver. "So did you guys."

Oliver jumped to his feet, his eyes glared, then narrowed. "No way. I was there," Oliver declared, his mouth open in awe. "That place was gone over with a fine-tooth comb," his brows gathered and wrinkled creasing between his eyes. He shook his head. His shoulders dropped as he realized his team had failed. "Where was it?"

Art shifted his weight, then smiled. "It was in the living room. The reason you didn't see it is because it's disguised as heat and air duct."

"Jesus. That's sweet, huh," Oliver said. He gave it some consideration, then looked at Walt and asked, "Shall we go see Kenneth Ward? He doesn't know it yet, but he's waiting for us. Let's see what he knows about the night of June 28th." Oliver stood and slipped on his jacket.

"Good." Art said as he headed for his office feeling more content than he had since this homicide hit his desk. *Finally, this case seems to be coming together. If we're lucky, and that's a big if, the Nelson case might just get cleaned off our desks.*

Art turned and noticed Tracy waving to him. "What you got?" he asked as he walked up to her.

"This came in for you, and I thought you'd be interested." She said and handed him a detective's report from the Nelson investigation on Reese Gainey. "Art if you want a warrant remember the judge is going out of town Thursday through Sunday," she said backing away.

"Right," Art said as though he was not listening to her. He looked up and said, "Let me look this over real quick, and I'll get back to you." He slipped the file under his arm and wiped then adjusted his glasses on his way to his desk.

Tracy just arrived back at her desk, but before she could sit, Art called out, "Hey, Tracy, we got anything to eat around here?"

She had bent her knees to sit but straightened and said, "Yeah, There're some donuts left. I can get you a couple. Want coffee, too?"

"That'd be good, thanks." Art called out and sat back in his leather chair reading. He turned the pages of the Nelson report.

This new report indicated an interview took place July 3rd, with Sam Nelson's bookkeeper's father, a Peter Vinson Gainey, age 69. It went into detail explaining that the father hadn't seen his son, Peter Reese Gainey, age 29, since June 28th, when they had dinner together at the father's home. *It's missing persons, not a homicide matter.* Art thought. *Why'd this hit my desk?*

Art scanned the statement to find out the significance of the report for his office. By the time he finished the two-page report, he had questions of his own.

Okay, Peter Vinson Gainey owned the bookkeeping business, and Junior is working for him. It was the father who had been Sam Nelson's accountant. After suffering a slight stroke, he had backed away from the office on doctor's orders and let his son take over more of the business. That was, according to the statement, two years ago. At that point, Peter Reese Gainey controlled the daily business, and Poppa became a figurehead. There's nothing strange about that. Art continued reading.

Peter Reese Gainey, known by his business card as Reese Gainey went missing June 28th sometime after 8 p.m. No apparent reason for the disappearance. The father was worried that something unsavory might have happened to his son since they handled large accounts for several important companies in the northern California area.

The secretary at the bookkeeping business stated that Reese was at work the morning of June 28th. He met with Sam Nelson for about a half hour, from 9:30 to 10 am. She said Mr. Nelson brought in several containers of personal papers and left them with Mr. Gainey, that Mr. Gainey left the office around 11:00 a.m. and had not returned. He didn't indicate to her where he was going or when he would be back. She said that Mr. Gainey wasn't in the habit of telling her what he would be doing.

Tracy placed the donuts on Art's desk with a hot cup of coffee and cream. She tapped the stir stick twice and smiled at Art. Art picked up the mug, bringing it to his mouth. He glanced up and said, "Thanks, Tracy."

She nodded and sat in the chair opposite him.

He knew she was there, but kept his eyes on the report. "You want something?" he asked.

"I just wanted to remind you of the time. It's almost 5:30 p.m. Judge James said he'd be available until 6:45 p.m., and I'm out of here at seven tonight."

"Thanks for the heads up. I'll need a few more minutes here before I know what I want to do," he said.

"Okay." Tracy left his office.

With determination, Tracy entered his space again and extended the papers toward him, waiting. Art stopped reading and took them from her.

"Now this is interesting." Art looked at her and said, "Good work. Did you request this?"

The fax she handed him came from court records of one Peter Reese Gainey from Florida, 1986. "Yes, I thought you might want to know. I figured it was getting late. We'd run out of time, and you wouldn't want to wait until tomorrow,"

"Isn't this interesting? Junior's a felon." He paused as he perused the report further. "With sticky fingers. I wonder if his father knows. It seems he worked his way into a two-year stay at the Gray Bar Hotel by taking money from his then employer. Now, just how in the hell can he be working as a bookkeeper with this kind of record?"

If his dad knows of his background, he could lose his business. He might not be aware of his past, Art reasoned. "Tracy, get DMV. I want a picture ID ASAP of young Mr. Gainey, and try the prison for picture ID, too."

She turned on her heels and headed for her work area where she requested the information from dispatch. The Motor Vehicle Bureau's answer took about four minutes to come over the lines, and she took the new fax into Art just before 5:39 p.m. She told him that the information from the Florida Police wouldn't arrive until sometime tomorrow morning.

Art took one look at the general description and a mug shot, and his hand grabbed the Nelson file. He flipped over four pages and read the possible profile of the perpetrator. He would be about twenty to thirty years old, more likely younger. Around five-foot-eight to ten, closer to ten. He had size ten and a half shoes and a medium sized hand print with average finger length. About 150 pounds, Caucasian with a hair trigger temper. Art studied the DMV printout, worked his lower lip up over his upper before saying, "Looks like Gainey's thirty-five now. It's close enough to be a match. Junior has the same characteristics. Tracy put out an APB on young Gainey, then get Judge James on the line for me."

After a long moment, she buzzed and picked up his phone." Judge James, Lieutenant Franklin here. I need a search warrant for the premises of one Peter Reese Gainey."

Tracy checked her watch, then edged closer, listening to Art's side of the conversation. She gave Art a look that said he was asking for the impossible.

He watched her point to her wrist.

Art gave her the nod.

Tracy raced off to fax the information to the judge as Walt and Oliver entered Art's office.

Oliver slid into the chair. "Kenneth Allen Ward isn't our guy," Oliver said.

Walt took the fax papers and the report Art offered and read them over. As he looked up, he handed them to Oliver, and they listened as Art explained he had requested a warrant for the home and workplace of Reese Gainey from the judge.

Walt shook his head and said, "Right now, all you got is a missing person."

Art looked from Walt to Oliver and back, "No, he's missing, and he's a felon. Nelson is dead, and we have a solid connection between them. Mr. Nelson met with Mr. Gainey the morning of his death."

A long moment passed between them. Oliver moved around in the chair and said, "I can't see a bean counter using a hoe as a murder weapon."

"He's certainly not going to kill with an adding machine," Walt said.

"I can't see anyone using a hoe. Seems way too clumsy, but think about it. Accountants push pencils all their lives. They're not violent types who carry weapons around as everyday business tools, so he would use something within reach. The hoe was probably just lying there, convenient," Art said.

"He snapped," Walt said. "It may be that simple." They stood quietly for a moment. "Would a bookkeeper tear up someone's house looking for money when he knows where it is? That's an act of a person out of control.

Accountants, God they have to be the most controlled souls on earth."

Art placed his hands on his hips. "Good question. The answer is, we don't know. Right now, I want to have a talk with Reese Gainey and find out what he does know about the night of the 28th of June." Art pulled a stick of gum from the package, opened it, and wadded up the wrapper. "Make sure we've got a crew to go to both places as soon as the warrants are issued."

Chapter Twenty-One

11 P.M. Deep in the Oregon Forest

Ray battled to keep his eyes open. Driving all day long and well into the night led him to a darkened, creepy, forest. On edge as he came to an intersection, he reluctantly rolled down his window. The air felt heavy with rain, and a cold breeze brushed a chill across his cheek. His flashlight shook sending the beam in jerks as he illuminated the words Ranger Station on a sign.

Five miles ahead.

He rolled up his window, his teeth chattering as he backed the car away and turned westward until he spotted a break in the forest. Ray trained the beam, flashing on one pine tree after the next until he caught a signpost in his spotlight. *Skyline Road, that's it, finally.*

He turned onto the road and within seconds, it became a swallowing, narrow blackness, a canyon between towering pines. He had asked specific directions from a young couple at the hamburger joint where he ate dinner, and they acquainted him with the Cove Campground, but they failed to inform him about the lack of light. They let him know it was their favorite campground for tenting. *If they told me right, it should be ten more miles until the turnoff to Timothy Lakes Campground.*

Storm clouds covered the sky, blocking the moonlight. High beams brightened shapes of fallen logs, death gray and still, lying on the side of the roadway, holding them for mere seconds before releasing them back to the dark. Once more Ray felt consumed by the menacing black. His eyes burned with exhaustion as he rolled the window down and stuck his face out into the fresh air. He sniffed the moisture, thinking, *rain would fall soon. Great, just great.*

He hoped to get his tent set up first, but more and more, he just wanted to get out of the car to walk around. A sign to the right caught his eye, Horse Camp. *It'll be five more miles to the camp, then a right at the Y.*

A sign directed him to turn right into more intense blackness. He sat at the intersection for a long moment gripping and releasing the steering wheel. Ray pressed the accelerator with the sense that if he went forward, he might just fall off into nothingness. His heart pounded as he proceeded into the unknown. *Tomorrow, just get me to tomorrow and daylight.*

Finally, his headlights illuminated the sign for the campground. Ray located the parking area. On exhausted legs, he pulled the tent from the trunk. Thus, he followed his flashlight's beam over a pathway into the trees and past some logs set up as a gateway to the camp area until he found an open tent site near the lake edge.

He had put the tent up a hundred times before, and he could do it in the dark, no problem. Just as Ray aligned all the parts for the tent, the clouds moved aside, allowing the moonlight to brighten the area. A crack of thunder warned Ray to be fast, so in less than ten minutes, he was pulling the stuff from the car and pushing it into the tiny home he'd made for himself.

A yawn stretched across his face as moisture filled his eyes. The humming of bugs built, filling the night; he was too tired to care. Twenty minutes later, he lay down on the sleeping bag. Pulling the cover over him, he fell into a deep sleep as rain plunked its first drops on the taut canvas.

The morning brought kids' voices, dogs barking, and sounds of axes biting into logs. Ray rolled over and got out of the sleeping bag. He stepped out into the early morning and pulled on his lightweight jacket. It failed to warm him. The heavy wooden table and benches in his campsite had puddles of rainwater standing on them, so he strolled down to the water's edge. Smoke hung low over the gleaming surface carrying the fragrance of bacon frying. Ray scratched his head, rolled his shoulders, then yawned. It was time to get going. The first thing to do was pay for the site.

The sun began warming the area as Ray walked the path to the main campground. Steam radiated from the ground and vegetation as he moved through to the roadbed. He watched several boaters already out on the lake at their favorite fishing holes. Innocently, Ray carried an empty bottle for drinking water and found the campground host dressed as a park ranger.

The man took the money for the two nights Ray expected to stay. "I see you need drinking water. You can use any of the spigots along the roadway for your water." The host pointed to one about twenty feet away. "The bathrooms may be a bit of a problem for you. The one in the Cove Campground needs replacing. You'll want to come up here. Just to let you know, we're getting ready to pump them out."

"What do you mean?" Ray asked.

"We'll close the bathrooms temporarily while we put some chemical down into the cesspool, it eats everything into a mush, then in a couple of days a company comes to pump them out. You just need to be aware of which bathrooms we're working. They'll be closed for a short time. Nothing will hurt you. It's just a little inconvenient. We'll be opening the bathrooms in about an hour after we

122

put the chemical down then you can use them like usual," he said.

Ray wanted to ask all kinds of questions about this chemistry that eats the stuff up, but he was smart enough to keep his mouth shut. *Now, how could anything be better?* Instead of putting the plastic bag into the trash container, he would put the clothing down the toilet. *Friggin' fantastic.*

Ray thanked him and moved to fill his bottle. Then he entered a rustic bathroom. They had told Ray that this was a percolating design that kept the smell down from open cesspools. Ray didn't think the idea was working. A zillion flies proved his point. Gingerly, he lifted the lid and leaned over to look down into the sludge. His lips tightly held together as his mind warned him that the floor might not hold his weight and, if it didn't, he could be up to his neck in stinking shit. It smelled. He could make out Coke cans, a baby's diaper, and a fishing pole. *It already looks soupy to me.* Ray put the lid down and walked out into the fresh air. Suddenly a chill raced through him, partly from the thrill of knowing how close he'd come to ridding himself of the damning evidence, but mostly from the morning temperatures. *I need my hunting jacket.* It was time to deal with the bloody clothes.

He walked back to his camp area and then to the car. He carried both the bags from the trunk of his car into his tent. Ray squatted, pushing aside the bag with the gun and jewelry. The hunting jacket came out of the bag first. He looked it over. *There're no blood spots that I can see. It doesn't make any sense to throw it away, and I know it'll be warmer than this thin old thing.* From his small camping toolbox, Ray removed a pair of scissors. His plan seemed simple enough, cut all the cloth into four-inch squares.

Ray dreaded handling the pants and shirt, but he pulled them from the bag and began cutting them up. An

123

hour later, his hand cramping from working the scissors, Ray finished. He put the pieces of material back inside the trash bag and rolled it into as small a package as possible. Ray looked at the socks, studying the brown stains. *These running shoes will float.* Ray placed the shoes inside the socks then weighed them down with small rocks and tied them off. He studied them for a time. *They'll sink to the bottom and stay there forever.*

He remembered that there were some candy bars, a box of crackers, and a can of tuna; nothing else. None of it sounded good, but he ripped open a candy bar and ate it in three bites. Ray walked to the car and brought the blow-up boat to the camp table where he attached the bicycle pump and pushed down on the plunger, again and again, inflating the boat. At one point he stopped and squeezed the edge of the boat feeling the firmness.

Everything was ready. With the black bag tucked under his left arm and the shoes under the sleeping bag ready for their boat ride, Ray surveyed his camp site. It looked okay. There was always a chance someone might nose around while he was away. Slowly, he walked toward the main campground. All the dread he'd been feeling seemed replaced by a sense of sheer excitement. *Once the "trash" is gone, they'll have nothing on me.*

He climbed the last, long, hilly walk into the campground and followed the circular layout of the parking area. Every campsite seemed busy. He approached one of the dark brown buildings as a woman walked out of it and said to him, "That one's open. They just finished it about ten minutes ago."

"Thanks," Ray said in his nicest voice. The door banged shut as he went inside. The smell didn't seem all that much better in this bathroom. Ray unrolled the plastic bag and opened the lid to the toilet, looking over the edge. It did look like something was boiling down there. He managed to get the opening of the bag over the toilet and let the whole mess drop away. Ray looked again to make sure it wasn't visible and saw it laying there in a lump on top of the mire. *Aw shit.* Slowly he backed away from the toilet and opened the door. No one was around, so he picked up a rock and took it back inside, dropping it into the middle of his cloth pieces. He jumped back so nothing could splash on him, then gingerly peeked over the edge and with pleasure saw the rock had pushed most of the evidence safely under the muck.

He left the bathroom and pushed the empty black bag into the trash container by the bathroom. Looking around and not seeing anyone looking at him he walked the lakeside trail back to his campsite. Now the shoes. He lifted the rubber boat and pushed it into the water. Ray grabbed his fishing pole and the shoes, jumped into the vessel and paddled his way to the middle of the lake. He looked over the side past the shine and sparkle of the water into the lake grasses reaching for the sun. Ray picked up the first socked shoe and dropped it over. He picked up the second and let it go into the water. Leaning over the edge of the boat and watching as they disappeared under the murky water gave him satisfaction. A smile spread across his face as the lake grasses waved slowly back and forth, accepting the shoes and hiding them securely. Ray lay back in the craft, stretched his legs so his feet reached up into the fresh air. His head back on the rubber sunning himself, he felt free at last.

Chapter Twenty-Two

9:00 P.M. July 7, Lodi Lake

Crickets rubbed their legs filling the evening with their music as Roland and Allison waited on top of one of the wooden picnic tables at Lodi Lake. Their bodies silhouetted against the lake. Tall cattails stood sentinels around them as geese quacked their soft night talk.

Ray recognized them as they sat back to back. He drove straight to them. They turned toward the old blue Ford just as Ray brought it to a stop.

As the headlights went out, Ray stepped out of the car. "I'm glad to be back but exhausted," he said. A yawn spread across his face, and he almost didn't hear Allison greet him. He nodded to her.

"You get everything taken care of?" Roland asked.

"Yeah," Ray said as he sat heavily next to Allison. "I've got to get some sleep, though." He yawned again. "Where can I meet you guys later, tomorrow sometime?"

"We've rented an old house out in the country. Allison and I talked it over, and we think it would make it a lot easier all the way around if you stayed with us. What do you think?"

Ray hadn't expected this invitation. He stifled another yawn while he thought. *I'm finished with my grandparents and done with the evidence.* "When do you want me to come?" he asked.

"Right now. We could all use some sleep. It's not the greatest place. In fact, it needs lots of work before we can even use it," Allison said.

Roland stood and said. "If you've got a sleeping bag, you've got everything you need."

"Yeah, I've got one in the car. You want a ride?" Ray asked.

"We've got our bikes, can we put them into the car?" Allison asked.

"No. It's too full of my camping gear." Ray said.

"Go on East Highway Twelve. Wait for us there, across from the Burger King. Then follow us to the house," Roland said.

Ray sat in his vehicle and called to them, "I'm hungry. I'll get something to eat. Do you want anything?"

"Pick me up an apple pie and large Coke," Roland said.

"Me, too," Allison said as she buckled on her helmet, and forcefully pushed the bike off directing it toward the lake exit. Roland headed out right behind her. Ray drove around them and out Lodi Lake gate to Burger King.

Ray, carrying the food out, waved as they passed. Roland rose up on his pedals and waved. Ray pulled his car onto the street and headed in their direction. They were riding fast now. He hit his accelerator and fell in behind them. His mind was already on collecting his belongings from his grandparents' home. He figured there would be one hell of a fight.

The couple leaned their bikes, turning onto a dirt road. He saw them bend to the left and followed. There were no streetlights along this stretch. It seemed more a path to him. He watched them enter a thick growth of trees and didn't see them again until he brought the car through the trees. They had turned to the right following the path, so he did the same. His headlights spotlighted

127

them leaning their bikes against an old farmhouse with weathered boards. Ray brought his car to a stop as Roland walked up to him.

"This is it, home-suck-home." He opened Ray's car door and took the bag of food.

"It's not much," Allison chimed in. "But you'll learn to love it." The three walked into the house, and Roland turned on the lights. Ray thought his grandparents' home was a shack. This old farmhouse made their house look like a mansion. He figured the house was built in the early nineteen hundreds and never repaired. He noticed there were no carpets, just wood floors that creaked as they walked.

"You can take this room. Roland and I will be in here." She turned on the lights, and Ray saw his new room, a nine by nine with one window. There was no decent furniture in the whole house. His heart sank.

Allison said, "Don't worry, Ray, we'll fix it up. Come on, let's chow down and get to bed." They walked into the kitchen and sat at a card table. Within minutes they wadded up the wrappers and stood.

"Yeah, shithead, when we get the money from the scam, this place will be history."

"It can't be soon enough," Ray said His voice sounded hollow. He walked back out to the car and pulled the sleeping bag from the trunk. Slowly, he rolled his head around on his neck to loosen all the tension. The yard lay in darkness, but Ray could hear the Mokelumne River. It couldn't be far away. He was about to go into the house when he remembered his newspaper. He reached back into the car and picked it up.

Roland and Allison had shut the door to their room. He could make out the sounds of their voices, but not the words. A yawn had his eyes watering. He unrolled his sleeping bag. His hand smoothed the wrinkles out. Then he turned the top back. Ray pulled his pants off, rolled

128

them up and used them for a pillow as he stretched out. It was warm. His belly was full, so Ray relaxed on top without covering himself. His eyes kept closing. He gave up and let the newspaper rest on his stomach as he drifted off.

Morning came without his having gathered the information about the cop and his kid. It didn't matter. Ray extended his arms and sat up. There wasn't a bone in his body that didn't ache. He'd driven fifteen hours yesterday and slept most the night fitfully on a hard, unforgiving surface.

I killed a man. Shit. That could be real trouble. I'm not going to think about it. After all, it was the old coot's fault. Anyone with half a brain would understand that.

He crossed his legs, spread the paper out in front of him on the floor, leaned over, and studied the picture. *The girl is in high school. He's the lieutenant of something.* His finger outlined the text until he found, *Homicide. Shit, he'll be looking for me.* She stood under a sign identifying the Lodi Police Department. The article said she had lived most her life in Lodi, was a member of several clubs and rode her horse in local Gymkhanas.

"Ray, you up?" Allison said.

"Yeah?" He answered and looked up as Allison opened his door.

"Roland wants you to help him out back. You want something to eat?" she asked, leaning against the doorjamb.

"I am hungry. What is there?"

"Not much. We have to shop. But there's some cold cereal and milk in the refrigerator." Allison had dressed this morning in jeans and a red T-shirt, catching her hair up in a ponytail with a red ribbon. She appeared fresh and peppy.

He reached up, scratched his head, and asked. "Roland's already outside?"

"Yep." She said, then shut his door.

He listened to the floor creak as she walked away. Ray folded the newspaper and dressed, then walked into the cheerless kitchen and ate a bowl of cereal. At the kitchen door, he caught sight of Roland standing at the edge of the river.

He looked down, then up at the house. He spotted Ray and yelled, "Bring the rope."

Ray stuck his head back into the kitchen and said. "Allison, Roland wants the rope."

"There's one in the living room," Allison said.

Ray went back inside and saw that Roland and Allison seemed to have placed everything from their storage shed in this room. The rope lay in a box near the door. He grabbed it and headed back outside.

"Take a look at this," Roland said as he reached up, taking the coiled hemp from Ray. Roland's right foot rested on two rather large roots. Behind him, the olive-green Mokelumne River raced past. He stood that way as he undid the rope and handed the end to Ray.

Roland could be washed away with one wrong step, Ray thought.

"Go toward the house, as far as you can," Roland said.

Ray glanced at the house. He furled his forehead, wondering what this was all about, but he did as Roland asked, dragging the rope behind as he walked over scrub grasses until he reached the peeling slat-board house." Okay, now what?" he called.

"How much rope's left?" Roland asked.

"None," Ray said as he held the end up.

"The house is fifty feet away. That's how long the rope is. Come and look at this cave. I think it goes to the house. It looks to me like a bunch of junk's caught up in there. We could get it out," Roland said.

"Why?" Ray asked.

130

"Well, I think we might be able to make a tunnel from the house to here. What we're doing now is setting up the house for an office to run a scam. If something goes wrong, we could get out this way."

"Yeah, I guess," Ray said looking around at the debris caught up in that opening in the cliff.

"Allison will start mailing out in about a week. She said something about going into town to get a list of everyone with the last name Nelson." Roland said as he worked at recoiling the rope.

"You and I are going to clean out the cellar and see what we can do to open the floor into the cellar. All the files she's working up will be stored down there out of sight."

"So, how's this scam work? What's with the names?" Ray asked watching Roland' arm jerk and wind the rope.

"We approach people with the same last name as this guy you told us about, asking if they're relatives of the old geezer. They're not, but they want to be, see, because, everyone is greedy. Our letter tells them that a relative, Sam Nelson, died after winning a lottery of eleven million dollars, and it could all belong to them. If they want our law firm to determine that for them, they need to send two hundred dollars. We'll send out hundreds of these letters, and people will answer them, you'll see. Allison will get more names from other towns, and we'll keep sending out letters. Get the idea?" Roland asked tying the rope together.

"Yeah," Ray said. "I'm not so sure I do." He looked at the river and back at Roland. "I have to tell my grandparents I'm moving out and clean things out of their place."

"Make it fast, shithead so that you can help me here. There's a lot to do." Roland said.

"Is the river always this fast?" Ray asked. The water by his private eddy always moved, but Ray could not see it flowing as he did here.

"I don't know," Roland answered.

Ray felt captivated by the river. Moments had passed before he said, "I guess I'll get going."

"Okay, hurry, so we can start cleaning this tunnel out."

"Where are we going to put the junk?" Ray asked.

"Upon the bank for now."

"That'll work."

"And, Ray, we've got to get more money, this dump cost more than we expected. There's a fair going on in the Gold Country this weekend, and we're all going. You haven't worked burglary with us before. Make sure you get back here so we can over our rules."

Ray nodded, glad that they were going out, and they included him.

Chapter Twenty-Three

9:00 A.M. Old Farm House.

Bright sun lit the outside edges of the trees growing along the river's edge. Birds sang as though the gentle morning was just for them. Angus cows grazed across the river. Their black hides shone through a cut in the trees.

The pastoral scene gave Ray a feeling of peace, one he hadn't felt for several days. He sat in the car and turned his attention to the eucalyptus trees circling the far side and front of the old farmhouse. They grew tall forming a hedge that walled the perimeter of the house. He was learning to love this house, after all. A smile parted his lips. He straightened his shoulders and pulled his car keys out of his pocket and checked the time.

There were things to accomplish and to sit here listening to the birds, or admiring those backlit trees, wasn't going to get them done. Ray needed a phone book to learn how many horse stables there were around Lodi. He figured to show up at the stables one afternoon soon to meet that girl. If all went well, she'd take a liking to him. With luck, he could keep abreast of the police's progress.

He headed his Ford toward the opening in the thicket, moved through the growth, and out onto the dirt path of a road he'd come in on late last night. It was a long way to the main road, a real good hideout.

He pulled the car over at the liquor store on the corner of Cherokee Lane and East Highway 12, walked into the store, and asked for the phone book. He opened it, found three listings, and scribbled them down circling Rocking Horse Ranch, its address, and a phone number since it was the closest to Lodi before closing the book and pushing it back toward the clerk. "Thanks," he said and walked out of the store. Ray grabbed the door handle on his car and jerked it open, then headed for the senior McNamares.

Full of resolution, Ray headed up the driveway, stopping in front of the opened garage. His Grandfather's car was gone. Relief washed over him. He walked through the back door, stopping at the sink for a glass of water. The house was quiet. Ray thought he was alone, he drew the water, drank thirstily, then placed the empty glass on the kitchen counter. He turned around and about jumped out of his skin when he saw his grandmother standing in the doorway.

"Raymond McNamare, where in hell have you been?"

You old war horse, Ray thought. "Nowhere."

Her hands were firmly planted on her hips as she said. "I want to know what you're up to."

"Nothing," he said. He stopped as she barred the passageway. Ray stared at her. They were inches apart at the doorway leading to the bedrooms.

Emily held her ground. Her face was stern as her eyes bore into his soul.

It unnerved him. "Move or I'll move you," he yelled at her face.

"I've had about enough of your lip, Raymond. I know you've been up to something. You'd better tell me about it right now."

"There's nothing to tell." He paused, and said, "Except I'm moving out."

134

"You're what?" she said.

Ray managed to move past her and head to his room. When he opened his door, he felt a stab of fear. The room was neat as a pin. "Where's all my things?" he asked not masking the anger he felt.

"Want to tell me about this?" she asked as she reached into her apron pocket and held up a little gold bowl.

Ray stared at it. Somewhere deep inside a rage built, casting a film over his vision. She'd gone through his personal belongings in his bedroom. Ray's breathing deepened, and his eyes bore holes into Emily.

"I told you it was time to do the cleaning."

She had that look on her face that said, what are you going to do about it?

"You took off, and I decided your room was as good a place to start as any."

"Where is everything?" He said as he hissed out the words.

"Some of it's boxed up, mostly things I don't know how you got, like this." She brought the golden bowl up again for him to see." Other than that, everything else is just put away. The bowl was my sister's." Her voice had an edge. "Did you take it, Raymond Michael McNamare?"

Ray felt his control slipping away. He could just as easy grab her by the throat and shake her senseless, just to shut her up, it would be so easy. He wanted to. Oh, how he wanted to feel his hands circling her neck. Some thin thread of control held him back, and he managed to say, "I'm taking off, so just leave me the fuck alone."

"What do you mean, you're taking off? Ray, I asked you a question, and I'm waiting for your answer," Emily said.

He took one of the pillowcases off the pillow and stuffed his underwear and socks inside. He grabbed his camera, shoved it into his pocket, then hung his binoculars around his neck.

"You can't have thought this through, Ray," Emily said dodging his brash movements.

"Things have changed." Ray dumped his hanging clothes onto the bed, searching the empty closet for anything he needed. Finding nothing else, he returned to his clothing. Pushing his arm under and around the clothes, he lifted them, grabbed the pillowcase filled with his underwear and socks and slung it over his shoulder. It was done, and he couldn't get out of there soon enough. He came to her as she barred the doorway out of his room.

"That's my pillow case," Emily said holding her hand out for its return.

Ray pushed himself, clothing and all, into her body, shoving her backward. His movement forced her fingers off the door jamb and made her lose her balance. The little gold bowl dislodged from her grip and hit the wall, shattering into tiny pieces. "Come back here, right now," she yelled.

"Up yours," he answered.

Anger flashed across his Grandmother's face as she righted herself and came after him. She pulled her skirt down with her left hand, pushed against the wall with her right. Her stocking twisted around her right leg leaving folds near her ankle. He heard the wooden floor under her feet groan as she marched after him. He turned and rushed toward the back door.

Once there he flung his armload onto the floor and whirled on her. "You want a fight, old woman. You've got one," he yelled. He stood his ground, his chin out, his eyes were boring into hers.

Emily made a low groan from deep in her throat. She swung her arm stiffly to the back, holding her fist tight. She gathered herself to produce a swing that would plant such a smack on Ray. She swung, bringing her arm around so it could connect with his face, but it wasn't there when her hand arrived. Her momentum carried her completely around. She was breathing fire now, her face bright red, the whites of her eyes contrasting with the brown irises.

Ray laughed as he put his hand on the top of her head.

She grew angrier as she fought to catch her balance. She swung again, hearing his laughter. She was huffing, puffing, and wearing herself out flaying the air. She stopped and stood with his hand still on the top of her head. She jerked away.

"Stop laughing at me. I said no. Now, you put those things back in your room. I want an explanation for everything that's been happening, and I want it now!"

Ray watched her cheeks turn even redder as she adjusted her dress and hair.

He screamed his answer. "Get out of my face."

She grabbed him with both hands clutching his shirt." You'll listen to me, Raymond if I have anything to say about it."

Ray slapped her until she sank to the floor. "Leave me the fuck alone."

Certainly no match for him, she kicked him, and he at her, causing more harm to her body than she to his.

He straddled her prone body yelling for her to leave him alone. Emily lay still, taking the blows. All of a sudden, he pushed himself away from her. He stood, stared and saw she was okay, stubbornly he grabbed his clothing and ran from the house.

Chapter Twenty-Four

10:30 A.M. Art's Office

"Okay, girl, my office." Art said as he walked by Tracy, carrying a box of donuts. Tracy grabbed her pad and hurried to follow Art to his desk. They both sat at the same time, an expectant expression on her face.

A smile broadened on his face as he said, "Thanks for making a pot of coffee. Would you like a cup?"

"You're welcome. Just one sugar for me. I'm cutting back." Tracy leaned forward. "And I'll have one of those donuts, the powdered one, please," she said as she sat back.

He began pouring the fragrant coffee into two mugs. Then stirred one spoon of sugar into hers and set it on the edge of the desk within reach for her. He held the box out to her, and she selected her donut.

He sat and looked at her saying, "Give. I want everything on Raven and his girlfriend. What's her name?" He turned to pick the glazed donut.

Tracy realized she would not be taking notes, and she placed her pad and pen on the desk near her coffee mug. She fingered the powdered donut, looked up and said, "What on earth possessed me to take this donut, it's going to get all over my dress." She held up her fingers covered in powdered sugar for him to see.

Art reached for a napkin and handed it to her.

She held up her fingers indicating she wanted two napkins.

He turned to the side table and picked up the pile of napkins and placed them within easy reach on his desk.

She bit into her donut, then sipped her coffee. "Good to the last drop," she said through snow-white lips. "Nancy Sue Dexter. I don't know Steven all that well. I get the impression that things were hot and heavy between them. Nancy talks like they're going to get married. I do know they've had some knock-down-drag-out fights. I think she can give as well as she gets. She's into weight training." Tracy rubbed her bicep. "She's got muscles like rocks. That's how they met, at a wrestling meet a couple of years ago."

Art watched as she talked the sugar dusting down each time the donut swung through the air. "Do you know if she knows anything about his job?" Art asked holding his mug with both hands.

"I'm sure she does. I don't think he could pull it off without her knowing what he's doing. Especially since he looks like a scrounge most of the time." Tracy wiped her mouth.

Art studied his donut. He abandoned the donut on a napkin and looked up. "You like him?" Art asked sipping.

Tracy nodded and said, "Yeah, well, what I know of him. He's a nice guy, but intense, you know what I mean?"

"Tell me." Art asked.

"Extreme, you know, nose to the grindstone. He's maybe one cookie short of a dozen. I don't know, Art. He's like all of you cops. You're wound too tight," she paused, and asked, "Your donut too dry?"

"No," he looked straight at her, his brows working.

"I love you, too, kid."

"Well, you asked." She spotted the playful sparkle in his eye, "What's the problem, or can I ask?"

139

"Well, Gil had a bust scheduled for the night of June 28th and Raven went missing. Seems he's been running some guys and the department decided they had enough to close them down for good. There was a house over on Garnet that the perps were using." Art's expression changed to concern. "And that's where Raven was the last time any of us knew anything about him."

Tracy's eyes narrowed; she knew how Art's mind worked. "So, do you think there might be some connection between Nelson, the house on Garnet, and Raven? Strange Nancy hasn't said a word." She looked off into space.

A smile crept across Art's face, "Don't know yet." He cleaned up his desk of the donut and extra napkins leaving them with the coffee tray. He checked his mug: it was half-full. Art turned and looked at her.

Tracy nodded as she read Art's mood. He was done with this conversation. She began picking up what remained of her donut the half mug of coffee, and her pad and pen to go back to her desk.

"Okay, Tracy. Let me know if you hear anything about him from any source. Until then, run a credit check on Reese Gainey. Put a watch on his credit card use. We'll track his whereabouts. Use June 28th as the beginning date for your search," he said.

She wiped her mouth and smoothed her skirt looking for any powdered sugar that might be clinging there as she said, "I'll put it into the database now. I'll probably have something on him in about an hour."

"Good. I want anything and everything on that bean counter, and I wanted it yesterday."

"Gotcha," she said as she walked away.

Art turned his attention from Tracy to Detective Oliver, who, smiling from ear to ear, strolled into Art's office and took a seat. "What's up?" Art asked.

"You're going to love this. We've got Gainey's prints on a soda pop can found in the Vic's kitchen."

Art sat back a pleased expression showing in his eyes. "No other prints of Gainey's found in the house?" They knew Sam Nelson had been at the bookkeeper's office the morning of his death. Now the detectives had more evidence pointing to Gainey. One piece of evidence found at the bookkeepers business, and the other at the Nelson crime scene. "When will the search of Gainey's residence and office be completed?"

"No, just on the can. It should be finished in the next hour or so. We have crews at both places right now," Oliver said.

Just as Detective Oliver spoke, Tracy stepped through the doorway of Art's office.

She said, "He's used two cards. We've flagged the accounts for any activity. The information will be forwarded to us as it happens."

"Great," Art said and drank the last of his coffee. He put the spoon he'd used for sugar into his mug. He wadded up the used napkins and tossed them into the trashcan." What about the druggy, what's his name, Kenneth Ward, you were looking at for this crime?"

"He has an alibi, we cut him loose," Oliver said as he crossed his legs and got comfortable.

"Okay Gainey's our guy," Art said turning to Oliver. "Good work."

Oliver took his pack of cigarettes from his shirt pocket and pulled one out. He lit it and let the smoke out as he said, "What we have so far on Mr. Reese Gainey says he's just a regular Joe. He's not been in any real trouble here in Lodi. Seems he did his time and then came here to turn over a new leaf."

"Yeah, sure, and there's this tooth fairy." Art pulled his rolling chair around and sat down, opened his top drawer. "I'd just as soon you smoked somewhere else. All of my areas are smoke-free now."

"Don't buy it? That Gainey is innocent?" Oliver asked.

"Once a duck, always a duck. I want to talk to Gainey senior. Do you know how bad off he is? I mean, is the stroke hindering him?"

Oliver took another drag, thereupon snubbed the cigarette out in the ashtray Art brought out of his desk drawer. "No, you wouldn't even know he's had a stroke. At least, I didn't. He could come in."

"Then, let's get the old fellow in here and see what he knows about his son."

"You want me to give him a ride downtown?" Oliver asked.

Art nodded. "Do that. I'd like to get that done before lunch, if possible."

"I've got to get a move on," Oliver said as he rose and left Art sitting in his office alone.

Art breathed deeply. He could smell the smoke. His eyes closed, savoring the aroma. Correspondingly, they flashed open upon hearing Tracy's heels click on the hard surface.

"Hey, boss," Tracy said as she flowed into the room, her mouth drawn into an oval, her eyes big and round behind her glasses, her voice high. "Ooooh." Her eyes sparkled. "We've got him."

Art busied himself cleaning out the ashtray filled with Oliver's left overs. He stiffened and asked. "Where?"

"Tahoe, Nevada side. He just used his card for lunch. Looks like lunch for two, twenty-four dollars worth," Tracy said.

"I want Wilburn and Williams headed up there now. Get them started, have them locate Gainey and check in with Tahoe PD. Then I want updates. We don't know if this guy's dangerous but treat him as such."

142

"Got it." Tracy raced from the room just as Walt entered.

"What?" Art asked eagerly.

"There's a partial list from the Gainey residence."

Art's mustache twitched as he moved his lower lip, pushing it against his top. "I can feel it, Walt, right here in my gut. We're getting close to buttoning this baby up."

"I hope so, Art."

"You have reservations?"

"I won't have, once all the I's are dotted and the T's crossed," Walt answered.

Art told Walt that Oliver was bringing Peter Vinson Gainey, the father, into headquarters. That he wanted to find out what the old man knew of his son's whereabouts during the time young Gainey was in prison for embezzlement in Florida.

At eleven-thirty Detective Oliver and Peter Gainey walked into Art's office. Art looked up from the report he was reading. A poised but slightly overweight gray-haired man stood before him. There were no outward nervous movements, but concern showed clearly in his facial expression. Art knew that being brought into the station could be disturbing. Worry about his missing son could also explain the look.

"This is Mr. Gainey. Mr. Gainey, this is Lieutenant of Homicide Arthur Franklin."

Oliver remained by the doorway as Art and Gainey shook hands.

Senior Gainey was a neat-appearing man wearing a gray tweed suit, silver tie, and white shirt. His fingers held gold rings, and he had a gold chain around his neck. He was clean-shaven and looked healthy as he stood before Art.

"Please sit. I understand your son is missing. I'm as concerned as you are, and we're trying to find him right now," Art said.

"Why is the Homicide Department looking for my son?" Senior Gainey's eyes narrowed as he settled himself in the personnel chair across from Art.

Art squared his body toward Mr. Gainey, his expression serious. "Your son's disappearance coincides with the homicide of Sam Nelson. That puts him on our radar. Can you tell us the last time you saw your son?"

Senior Gainey sat straighter, his eyes looking off to the right. Slowly he answered, "Around 8:00 pm on the 27th of June. We had dinner together, and then he left. He didn't say anything to me about leaving, so I don't have any idea where he is or, for that matter when he left."

Art watched the unsettled expression deepen.

"You don't think he's dead, do you? Oh, God, no.... You don't think he killed Mr. Nelson?" he said, his mouth open waiting for Art's answer.

Art didn't want to tell the father that the department was considering young Gainey as a prime suspect. Guardedly, he said, "No. No, not at all. In fact, we believe he's currently in Nevada at Lake Tahoe. Is your son a gambling man?"

Senior Gainey gave thought to his answer, taking a few moments before saying, "Peter's had some problems before, but he's over it now."

"When was that?" Art asked sitting back in his chair his eyes still on Senior Gainey.

"Oh. A few years ago," Mr. Gainey answered while shifting his weight and crossing his ankles.

Art pushed his lips together judging the man sitting across from him. "Can you tell us what happened?" He sat forward and took up his pen to write on his pad.

Art could see by the expression on senior Gainey's face that he knew the police were after something. He just

144

wasn't sure what and how it affected Peter. "I'm not too sure, but he got into some trouble and went to a rehab place for compulsive gamblers. He told me he couldn't contact me or I him for two years, but that it was what he had to do to beat the habit."

Hum, Papa didn't know about the prison term, or he wants me to believe he wasn't aware, Art thought, then added, "How did it work for him?"

Mr. Gainey had his hands over his mouth as though to keep himself from saying anything more. Before long, he said, "He seemed cured. That's why I was surprised when you said he was on the Nevada side of Tahoe."

"How long has he been working in your service?" Art asked.

"Since he came back, about a year and a half. He needed work, and I needed him to work for me. I had just had a stroke, and the doctors wanted me to rest. The problem with bookkeeping is it never ends; it's a month-to-month business. Then income tax time rolls around. I needed him."

"Then he's been good at his job, no complaints?" Art asked.

"No, none. Why?" Senior Gainey asked.

"Well, I thought you might have had a falling out. Maybe he just took off to cool off and ended up in Tahoe."

"I see. Well, no, everything was all right as far as I know. He was elated that Mr. Nelson... I'm sorry about what happened to him, poor man. He won such a large amount of money. We were setting him up with one of the investment houses here in town that would help fund some charities he liked. Reese had a lot of good ideas and was looking forward to directing Mr. Nelson in the investments."

Art thought that maybe one of the charities was Reese himself. He felt there was nothing more he needed from the father. With that thought, Art rose, extended his hand and said, "Thank you for coming down."

Senior Gainey stood, reached for Art's hand and said. "Thank you, Lieutenant, my pleasure to help. When you get information or find my son, you will let me know?"

"Of course."

Chapter Twenty-Five

1:00 P.M. Ray's Car

The afternoon of July 8th, Ray's eyes dropped to the newspaper waiting in the passenger's seat across from him. Eagerly, he grabbed it and smoothed the paper. Just as he found his place in the article, the car in front of him moved forward. He put the paper aside, followed the traffic until he could pull over by Oak Park to read about Melissa Franklin.

Slowly, he pulled the note carrying the stable addresses from his pocket. This one's in Lockeford. Ray smiled. It would all work in his favor. *Dear old Dad won't know what hit him.* The thought put a sparkle in Ray's eyes.

Back at the old house and in a much better mood, Ray stepped out of the car and called, "Roland."

Allison, in blue jeans and a red checkered blouse, walked out of the kitchen door onto the porch and pointed toward the river, "He's over there."

Ray walked to the edge of the land just before it dropped off into the Mokelumne River and yelled.

"Down here," came Roland's muffled answer.

Ray made his way down the embankment until he could look into the man-sized hole.

Roland had moved a lot of the debris out, proving that a person could travel quite far back. "You're doing pretty good, man," Ray yelled over the roar of the river.

"Yeah, I'm removing all the loose stuff that's caught up down here. Come on, help me," Roland said.

Ray looked at the rushing water just inches away, then he bent his body and started slowly, carefully placing his foot and working his way over the exposed roots into the tunnel. Ray hunched over even more to duck the roots that reached down from the top and sides.

Roland adjusted the light beam to focus on a pile near Ray's feet. "Take that stuff and throw it into the river, then come back and get this," Roland pointed to a pile of dead branches, twigs, and some paper near his feet. "I'll keep working back toward the house while you get rid of what I pile up, okay?"

"Whatever," Ray said, not at all pleased. He reached down and picked up an armload.

Together, they worked all afternoon clearing most of the cave and tunnel. "Do you think someone would want to get into the house from the river?" Ray asked as he filled his arms with dried paper and twigs.

"I like to cover my ass. It's better to have an alternate way out and if you can have a way out no one else knows about, all the better." Roland said as he pulled more twigs free.

Ray wished he could stand up. Every time he moved some root punched him, and it hurt. "Are we worrying about the police?" Ray asked.

"Them and anyone else," Roland said.

"Like who?" Ray asked on his way back outside with another load.

"Anyone I want to get away from, Ray, that's who. I'm just trying to cover any and all possibilities." Roland said starting a new pile of twigs and moldy paper.

Ray let another armful fall away from him into the river. He watched in wonder at the stuff as it washed away and out of sight. Working his way back to Roland, Ray asked, "If I understand this whole process, we open this tunnel..." He took an armload from Roland. "Then dig a connection into the house in the cellar?"

"Yep." Roland stopped to mop his head. "Allison is setting up the office now, and we're setting up an escape route. All the files necessary for the scam will be in the cellar." Roland said as he picked up his flashlight and forced his body deeper into the tunnel, pulling debris free.

"What's going to stop them from looking in the cellar?" Ray asked now working in the dimmest part of the tunnel.

Roland stopped, turned to look at Ray with impatience. "We're going to cut a hole into the floor of the living room. We'll put a trap door in, and cover it with a rug," Roland answered giving the impression that he was done talking about this with Ray.

"Oh," Ray said. He couldn't help but wonder why the rug couldn't be moved, and the trap door opened, but he didn't ask. *I don't want to rock the boat just yet.*

"Let's get out of here and check out the cellar," Roland said.

Ray picked up two pretty good-sized branches, turned, and moved toward the opening.

Roland followed. They tossed the debris into the dark green water. Roland pointed at the river bank. "Go up that way. Let's have a beer." Together they walked back to the house. Roland called to Allison, "Come on out and bring some beer."

The three sat at a makeshift table on folding chairs, snapped open the tops, and relaxed.

Roland put the chilled can to his forehead, rolled it from side to side, and said, "I've got one hell of a headache. When we go into the cellar later, we've got to connect the cellar and the tunnel. I don't think we have far to dig." Roland drained his beer, crimped the can, and tossed it into the air. It hit the ground and bounced as he stood.

Lethargically, Ray got up. He checked his can and found it empty. His hand squeezed and crushed it and with one smooth motion, he tossed it to rest with Roland's. Subsequently, he followed listlessly toward the cellar door.

Roland pulled the door open. The hinges protested with a groaning whine. "No one's been down here in ages." He picked up an old broom leaning against the house and knocked the cobwebs out of the way. The two men tested the old steps and gingerly walked down into the ten-by-ten-foot space.

Roland stood in the middle of the room, looked at the door into the cellar, and announced, "The tunnel has to come in right about here." He rested his right hand on the dirt wall.

They surveyed the ceiling. "We'll cut a hole into the floor about there. Ray, hand me that broom." He took it, broke away a piece of the straw. "Give me a leg up."

Ray raised Roland high enough to stuff a piece of straw through the crack in the floor. It stayed in place as Roland carefully took his hand away. "Let me down." He stepped back, nodding his head, and without further ado, he headed upstairs.

As they came through the back door, they saw Allison working on the scam project in the living room. "Don't move," Roland's voice startled her.

Turning toward his voice, she asked,"What?"

"I pushed a piece of the broom up through the floor; you were about to step on it." Roland pointed at the floor as he walked across the room.

"So, what's that for?"

"That's where the opening into the cellar is going to go."

150

Her shoulders dropped. She had worked all morning long on organizing, and now it was going to be messed up with sawing and sawdust. "When are you going to cut that?"

"My guess is tomorrow. Is that okay with you?" Roland asked, aware he was stepping on her toes. He picked up a marking pen from her card table desk, knelt down, and marked the floor. He capped the pen and handed it back to her.

She nodded her head. "Yeah, that'll work. I'm going to town tomorrow to see what I can find on Sam Nelson."

Roland looked to Ray and gave him the "let's go" tilt of the head, they started for the kitchen door. The rest of the afternoon, they removed the shelves and pickaxed the dirt wall until they had a hole started. Roland worked from the tunnel side and Ray from the cellar side.

"We're through!" Roland yelled.

Ray used the pick's blunt edge to break the hole wider.

"Finally. Ray, clear all this dirt out and dump it into the river. I've got to find something to put over that hole," Roland said as he stepped through the opening.

Ray leaned on the pick handle, his shoulders dropping as he understood he had the job of removing a pile of dirt. Another thankless heavy labor job he thought. "You opened it up to close it?"

"Yeah, dummy. Some sort of door," Roland answered.

Looking with dismay at all the dirt, Ray asked, "How am I going to move all that dirt?"

"With a bucket," Roland said.

151

Chapter Twenty-Six

10:00 A.M. July 12

Sandy asked, "What's Midnight doing?"
Melissa let the horse's hind foot drop to the ground. She stepped back to get a better view. Midnight's muzzle wrapped around an open can of Coke sitting on a shelf. "Hey, you're in training," she said as she smacked his fanny, and he swatted her smartly with his tail. Melissa, covered with stable dust over her blue shirt, blue jeans, and brown cowboy boots pushed the last of the tail hairs away and explained to her friend, Sandy, "He's into sodas."

"You're kidding," Sandy said. It was Sandy's first time at the stables. The horse seemed overpowering to her. The surroundings were strange and surprising. She sat on some bales of straw that were piled together off to the side of the stable door. She wore a green halter-top and cut off shorts. White sandals slipped on the straw each time she moved her feet. She had watched Midnight since she arrived at the stable. He had a halter and lead rope, but was free to roam if the mood struck. Knowing that worried Sandy, whose senses were being assaulted with the pungent odors only a stable can produce. Wrinkling her nose up, Sandy asked, "So you come here and clean out all that crap every day?"

Melissa smiled and answered, "I try, but sometimes it's hard, especially now that I'm taking care of Nicole's kids. She stayed home today, so I took off."

Sandy gazed around the stable area looking into the darkened space Midnight called home. She studied the bridle hanging on a hook. The bit appeared uncomfortable to Sandy. She moved her tongue around in her mouth in response to the thought that she wouldn't like to have a bit in her mouth. "Does your Dad know the invitation for the endurance ride came?" Sandy asked turning her attention to Melissa.

Melissa's hand moved down the long back of the horse rubbing with a soft cloth. "Not yet. We haven't done any real talking for a long time."

"Are you still mad at him?" Sandy asked and fiddled with the straw packed in one of the hay bales. Her hand pulled until a long piece broke free. She used it to poke at Midnight's muscular rump and watched with wonder as his hide shivered. Instantly, his tail whipped past her face, the tips stinging her cheek. Sandy's hand responded, covering her smarting skin as she leaned back.

Melissa finished cleaning the hooves and picked up a soft brush, rubbing Midnight's back and rump with long sweeping strokes.

"Tell me how you do that stall thing," Sandy asked.

"I take the old straw out and spread new. He goes, you know, in one corner, so the whole place isn't messed up. It's not bad; you're a pretty clean horse, aren't you?" She said and smacked him on the rump. "You like things clean, don't you, boy?" Melissa asked.

Midnight brought his head around to her 501's and nuzzled her back pocket.

Sandy's eyes went wide. "He's biting you," she said, her voice a squeal.

"Yeah, I made a mistake a long time ago and put some carrots in my back pocket. You're not going to forget that are you?"

Midnight made a low rumbling, throaty sound, then snorted, blowing dust along the ground. He stepped to the side and the movement of his hooves made a hollow resonance on the packed surface.

Sandy jerked back rigidly. "What's he doing?" She asked, expecting all hell to break loose at any moment.

"Nothing. He does that all the time. Don't worry. He won't kick you or anything," Melissa said. She bent to pick up her things and place them in the tack box. Seeing she had everything picked up, she lowered the lid and sat on the container.

"Kick me? You mean he kicks?" Sandy asked looking seriously at Melissa.

"No, don't worry. He's okay," Melissa said.

"When are you going to tell your Dad about the endurance ride?" Sandy asked keeping a close eye on the horse's rear end.

"This weekend; I'm going home for a couple of days. Sandy, this mom thing is great and all, but, rug rats twenty-four seven?" Melissa shook her head. "The police force is looking pretty good," Melissa said as she stood up and pulled Midnight's tail hairs together smoothing them.

"Yeah, you say that now, but wait until you meet mister right," Sandy said pulling another straw and putting it between her lips.

Ray came through the entry into the barn from the parking area. The bright sun backlit him, and he presented a solid black silhouette moving slowly toward the girls. Roland's hat was tipped back on his head. With each stride, he purposely swung his legs and bowed them out, and the cadence of his step added a rhythm to the girls' beating hearts.

154

Sandy and Melissa stopped talking to watch.

He looked from one girl to the next. The blonde was sharp, the straw sticking out of her mouth corny. The redhead just had to be the Franklin kid. Her hair was tied back at the nape of her neck with a blue bow; her shirt fit perfectly. The faded blue jeans were snug, and her cowboy boots gave her that cute style. "Hey," he said to her.

"Hi." Both girls answered him at the same time.

"I'm thinking about getting a horse and wondered if you know anything about this stable, how they treat the animals and all. It's a good idea to talk with people who use the stable you're interested in, don't you think?" Ray said as he used a warm, deep-bodied male voice.

"I don't have a horse yet," Sandy said, sitting forward and doing her best to garner his attention.

"It's a good place to keep your horse. Charlie, he's the wrangler here, watches them real close. And, if you can't get here to feed, he'll do it." Melissa said as she rubbed Midnight's rump and gathered his tail hairs up in her hands.

"You've had your horse here a long time?" Ray asked.

"About a year," Melissa answered.

"You're just the person I need to talk to," he said. His body shifted to the right as he bent his left leg and placed his fist on his hip. "Name's Ray."

"Midnight and I will be entering the endurance ride soon," It sounded lame even to Melissa as she spoke, and she wished she could just fall into a hole.

"That sounds great. So, you can find good horses around here?" Ray asked.

"Oh, yeah. Go to the feed store. You'll find all kinds of listings on the board," Melissa said.

"I can do that, thanks. Are you here a lot? I mean, do you have a certain time you come to the stables?" He asked.

155

"Most any time in the summer," Melissa answered.

"Ah, would it be possible for me to give you a call later today, and we could talk some more?" Ray asked raising his eyebrows.

"Yeah, that'd be okay. My name's Melissa." She said as she pulled a business card container from her pants pocket, pulled one free, and reached over Midnight's back, extending it toward Ray.

"You have a business card?" Ray said as he took the card.

"My Dad taught me to have my information ready in case," Melissa said.

Ray wrinkled his brow deeply, his teeth sparkled as he said, "Well, okay." Ray studied the card, then looked up into her eyes. "Melissa Franklin," he said in a whisper and let his most winning smile stay a little longer on his face. "I'll call you later." He said and bowed.

Neither girl moved as they watched Ray walk away back out into the bright sunlight. They listened to his car start and roll down the gravel driveway toward the road.

"Geez Louise, talk about Mister right," Sandy said.

Ray made his way to the Franklin residence. He made certain the house was empty and walked around looking for a monitoring system, but found none. He went back to the window and using one of his many tools, managed to force the window. He climbed through the opening, roamed quickly through the lower level, then started up the stairs to the bedrooms.

The house had a quiet, rich quality about it. The colors throughout the house were beige and brown with splashes of bright white. He opened several doors, closing each until he found Melissa's room. It had pictures on the walls of her and the horse. The room, all done in aquamarine and white looked like her. Ray moved around, touching her things. Ray snapped some pictures of her room, smelled her perfume, and found a black and white checked scarf in her dresser drawer like the one around her neck in the photo of her at a horse show. *She's competitive; I like that.*

He used the scarf to wipe everything he touched then Ray pushed the silk scarf into his front pocket and closed the drawers carefully. He glanced into the bathroom, then walked to the window and looked out into the back yard. The grounds were neat. He longed for a plunge in the pool and decided one day he would have a place like this.

The carpet felt thick underfoot as he walked down the stairs and to the window he'd used to enter the house. He took one last look around the room and crawled back outside.

Chapter Twenty-seven

5:35 P.M. July 12

Roland had the skill saw singing when Allison arrived home. He watched out of the corner of his eye as she put her things in the house, then came out to be near him. He killed the saw and looked up. He caught that lovey-dovey look on her face. "What?" he asked as he smiled.

She just smiled at him. He looked soft to the touch with a covering of sawdust. "I did okay. I got everything on Nelson we need. There's just one thing." A long silent moment passed where she looked toward the river. "I went over to the Nelson property."

He let go of the saw; it rocked to a stop on the saw table as he turned toward her. His jaw dropped open, his fists clenched as he said, "Shit, Allison. I've told you a thousand times."

She cut him off and said. "I had a talk with an old woman who found Nelson's body. Don't worry. It'll be okay." Allison looked around for Ray's car. "Where's Ray?"

Roland answered, "He borrowed my cowboy hat and said he had an errand to run; he said he'd be here later this afternoon." Roland looked at his watch. "He should be rolling in here any minute, and I need to get this all marked and cut so he can help me put them into place. Tonight, love, we'll have access to the cellar."

"Can't be soon enough for me. That saw drives me nuts." Allison, determined to tell him what she had learned today, began. "Roland, I think Ray killed that old man."

Roland drew a pencil down the straight edge sitting on a stringer and answered her absentmindedly. "What old man?"

"Duh." She paused. "Stay with me, Roland, Nelson."

"Shithead." Roland pulled his red bandana from his back pocket and wiped his face.

"But, Roland, before I tell you, promise me you won't be mad."

Fear stabbed Roland's heart. *What'd Allison do?* Guardedly he said, "Okay." He stepped back narrowed his eyes and fixed them on her.

"I think I learned some important information today," she said, her smile fading at his look.

His breathing deepened, and his face flushed.

Allison knew he might blow up any second, so she hurried. "Okay, get this." She sat more erect, telling with expressive hands,"I go to the old man's house."

Roland's eyes widened.

"I'm standing there, looking at the house when this whistle sounds. I turn and here's this old woman waving to me. I go over and sit with her. She tells me she found the body."

"Yeah, yeah. Does this have to be a long story?" Roland asked wanting to get back to his work.

"I've been thinking, how would Ray know so much about the old man's death?" Allison untied the bow from her ponytail and let her hair swing loose.

"Wait a minute. You think Ray killed the man just because he knows the man's dead? I'll bet most of Lodi knows about it." Roland began to settle down.

She swung her leg around and sat with her elbows on her knees. "I could never kill anyone. Could you?"

Her hand brushed the sawdust off her knee. "I'm getting hungry. Do you want anything?"

159

"Naw, not now." Roland bent, re-checking the measurement again.

Her chips and sandwich waited on the table. Ray's old Ford rolled out of the trees just as she poured some tomato juice into a small glass. He parked and followed the high-pitched singing of the saw. She watched as Ray joined Roland as she ate.

Allison finished her lunch and went to work on a business letter. The paper Allison chose to copy the letter onto was of rich quality, a gray parchment with envelopes to match. She ran her hand lovingly over a sheet. Now all she needed to do was come up with a law firm name, one that would clinch the illusion that this letter was the real deal.

She penciled some names, crossing them out almost as soon as she thought of them. Then one by one the names came to her. A sense of pleasure filled her as she realized that this scam had finally caught fire. She studied her practice letter. It looked so good she almost believed it herself.

Roland and Ray entered the house and were kneeling on the living room floor. Roland bent over his jig-saw, making the cut in the floor as square as possible.

Allison covered her ears enduring the screaming saw. The last of the oak planking gave way and tumbled down the new stairs onto the cellar's dirt floor.

Roland said, "Okay, now we have to board up the original opening into the basement. Then we're done."

"I'll get the broom. Are you going to leave a hole in the floor?" Allison asked as she headed for the back porch.

"No, we'll use the piece that fell through and make a trapdoor in the floor. Will that satisfy her Majesty?" Roland called out to her.

"Do what you have to do, just get done and turn that damn thing off. It hurts my ears and makes me want to scream."

"As your majesty commands," Roland said.

Chapter Twenty-Eight

8:00 A.M. Saturday, July 15

Ray slung his camera and binoculars around his neck as he began his journey through the thick brush surrounding a marsh known as Pig Lake. It had a furry, lime-green cast to the water as he passed. Nothing seemed to grow in it, and he doubted there were any fish. Blackberry vines grew abundantly around this back part of the wilderness area at Lodi Lake. Ray ate some of the sweet berries as he pushed through the mile-long trail. He came to a dirt path that went almost straight up. His feet slipped all the way to the top until he pushed through a bushy clump, and he could set his feet flat again. He came out upon a clearing that afforded him no protection. He darted across the clearing then worked his way through the brush until the Franklin property came into view. About 350 feet of river separated them.

Ray's eyes narrowed; he felt instant anger. *Father and daughter sitting on the back lawn having breakfast; how nice. Some people have all the luck.* Ray readied his camera for some pictures.

They were in their bathrobes, under a large shade tree, just back from the dock where their red and white boat bounced with the tide.

Boy, Ray thought. *Could you have a better lifestyle— a horse, a boat? The river and a swimming pool right in your backyard.*

162

Ray brought his binoculars to his eyes and looked at the orange juice in their glasses, the coffee cups, and the rolls on a plate. *The cop's reading the newspaper, and she's filing her nails.* He placed his binoculars on the ground and readied his viewfinder; made a couple of corrections to his setting on the camera.

Ray snapped several close-ups. He took three of Melissa and one of her Dad when he put the paper on his lap and laid his head back against the tall back of his chair. He snapped some of the back of the house, and the bedroom he was sure he'd been in, framing what he believed to be her window in the viewfinder. When he finished, he raised his binoculars for one last close-up of both their faces.

A glint of light flashed. Art saw, "There's something over there."

"Where?" Melissa looked up, then followed his direction.

They both studied the heavy growth across the river.

They saw something; Ray realized as he moved back. *Not yet, not yet, I'm not ready for you to know about me.* A calculating smile spread across his face.

"I don't see anything." Melissa scoured the opposite bank.

Art put the newspaper down and stood up. "Huh. Well, something shone brightly a second ago. I hope we don't have people climbing the fence to get in over there again."

"I thought the city posted it off limits," Melissa said coming to stand beside him.

"They did." Art put his arm protectively around her shoulders.

The phone rang, and Melissa ran to answer it and got it on the fourth ring.

Art watched her as she ran, pleased that they were talking again, even if it was superficial. They talked around, but not to the core of their disagreement.

He wondered if he would find the strength just to say it to her. *Melissa, I'm sorry; I messed up. Can you forgive me?* So far he let other matters get in the way; sleep, the newspaper, his pride, and now this phone call. He'd do it soon.

She talked at length, and Art laid his head back listening to her voice. The pool pump cycled; the breeze rustled the leaves. The boat bumped at its mooring. He loved that sound. *Sitting out here was nice. Life was good.* Art sighed.

The back door banged. Art jerked.

"The mail's in," she announced, "and, well, here, this is for you to look at," she said as she came to a stop holding out the envelopes.

He opened his eyes and took the bills and the envelope she'd put on top. "What's this all about?" he asked.

She sat on the edge of her chair. "You know, Dad, the endurance ride."

Art stiffened and got all negative inside. "Melissa, now just a minute. I thought we agreed that Midnight wasn't the kind of horse that should go on endurance rides. Didn't you tell me that the best horse for that race is the Arab?" *Maybe I can dance my way around this problem he hoped.*

Her red hair swished as she grabbed the letter from his hand. "Don't be dense, Dad. Midnight can do it, and it's not a race. That's the beauty of it. We all start from the same place when we choose to start and end up at the same place. We don't take off running like at a horse race. Everyone is going along as best they can. It's a timed

164

event. And veterinarians will check the horse's vitals three times during the race. In the end, the best vet check and the best time wins.

She went on and on, her voice getting louder her words coming faster.

Art knew it was a lost cause, something inside caved.

Her eyes were shining. "Oh, Dad, doesn't it sound wonderful?" she said, smiling as she read the advertisement off the brochure.

I've got to rent a horse trailer. The Bay Area's not that far, but it'll take some doing to get a horse from here to there. "So, when is this thing?" Art asked.

Ray watched Melissa be all wiggly; *I think she's working her Dad on something. Wonder what she's up to, a mystery to unravel.* Ray put his gear away. He needed to get back to the house to help Roland, but first, he would stop to print the pictures.

Chapter Twenty-Nine

10:00 A.M. July 15

A rt's hand moved and had the receiver up to his ear before the first ring ended.

"Franklin."

The news wasn't good. Art looked at his watch and calculated the team had been on the lookout for Gainey for seven days now. "Okay. Stay put, and we'll keep watching for credit card use at our end. He'll surface. I want you both there when he does."

A sense of sadness enveloped him as he placed the phone back into its cradle on the kitchen wall. He poured a cup of coffee and sipped. *Okay, it's me, Greeley, and Sacramento.* Art dialed the professor's number and listened as the phone rang six times. His shoulders dropped with disappointment. *Had he forgotten?*

"Hello?" Greeley said in his long slow drawl.

Art's eyes sparked, "Professor, I'm ready to head out for Sacramento. Shall I pick you up?"

"Well, son, I've been waiting for your call. You tell me when and I'll be curbside." His Southern drawl drew the words out melodically.

"About fifteen minutes," Art shot back. "I'll be out front."

"Ten-Four, son, Ten-Four," he said with obvious pleasure.

Art hung up, poured out the remainder of the coffee, rinsed the cup, and called to Melissa. "Honey, I'll be home late this evening."

He heard her run from her bedroom door to the railing near the top of the stairs. He walked into the foyer and looked up as she smiled down at him and said, "Okay, Dad. I'm going over to the stables for a while this morning. Then I'm back to Nicole's to babysit so I won't be home tonight."

"Take care," Art said, a smile blooming to showwhite teeth.

"I will."

They stood looking at each other. *There's so much to say, but I don't want to mess anything up.* "Bye," Art said as he checked for his keys, grabbed his sports jacket, and had the door open when she spoke.

"You look weird in those clothes."

He stopped, gazed down at his slacks. "Why, what's wrong with them?" His face was a mask of concern.

"Oh, nothing with the clothes. It's just you look funny, not like my Dad."

"It's not my usual cop attire?"

She nodded and said, "Yeah, that's it. I'm not used to seeing you look like a regular guy."

He gave her a big smile and waved, then closed the door behind him. He'd purchased these clothes thinking that sometime soon he'd be taking Doctor Amanda Deanna Burtoni, the psychiatrist the department used, out on the town. The salesperson at the haberdashery told him that the gray tones were good against his skin and hair coloring. Confidently, he swung the tweed jacket over his shoulder and sauntered toward the car.

The professor's ham of a hand gripped the car door handle. Dressed in his usual baggy dark blue slacks, white shirt, and red suspenders, he gave off the illusion of a

167

sweet old grandpa. His wavy white hair, a little flyaway, had been smoothed into place. His face was scrubbed clean; the chin hairs were smoothly combed. The old man hefted his bulk into the seat next to Art and buckled up. Then he broke into one big smile as he looked at Art. "Morning. I certainly thank ya, son, for bringing me in on this. Ah do hope we find Sam's ring today," his fingers gathering his goatee in hand and smoothing downward.

"Glad to have you along, Professor."

"Where are we gonna start?" Professor Greeley asked.

Art answered, "On the north and east sides of Sacramento, then work our way over to Old Town."

"Sounds like a plan," the professor's cheeks bloomed rosy as they puffed in a smile.

Art looked both ways as he exited the Academy parking lot. He turned his head briefly toward the professor. "Nice morning for this. Not quite so hot today."

"Yes, been G D Georgia hot here lately," Greeley said.

"Do you miss living in Georgia?" Art's head was turned, his attention on several cars that needed to pass.

"Hell, no. Ya ever were bitten by red ants?" The professor went on about the South and everything that grew bigger and prettier there.

Art listened to his drawl. "Finally." He saw an opening in traffic and he entered the roadway.

"No, I don't miss that," Greeley said.

"Can't say I have." Art checked the rearview mirror.

"Have what?" Greeley asked looking at Art.

"Been bit by red ants."

"They'd love your sorry arse." Professor Greeley looked at Art and grinned.

It was five-thirty when they reached Old Sacramento. Visitors randomly roamed the narrow streets, dodging the horse-drawn carriages while their kids ate ice cream cones. Old-time music drifted through the air. Baskets of flowers hung attractively, lining the streets. If they didn't locate the ring here, it would be the end of Art and Greeley's hunt. The few remaining shops they would visit were located in and around what had been the original township in Sacramento's early days. Now the buildings were fussed up, painted in mauves, blues, and deep greens, giving a sense of festiveness that Art didn't feel.

As they approached the last business on their list, Art took a place outside the pawnshop, letting Greeley enter alone. Even though Art's outfit seemed ordinary everything about Art cried cop. He knew that and gave Greeley free rein at the shops.

Inside, Professor Greeley approached the counter, smiling his full-cheeked rosiest grin. "Excuse me, Sir, ya-all the proprietor here?"

"No." A young man looked curiously at the rumpled, good-humored man standing before him. "Mr. Stone is. He's in the back. I can get him for you if you'd like?" he said.

"That would be wonderful, I thank ya kindly," Greeley said.

Greeley watched the young man go out of the room, and when he was alone, he looked around the shop, his mind storing every little detail. The room seemed crowded with discarded household items; dishes, pans, pictures, an old dusty violin, and a pair of roller skates complete with a key tied to the laces. The professor doubted the shop was doing much "out front" business.

Greeley spotted a two-way mirror on the wall behind the counter when he first came in. He figured the sales clerk and his boss were now watching him. He

169

wondered if he should fiddle with his mustache and stare back at whoever was on the other side. He decided against it. After a long moment, the proprietor came pleasantly into the room asking how he might be of help.

Greeley's drawl, even more, Southern now, spun the story of his friend who had fallen on hard times and who had pawned a family treasure. "It was a ring, a heavy ornate 24 karat gold band set with a rectangular cut gem, an almost perfect emerald," he said. He'd hoped to see a change in the storekeeper's eye, but he didn't. Greeley stroked his goatee slowly and said. "You have anything like that come in lately? I'd be pleased to buy it back for my friend."

The shopkeeper was a rather small man, with messy black hair and close-set dark eyes. The jeweler's loupe around his forehead swung back and forth, as he shook his head. "Wait a min; I do have an emerald ring."

Greeley walked to the door and signaled Art, who eagerly walked through the doorway.

As a tray filled with nice jewelry pieces slipped onto the counter, the jeweler spotted Art. The tension in the little room heightened as the shopkeeper started to withdraw the rings. "What's this all about?" he asked.

Greeley's only answer was a shake of his head, letting Art know the ring wasn't there.

They thanked the man and walked out of his shop.

Somewhere deep inside, Art knew they wouldn't find the ring today. "One day I will have that ring in the palm of my hand." He smiled at the professor and said. "I bet you're tired."

"Time enough to lay my head down, son. I'm still rearing to go." Greeley mopped his brow with his handkerchief.

"If that's the case, can I interest you in some dinner?" Art removed his jacket and tossed it over his shoulder with one finger.

The old man turned to Art, "On the Department?"

"On the Department," Art answered.

"Well, Sir, I wouldn't want to deprive them of the pleasure. Might I suggest a suitable watering hole? I know a place where gentlemen such as ourselves might enjoy the ending of our day with fine food and smooth drink." The professor said, and his heavy brush eyebrows lifted in anticipation, his eyes sparkled.

"Suggest away," Art said becoming a part of his duplicity.

With a hand flourish and a twist of his heavy body, he said, "Let's get our chariot and I'll direct you."

After a lengthy drive through heavy traffic, Art and Greeley drove up a winding driveway to a sprawling dark-green one story, massive Tudor hugging the greenest, smoothest, and most expansive lawn Art had ever seen. The backdrop for the building was the river and a heavy thicket of hardwood trees.

Art thought, *It's right out of a historical movie.*

"This is the Rusty Duck where a man may take his leisure," Professor Greeley said as the door opened for them.

Art smiled and pouted. *This place must cost a bundle.* "You come here often?" he asked.

Greeley's eyebrows rose into a shrewd look. "Once in a blue moon, Sir," Greeley said as he bowed and flared his arm to show the way. They'd just walked through the entry when a man approached.

"Professor, how nice to see you again." The suave older man dressed in black stretched out his hand and warmly shook the professor's. "Your usual table?"

Chapter Thirty

10:10 P.M. July 15

The heavy smell of precipitation hung in the air as clouds capped the sky. Ray felt the dampness in the air and knew it would rain soon. "Do you see her?" Ray asked as he squirmed, craning his neck looking around.

They parked at the curb on the east side of town. This part of town was quiet. Darkness had covered the buildings and trees dimming them.

A couple of hours ago the street lamps lit, and colorful neon lights flickered, announcing two bars and one cafe. Shades of red, then blue rhythmically colored Ray and Roland's faces.

Roland sat coolly in the driver's seat staring ahead and answered, "No."

No matter how hard Ray looked over the parking lot for Allison, he couldn't see her.

Allison had pulled her hair up and covered it with a baseball cap. She wore dark shoes and jeans and a loose fitting shirt over her T-shirt. She jogged slowly through a downtown parking lot with a pair of skin colored latex gloves pulled snuggly over her hands. They rubbed against vehicles as she came in contact with one driver's side window to the next. Two of the overhead lamps in the parking complex were out, making the area dim. It gave her an edge but made it much harder to see the lower dashboard inside the vehicles. So far, she'd located four possibilities, a small light brown pickup truck, and three older sedans, all with keys dangling from their ignitions. She decided on the truck.

Allison forced the pickup's door. She sat for a second resting her gloved hands on the steering wheel, then started the engine. The needle on the gauge pointed to the full mark. *It sounds okay; no knocks.* She put the truck into gear, hit the accelerator whipping the vehicle out of its spot. With wheels spinning, she headed off the parking lot right in front of Ray's Ford.

It was all the notice Roland would receive.

Ray yelled, "Go, go, go."

Roland gunned the Ford, and both vehicles left without headlights. A block away they turned their beams on, then headed out of town on Victor Road, toward the Gold Country. At first, Allison drove as though she had a score to settle.

Her wild driving caused Roland to cuss.

She must have heard him in her mind because she slowed to the speed limit and drove carefully to the next town.

They pulled off the road in Lockeford, stopping right by the same feed store Melissa was sending Ray to find his horse. He looked the store over and decided to come back later.

"We'll go to Plymouth then change the plates behind the laundry on the main street," Allison said looking at the heavens.

Roland knelt beside the truck. "Why not do it right here? It takes a Phillips; four screws and you're done." Roland said as he got to his feet. "It could be raining when we get to Plymouth."

"It's just smarter to do it back of the building in Plymouth; there's too much traffic along here," Allison said. She jumped back into the truck. "Well? Are you coming, or are you waiting for the rain?" she asked.

173

Roland and Ray raced for the Ford as the pickup's back wheels spewed grit their direction. Roland pushed the Ford to overtake her, running on the wrong side of the road until he passed her. He slowed and moved along moderately until pulling into the laundry parking lot. They drove around behind the brick building where large trees fenced the place and made it very private. *She was right; this is the best place.* It bugged him when she was right especially right now when he could take her head off for being so foolish. Roland turned on her as soon as she stepped out of the truck. "What in hell were you doing driving like that? You know better," he yelled at her.

"Yeah, I know," Allison looked around at the antique building and the parking lot, "it just felt. . ." She smiled and had a look on her face like everything in the whole world was perfect and said, "good."

He knew that feeling and loved it when he felt it. Roland turned his head so she wouldn't see him smile. "Don't do it again," he said. He opened his personal toolbox, took a Phillips screwdriver to the back of Ray's car and grumbled as he changed the plates.

They drove into the neighborhood at Plymouth they'd chosen and clasped hands. Three people covered in dark clothes, gloves to match.

"You know what to do?" Roland said to Ray.

"I know," Ray answered and said, "Be safe."

"You too," Roland said grabbing Ray's hand again, gripping and turning it loose.

He gave Allison a scouring look and said, "Let's go." Allison and Roland left disappearing into the night while Ray watched their black costumed bodies fade away. *If they don't come back in thirty minutes, I'm to drive the car to the next corner to pick them up. It feels like they've been gone ten minutes.* Ray glanced at his watch. *Shit, two*

174

minutes. Ray quietly opened the pickup truck's door and sat down.

Roland found an unoccupied house right off. Allison had to go down four houses. Both had entered through open windows at the backs of the houses. Individually they had done a quick search and found money lying around. They took only cash, never anything else of value.

Roland reasoned with money missing; the owner will believe he spent it and not remember where. On the other hand, take some item of value and the owner will hunt it to the ends of the earth.

Allison found a jewelry box open on the dresser of the second house she'd entered. Lovely pieces draped over the edge. The antique lamp's soft light shown on the jewelry making them appear even richer to her eye. She couldn't help hooking her index finger under a necklace lifting it to the light. *It's real.* Gently pulling her finger away, Allison let the necklace relax back in place. Her eyes caught a watch; its band studded with diamonds. *God, I love that.* Her hand hovered just inches away.

Slowly, she forced herself to move into the hallway and to the office or den. It was too dark, and she wasn't sure which. She let her eyes get accustomed to the gloom before moving into the room. Heavy drapes shut out any light from the windows; there stood a couch just ahead of her, then she saw an open door to a large safe. It startled her. "Who keeps a large safe practically in the middle of the room?" she said out loud, then listened to make sure she was alone in the room. Allison knelt in front of the opening; the cash had her mesmerized.

Carefully, she unzipped her bag and began stuffing the currency down inside. *The stacks were five across and*

175

twenty high. There is no way she could carry all of it now.
Allison could fit only one stack in her bag. She felt a stab
of uncertainty as she pushed the money down into her bag;
she forced the zipper to close. As she stood, a pair of men's
shoes caught her eye. They were weird since for them to be
up like that someone had to be in them.

Allison stiffened with fear. Slowly, she looked over
the couch into the face of a young man staring back at her.
She gasped. *It's not right, the way he looks;* she knew she
should check for a pulse, but jerked back in terror instead.
She pressed her hand over her mouth so she would not
make another sound. Slowly, she looked again at the
neatly dressed man in a business suit. The man seemed
freshly shaved and had a rose pinned to his lapel. *He's
dead. Someone put him there.*

Are we alone, this body lying on the floor and me?
Allison's eyes felt like they would pop out from straining.
A cold chill crept over her as she went back to the window.
Allison let her body slide over the sill. She hurried down
the driveway and spotted Roland. "Roland," her hoarse
voice reached across the street stopping Roland in his
tracks.

He came across the street at her frantic motion.
"What?" he asked looking into her stricken face.

Her voice came across in a hoarse whisper as she
pointed and said, "There's a dead guy in there, and enough
money to keep us for a long time. I've shoved as much of it
as I could in here." She patted the bag hanging over her
shoulder.

Without further discussion, he left her and slipped
through the window.

Allison's arms flew out from her sides, "Oh, great,
now what do I do, stand here?" she said to the driveway.

Roland flung his leg over the sill, emerged from the
house, then hurried back to her, "Come on," he said. They
ran to the truck.

Ray felt confused when they ran back to the truck. Because this was not supposed to happen, everyone was supposed to be calm and quiet. He started to ask questions.

Roland cut him off. "Allison, you're our driver now. Ray and I are going back inside. Pull these rubber gloves on Ray. Allison, you wait ten minutes, then come into the driveway backward, got that?"

Finally, Ray thought as he ran side by side with Roland to the open window. "What's up?" he asked.

"Get in there," Roland said and pointed, then followed Ray inside the house. "Come on." They made their way to the man lying on the floor.

"How comes he's dead?" Ray asked.

"I don't know, but look at all that loot. Allison boosted some of it, and we're taking the rest." Roland said. Roland found a bedroom and took a pillow case pulling the pillow free and tossing it aside. "Ray, we are going to fill this pillow case with all that money," He said, rushing back into the room. They worked fast and in a few minutes pushed the pillow through the window followed by themselves.

Roland and Ray were both carrying the pillowcase while running awkwardly toward the truck. Jumping into the front seat Roland shoved the pillowcase down into the foot well and said, "Move this thing."

"We should've looked at his wallet to find out who he was," Allison said putting the truck in gear.

"No way, I'm not getting near any stiff, man. You can forget that noise." Ray said as he settled into the seat and tried to find a place for his legs.

The pickup raced toward Plymouth Laundry and Dry Cleaning, turned on the south side of the lot, and came to a stop alongside the Ford. The lot was empty, but the three felt the need to hurry and not talk. Ray and

Roland changed the plates; then Allison drove off the lot heading for Lodi. By the time they caught up, she had made it to Lodi, left the stolen pickup in its place in the parking lot, and started walking down the block.

Roland spotted her and the oversized bag she carried over her shoulder. She had let her hair down and turned the baseball cap backward on her head.

He slowed, lowered the window, and called, "Hey, Cutie, want a ride?"

Chapter Thirty-One

10:00 A.M. July 16

Ray lay atop his sleeping bag wearing his dirty T-shirt and dusty jeans, much too excited to care about the uncomfortable hard floor. The black clothing he wore to the score tonight was now tucked inside his duffel bag in the corner of the room. He pressed his lips tightly to keep from shouting, Two Hundred Thousand Dollars. One night, one hit with Roland and Allison, and there's more money than he ever believed possible. He could buy that damn horse if he had to. He could show everyone who ever thought he wouldn't be somebody, how friggin' wrong they were, especially his grandparents.

The glow of confidence helped spread a smile over his face. Slowly, he brought his foot up and pulled the other shoe at the heel. It fell from his foot, then his big toe found the back of the other shoe and sent it clattering to the floor. Slowly, he stretched and wiggled his toes.

He daydreamed about opening that first package of twenty-dollar bills and how it felt to have that much money in his hand. Allison used a calculator to add the individual tallies, which totaled two-hundred thousand. He was rich, and the thought brought a broad smile.

Eventually, the money was divided, and Ray held exactly Sixty- six thousand six hundred sixty-six dollars. Over and over in his mind, he thought about how grandly he'd told Allison and Roland to keep the 66 cents. Ray lifted his legs, placing his feet flat on the flannel; then he slid his hands to cradle his head, more pleased and peaceful than he'd ever been in his life. He could hear their muffled voices. They couldn't sleep either.

In an instant he stood, eager to join them. He crept to their bedroom, cupped his hand around his ear, and pressed it to the door, just in case they were doing something he shouldn't invade. He smiled as he placed his ear against the wall.

"No, Roland," Allison said then paused for a long moment. "The old woman saw the guy. She told me the police took her to a hypnotist, and they made her remember everything about how he looked. You know that camouflage jacket Ray's got hanging on a nail in his room?"

"Yeah," Roland said in a muffled voice.

"She said the guy wore one like that the day of the murder," Allison said.

Little by little the smiled faded. Ray realized they were talking about Sam Nelson's murderer. *They're talking about me!* His eyes widened as he pressed harder, trying to hear every single word.

"And she said he wore a blond wig. The police know all about what he looks like. Do you think they'll come here? You know, to arrest him?" Allison asked.

Fear ate at Ray's heart. He had to leave here. For sure, he had to make a stab at the Franklin girl. She would know if her father was close to figuring the case out. Where would he go, back to his grandparents? The thought chilled him. Ray pressed harder.

"She said she found the body on July second. There's no way Ray could have known the guy was dead when we met him at the lake unless he killed him. It's that simple, Roland."

"So, he couldn't know from the newspaper because there wouldn't have been anything in the paper before the second. You may be right. Just be careful from now on," Roland said.

"Maybe we should ask him to leave?"

"He's not going to leave the eleven million dollar scam we've got going."

That's right. Ray's ear burned, no matter how he adjusted himself. Their voices muted, and he couldn't make out anymore. Slowly, he crept back to his room. He had to think. *Where does this old woman live? She's a neighbor to Nelson. Okay, he'd find her and take care of business.* Ray's shoulders dropped as though all the fun had gone out of the day.

The call pierced the darkened room. Art's lazy hand probed for the receiver. Finding it, he sleepily answered, "Yeah?" His eyes felt glued shut, and he fought a yawn that stretched his jaw wide. Groping the phone, he managed to get his ear in contact, and he heard a man's voice. He sat up. *I know that voice.* Art tried to focus on the alarm clock, but it was just out of range.

"Las Vegas P.D. has Gainey," Walt said again.

His voice clicked in Art's brain. He sat straight up, instantly wide awake.

"They want to know what we want to be done?" Walt said.

"See if they'll waive extradition. Try to get him on the next flight back here", Art answered while swinging his legs over the edge of the bed. *No point in going back to sleep. He was awake now. Finally a break in our favor.* Waiting for something to happen always took too long and

181

M.L.WEATHERINGTON

Art didn't think he had gotten any better at the job of killing time. At least for him, there's no more sitting stakeout. He was glad. That was for the younger guys. Art got up and headed for the bathroom.

The shower door clicked open, and Art reached for a towel, pulling it around him. He tucked it around his waist as he stepped onto the bathmat and burst into a rich baritone. His hand shook the shaving cream. Totally into the melody he sang out "Gainey will be going away."

Chapter Thirty-Two

11:00 A.M. July 16

R ay parked a few feet from the stable door and walked to the opening. He watched as Melissa lifted the mane and smoothed it over the black horse's browband. She slipped her finger under the straps near Midnight's ears just as the horse took two sideway steps riveting his eyes on Ray's entry.

Melissa lifted her saddle off the stand and heaved it up on the tall horse, catching the cinch as it swung under his belly. She discovered Ray's approach as she pulled the cinch strap tight.

"Hey," Ray said as he made his voice low and melodic, drawing the sound out as long as possible.

"Hi," she answered back. "You find a horse yet?"

"I've been busy." He leaned down and picked up some straw. "You have a great horse. I thought you might point me to a good one."

"No. I just got lucky with Midnight." Melissa finished checking all the buckles on the cinch. She pulled the stirrup to check the seat of the saddle. "I got Midnight over a year ago now. I don't think I've seen any of the horses that are listed." She turned toward Ray.

He took a relaxed stance, his smile a killer.

She smiled back at him. "I've got to get some miles in today." Melissa forced herself to study Midnight's mane

183

near the saddle horn, eventually allowing her eyes to center on Ray's. "When did you want to check those horses out?"

Ray cast his eyes down to the ground, then raised them, slowly leveling on hers. "I'm free now."

"Let me take Midnight around the ring for half an hour. Then I can go with you. I need to exercise him. He gets so excited when I saddle him; I wouldn't dare just put him back in the stall." She pulled a sugar cube from her pocket and offered it to Midnight. Turning her head she tried to hide the flush that had settled in her cheeks, but Ray saw and knew he was getting to her.

"Sure enough, I'll just watch if that's okay."

"That's great." She swung into the saddle, gathered the reins, and booted Midnight's ribs.

Ray watched them jog slowly out into the sunshine.

He called to her and asked, "Will it be okay if you go with me in my car to the feed store?"

Melissa kept her eyes straight ahead, her attention on Midnight while opening the gate and entering the arena.

Ray thought as she rounded the ring. *Maybe a hamburger; I'll keep the smile going and make as though I dig her.*

"Oh, sure," she yelled over her shoulder. She sat back in the saddle and Midnight responded by setting both rear feet forward and slid to a stop, she leaned her weight and swung the horse around, and trotted back to Ray. "I just have to be someplace by five this evening. I have a babysitting job."

"No problem," he said. *That works out for me, kiddo; I've got a date with an old lady.* Ray kept his pearliest smile on display. "I just didn't want you to get into trouble with your folks."

Charlie, the owner of the stable, drove his beat-up old Ford pickup into the paddock area near the barn, and

Melissa brought Midnight to a halt and called out, "Hey, Charlie."

"What can I do for ya?" Charlie answered as he looked in her direction. He worked on a well-chewed, unlit cigar protruding from his mouth as he sauntered toward the arena. He wore faded jeans, a blue checked shirt, and a hat dirty with years of handling. His tanned skin held deep wrinkles on a face with friendly brown eyes. He placed his callused hands over the railing.

"Can I put Midnight into the pasture until four today? I'd like him to get more exercise, and I need to go somewhere for a few hours." Melissa pointed toward Ray. "I'm going to help him find a horse." She smiled sweetly at Charlie, and his toothless grin matched hers.

"Sure," he said. "Be good for the old man." Charlie rubbed the horse's soft nose, swung a glance at Ray, nodded to him, after a moment he backed away to finish unloading his vehicle.

Ray watched her put the horse out. *Okay, all you want to do this time is get close.* He pulled his car keys out of his pocket and smiled as she ran toward him.

1 P.M.

"You're Peter Reese Gainey?" Art asked holding a file.

Gainey zeroed in on Art's mustache as it twitched, then on the file before looking up into the lieutenant's eyes.

"Yes," he answered in a voice that quivered. "What's this all about?"

"Tell us what you remember of June 28?" Art asked keeping his eyes on Gainey.

"June 28? Well, I don't know."

Art watched him process and thought it looked like the man's mind went blank. That's fear, he decided.

"I had a normal day, closed up after lunch. I had dinner with my Dad, then left town."

"You didn't tell your father you were leaving town?" Art asked.

"Hell no; the old fart plays the stroke card every time he gets a chance. You crunch numbers like I crunch them, you've got to drop out for a while."

"What can you tell us about Sam Nelson?"

Reese Gainey tensed.

Art had on his poker face. "You saw Mr. Nelson on the 28th?"

Reese Gainey squirmed in the chair. Art knew he needed the bathroom, using that need often helped get answers sooner so Reese Gainey would not be using the head anytime soon.

"Yes, he was my last client for the day."

"Did you go to his home?"

Gainey looked from Art to Walt. Gainey's brows came together, and he answered, "No, I've never been to his home."

Art looked from Gainey to Walt. A silent message passed between Walt and Art. *That's a flat out lie.*

"Mr. Gainey, you're under arrest for the murder of Sam Nelson," Walt said and moved toward Reese Gainey.

3:30 P.M.

"So you think the Bay is better than the Dun?" Ray said as he brought the hamburgers on a tray, setting them on a yellow, plastic table. "Want catsup?" He asked and looked her square in the eyes as she slid into the plastic seat.

"Yes, on both. I want lots of catsup." She said while she unwrapped one of the sandwiches, then shook the fries from the container onto a napkin. "My faves."

Ray grabbed a handful of the little pillow packages and sat across from her, letting the tomato sauce fall from his hand between them. "Why the bay over the other one?" Ray took a bite of his hamburger and followed it with a gulp of Coke.

She swabbed a long thin fry in a pool of catsup. "The bay's a gelding; you'll get more use out of him."

"I sure did like the dun's coloring. Boy, that stripe down her back, and a black mane and tail. She sure is beautiful."

"What's wrong with the Bay?" Melissa asked as she dabbed her mouth with a napkin. "It's got a black mane and tail."

"Nothing, I guess. They want a lot for him," Ray said.

"About what I paid for Midnight. Good horses aren't cheap."

Ray and Melissa ate in silence, finishing together they rolled up their papers, sipped the last of their sodas and left the hamburger joint.

4:30 P.M.

Ray pulled the car to a stop by some tall eucalyptus trees, his hand resting on the keys, ready to pull them from the ignition. He turned to Melissa. "I had a nice time."

"So did I."

Ray gave her his steady gaze. "You say when it's a good day for you, and we'll see that gelding." He said, then sighed. "I guess I'd better get your bike out of the trunk."

Both of them walked to the back of the car, and Ray pulled her bike free.

Before they could say anything else to each other, Nicole's children piled out of the house and raced across the lawn yelling at the top of their lungs, begging Melissa to come with them. Melissa reluctantly said, "See you."

Ray walked around to the driver's side of the car. "Tomorrow, at the stables, about ten?" He called over the top of the car.

"I'll be there." She flashed him her widest smile as he brought his two fingers to salute.

He had her attention–hook, line, and sinker.

"Naw, you promised you'd play with us today, and it's almost dinner time," a chorus of small people said.

"Just a minute, keep your socks on." She rolled her bike to the house and leaned it against the wall. Melissa pushed the screen door open and walked inside, her legs weighed down with two little ones clinging to them." Nicole, I'm here."

Nicole reclined on the couch a magazine on her lap. Something wonderful was cooking and filling the room with fragrance. "I can see that. When did you sprout those appendages?"

The boy's chin rose, and he indignantly said, "I'm not appendages, Mom. I'm J.R."

"Yes, you are," Nicole said as she looked lovingly at her son.

Melissa sniffed and asked, "Pork chops? With applesauce?" She loved Nicoles pork chops and could eat a couple even though she was stuffed with a hamburger. "How was your day?"

"Evidently not as good as yours. Want to tell me about the hunk?" Nicole said as she laid her magazine down.

Melissa smiled. "I think I have to play right now," she said as the children pulled on her arms and dragged her out onto the lawn.

Nicole checked her watch; there was time before dinner was ready, so she picked up her magazine. She crossed her feet at the ankles and settled back into the couch cushion while yelling at Melissa. "What a chicken way of getting out of telling me about him."

The screen door slammed, and the yard filled with laughter as Melissa joined in the fun with the kids. Her heart hummed a private tune.

Chapter Thirty-Three

5:00 P.M. July 16th, 1995

As soon as Ray turned the corner, his sweet boy smile faded, and he was all business. He had Melissa solid, and he felt pleased with himself. He drove to Highway Twelve and turned eastward.

Ray guided the car through the dirt path and the trees until he was up to the old, gray, clapboard house. Ray parked his Ford by the back porch. He pulled the keys from the ignition when a noise caused him to look at the back door.

Roland and Allison came busting out the door. "Good thing you're back. We're wigging out man," Roland said as he and Allison rushed up to his driver's side door.

"What's wrong?" Ray looked from one to the other. Clearly, they were worried about something, and he wondered if it had any implication for him.

"We've got to get back up to the Gold Country. Now!" Roland said. His facial expression filled with worry as the wind lifted his hair.

"Why?" Ray asked and looked first at Roland then Allison.

"Just drive this tub, will yah?"

Ray nodded that he could drive them. Then he asked, "Where are we going?"

"Back to Mickey's." Allison's voice displayed urgent need.

"Who's Mickey?" Ray twisted around watching as they circled the car to get into the front seat.

"You know, the stiff from last night," Allison said as though everyone should know who the dead guy was.

They were acting strange even for them, he thought. "You want to go back to that house?" Ray leaned forward looking past Allison and straight at Roland. "Isn't that dumb, Roland?" Ray asked with a sense of foreboding and anger mixing through his feelings. "Is this plan B?" he asked narrowing his eyes.

Allison settled in the middle of the seat and said, "Roland can't find his wallet. We figured he dropped it from his pants pocket when he stuffed some of the money into his pants."

Ray thought, *And they think I'm dumb.* He felt better about himself as they talked, but then the idea of his car being spotted didn't sit well with him. "Shit man. We've got to boost another car; I don't want the Ford seen around that house." His voice sounded confident.

Allison had her large bag. It was stuffed full, and she hugged the bag to her right side away from Ray. She did her best to make sure Ray didn't notice her movements, but he saw, he just didn't know what was going on with these two.

He didn't need to worry about that; it was her mouth that caught Ray's attention. She talked and talked until he wanted to shut her up. He clenched his left fist near his left knee. Ray asked, "What are you suggesting we do, drive there right now, in the middle of the day? You want to go through the house looking for a wallet now?" He looked straight at her.

Her head nodded as she turned her face to him and said, "You got a better idea?" She made a motion with her head that suggested let's go and said, "We've got to get it before the cops find it."

Ray sat there, his hand on his keys in the ignition and asked, "That's the only place it could be? You've gone through your things?" Ray questioned all the while thinking, that it would be better to wait until nightfall. Then go back to the Gold Country. "A storm is coming in tonight."

Allison nodded again squirming in her seat. "We went through the house over and over. It's not here," Allison said. "Can we just get going?"

Roland managed to fit his body into the front seat and closed the car door. He brought his hands to his forehead as though to hold his head. "I'm more worried whether they've found the body," Roland said as he nervously pushed his hair back over his head. "If they have, and I left my wallet they've got my ID, I'm history. They'll try to pin that stiff on me for sure. We've got to get out of here today," Roland said leaning a bit forward to see Ray better.

Stabbing fear raced through Ray. *What are they saying?* "Everything's just coming together now, and you want to bail?" He looked from Roland's face to Allison's. "What about the scam? Are you just forgetting about that money?"

Roland's face changed two shades of red and looked like he wanted to explode. "Just drive us, Ray, now!"

"Ray, just drive," Allison said her voice high and tight.

"We can't take this car into that housing area."

Ray didn't want the Ford associated with that area period. *Not another body, shit.* He had enough trouble going on right now and didn't want anymore. Ray didn't see any other way but to drive them back out there.

"Where do you want to go to boost the car?" A quiet moment passed. "Because we are not using this one." Then the thought came to him. *They think I killed the old man. Are they trying to pin this Mickey on me?*

Allison looking at Ray's eyes said, "The parking lot by the movie theater on Elm Street. Go!"

Fuming, Ray hit the accelerator, and the Ford shot backward.

Chapter Thirty-four

5:15 P.M. July 16

Angry steel gray clouds scudded together hiding the azure sky. Wind-whipped trees sent an eerie whistle to the ear. Downtown Lodi lay hunkered down and still. The century-old brick building stood sentinel over the parking lot. In a few hours, the night would come and, with it, a summer electrical storm of major proportions. Ray sat quietly next to Roland as the wind whistled in his ear, his mouth set, his mind working.

He could see Allison pushing through forceful wind gusts. Missing her latex gloves, she hunted, leaving fingerprints on several vehicles in the parking lot. Finally, she settled on a blue sedan.

She turned waving frantically. They left Ray's Ford and ran to the blue sedan. Ray, his breath shortened, worried about their intentions. His Grandmother's words circled in his mind, 'Hang with those two and you'll end up in trouble.'

They drove at the speed limit to the area where they'd burgled the money. While cruising slowly past the house, Allison said, "Everyone must be inside because of the wind."

"Yeah," Roland said. "Let's go around to the next block, and I'll get out there."

"You still think it's a good idea to go back to that house in daylight?" Ray watched Roland as he waited for an answer. Usually, he was the careful one. He's the one always looking for another way out and watching your back. Ray saw how jumpy Roland acted and asked, "So, what's the plan?"

Roland answered, "This plan's going to be made up as we go along. Except..." he paused for a long moment, and the wind whistled through the slightly opened window. "You guys stay here. I'll see if I can get in and if I can." He paused looking around the neighborhood, then checked at his watch, and said, "Give me ten minutes if I'm not back then take off."

"Leave you here?" Allison's hand grabbed at his arm. "I'm not leaving you."

He pulled away. "Don't go nuts on me, Al. If the cops get me, I'll toss my phone if I can. That way they won't find you right off. You have to go. Allison that stiff's going to be tagged on someone. It's best if it's just me." With that, he left them and ran across the street, disappearing into the bushes next to the house.

He's got more balls than a golf course water-trap, Ray thought, as he slid his arm over the backrest. "The wind's picking up," he said to Allison, who focused on the direction Roland had taken.

Art looked at Tracy and called out. "Get Gainey senior on the line."

She had her head down studying something on her desk. Tracy sat back, turned from her computer work to look up the number. She dialed, listened a second, then turned to look at Art and nodded for him to pick up.

"Mr. Gainey, Art Franklin here." Art rubbed his temples with his fingertips. That headache lingered. He could use a nap, hell; he could use a stiff drink.

Senior Gainey cleared his throat and asked, "Have you any word on my son?"

"Yes sir, he's fine, and he's here right now." Art said then guarded his speech and said the words that were going to hurt and shock any parent. "Mr. Gainey, he is under arrest for the murder of Sam Nelson." His lower lip covered his mustache, and he drew the lip down smoothing the hairs waiting for the expected reply. It came just as Art knew it would.

"What?" Senior Gainey's strident voice expressed his alarm. "What did you say?"

Ray spotted Roland before Allison, but she had the door open before Ray could tell her. Roland hit the seat, and Ray pressed the accelerator. "Well?" Ray asked as Roland shoved Allison more toward Ray, and the car began to roll.

Roland settled into the seat and closed the car door. "No good. I couldn't find the wallet."

Allison looked at him. "Is Mickey still there?" she asked.

"Yeah, nothing's different," Roland answered.

High winds beat at the trees and swayed wooden power poles. "Until the stiff's found I'm safe. Until I find my wallet, I'm not safe." It was a quandary for all of them. "Let's take off up the hill and find a motel to stay in for the night. We can decide what to do once we're there."

"We need to make up our minds or buy more gas," Ray said looking at the gauge.

Allison leaned toward Roland and said, "What about the house and all the scam mail that's ready to go out? We can't just leave it there."

Roland shook his head, lowered it, and said, "Well, it looks to me like it's going to sit there until we figure out if it's safe to go back."

"I've got to go back," Ray said taking his eyes off the road momentarily to get eye contact with Roland.

"Why?" Allison asked as she looked at Ray.

196

"I just do," Ray said. "Oh, there's a station, I'll get gas for this buggy. Regular okay?"

"Yeah, it's okay."

"Who's paying?"

"Well, dickhead, I will as soon as I find my wallet."

As he pulled to a stop, he stepped out and engaged the pump. He stood thinking; *I want to retrieve the handgun and other evidence in my jacket, as well as get my share of the money from the burglary.* He leaned in the window, "I left the money in my sleeping bag."

Roland looked at Allison.

She tightened her arms closer to her side, Ray barely heard the exchange between them, but saw the movement and wondered what was happening that they weren't sharing with him.

Roland still whispering into her ear as Allison shook her head in reply to his words. She whispered something back, and Roland whispered to her again.

Ray was fed up and just about to let them know he didn't like it one bit when they whispered. It left him to think all kinds of things, none of them good. Ray ran into the station and paid for the gas. He slid back into his seat as Roland looked at Ray and then out the window at the trees beaten by the wind and said. "I don't know, Al. Let me think, Okay?"

She moved away from Roland and said loud enough for Ray to hear "Okay!" she said, "How about Jackson?"

"Yeah, that's good; we can go to the casino," Roland said.

"I'd like to go back and get my car and drop this car off," Ray said. "This car still has its plates, I just think..."

"Not tonight, shit face," Roland snapped back his reply.

Ray looked at the car's floorboard as he reasoned. *Melissa will be looking for me tomorrow at the stables. If I go to Jackson now, how can I be back here at ten o'clock in the morning?*

Ray couldn't figure a way out of his troubles. *I've got to get over to the old lady's and get rid of her.* Sluggishly, he started the blue sedan for the casino in Jackson. The vehicle rode smoothly over the undulating back country road now dim in the evening light. Moments later the heavens to the west lit up, giving the clouds a ghost-like appearance. Every few minutes he checked the rearview mirror for cop cars. So far so good, he thought as he gripped the steering wheel tighter.

They managed to stay out of the heavy rain most of the way to Jackson and found the casino easy enough. "Okay," Allison said, "Let's get a shower and come back down here for dinner in an hour and a half. Then we'll feel like figuring this out."

Ray firmly pressed the elevator up button. He didn't like this one bit.

Chapter Thirty-Five

9:30 A.M. July 17

Midnight's hooves danced with impatience. They should be out in the crisp morning air. He snorted his disproval at being tied to his stall door. His eye watched while she hung out at the opening of the barn. He swung his rump around, snorted again, and pawed the ground.

Ray hadn't come by this morning as he had promised. Melissa's shoulders slumped as she walked to Midnight and freed the reins. His muscles shivered with excitement as she jumped into the stirrup, then raised herself onto the saddle. She felt his sides swell as they jogged slowly out of the barn. Melissa watched clouds for the next storm forming, but right now it was dry enough to get some exercise. "Hey, Charlie, how'd you like last night's storm?"

The man leaned over, grabbed a bale of hay by the wires, and hefted it off the back of the hay truck to the ground. "Had my hands full, that's what I thought. We got plenty of lightning with that one, and I figured, for a while, that the barn might fall over from the wind."

Melissa held Midnight back as she talked with Charlie. She looked the barn over and said, "I love this old barn, and I hope it's here forever."

He jumped down from the truck, picked up a shovel, rested his hands on the top of the shovel handle, and set his chin on top of his hands. He smiled at her, looked at the barn and said, "That's asking a lot."

She gathered the reins and sat straighter. "We're going to do ten miles today before the next storm comes in."

Charlie looked skyward and studied the clouds then said, "I expect that'll be about five."

"I'll have Midnight bedded down by then. I'm babysitting this evening again."

"You're sure a busy gal, Miss Melissa. Sure you got time for a boyfriend?" Charlie asked through a smile.

"I don't have a boyfriend." Her cheeks reddened as she answered him.

Charlie's cheeks swelled up as he bit down on his unlit cigar. "Sure looked that way to me," he said casting his eyes away not to notice the reddening of her face.

She lowered her head for a moment to hide the embarrassment although she allowed the corners of her mouth to turn up a bit as her eyes looked once more for Ray's car. She bit her bottom lip, nudged Midnight, and said, "Later Charlie."

10:16 A.M.

Ray stood at the casino information counter listening as a young female clerk explained, "There's a shuttle bus that runs to Lodi from here. You can catch the next one at 10:30 a.m."

Ray nodded and said, "Thank you. How much is it?"

"It's a free service," she said. She reached for a card and slid it across the polished counter to Ray, "Just show the driver this pass and he'll know you're staying with us."

"Thanks," he said and picked up the pass.

An hour later, after bidding a quick goodbye to Roland and Allison, Ray arrived at the Lodi Senior Center.

Two tree service trucks parked on the street had their equipment chewing up downed limbs and sang a high pitch whine as the wood met the blades. Ray stepped from the shuttle and walked briskly.

A block away from his car a shiver of fear shook him. *There's a police car at the curb near my car.*

Ray stopped.

He searched the parking lot. A man, woman, and a teenage girl standing with the cop in the lot right where the blue car they'd stolen were parked. Ray ignored them and continued to his Ford.

"Excuse me, sir," the cop turned toward him and spoke.

Ray's eyes closed for an instant. *I have to respond.*

"Yes?"

Ray turned looking at the family, trying not to look into the cop's face.

The officer walked toward Ray. "Is this your car?" he asked Ray.

"Yes."

He saw the notation of his license plate number going into the cop's notes.

Shit!

The officer looked up, "When did you park here?"

Ray looked at him, every nerve in his body telling him to run. "Yesterday. I went up to the casino for the evening."

"Did you see anyone hanging around the parking lot when you left your car?"

Ray's legs, eager to move, shook, but his voice was firm, "No."

"Did you see a Blue sedan parked here when you left your vehicle?"

Ray shook his head and said sharply, "No."

The officer turned toward the family, "Well, it seems the young lady there received a car as a gift yesterday. She left the keys in the ignition, and it's missing. Just wondered if you saw anyone around the car?"

"I didn't." Ray watched the girl wiping her eyes.

The officer thanked him, nodded, and backed away.

Ray drove his car off the lot. A block away, Ray pulled over and looked in his rearview mirror to see if the cop followed him. His hands shook as he clenched and unclenched the steering wheel to settle down. The road was clear. He'd go to the house, get the money, pick up the mail, then do the old lady.

In the daylight? Shit! Once in my life could something work out? After the old witch is gone, he'd find Melissa and try to make up with her.

Right now, he needed to get the money, so focus on that he told himself. Everything else will fall into place. As he turned onto a dirt path to the farmhouse, Ray decided to park among the trees and go on foot to the house.

The wind picked up, shaking the leaves, and creating enough noise to cover his passage. Ray made it to the side of the house and peered into each window as he moved around to the door.

The house was clear. Confidence filled him, and he walked into the farmhouse and directly to his sleeping bag. He jerked it up from the floor. Ray searched his room. He went through his jacket then tossed it on the floor. The money was gone!

He walked to Roland and Allison's room; it looked tossed. Ray searched through the whole house. He lifted the trap door, leaving it precariously against the chair, then looked down into the basement. Through the dimness, he could see it was empty. Anger raced through him as he flashed on Allison holding their bag close to her when they left here. *They've got it. They've got my money. That's what's in her bag.*

Ray forgot about the scam material while lumbering out the door, racing to his car, and the casino. He gave no

202

thought to the evidence in his room. Ray wanted one thing only, Allison's neck!

Melissa was startled by Ray's Ford as it careened out of the copse just ahead of her. It's wheels spraying grit. Midnight reared and whinnied. She stood in the stirrups, lifted the reins, and yelled, "Yaw, yaw." The horse stretched his legs in a hard run toward Victor Road.

Ray raced away never looking back.

"Ray!" She yelled over and over. Midnight couldn't keep up this pace, and Melissa knew it. Disappointed, she sat back in the saddle and let the horse slow down. The animal, invigorated by the run, snorted disapproval. She stroked his neck to calm him. She then turned back, curious about the pathway they had just raced over.

Two sharp jabs sent Midnight to canter. She wanted to see where Ray had been. She came through the trees noticing tire marks on the dirt leading to an old farm house. The back door stood open.

Melissa jumped down from Midnight, tied him securely to a branch. Cautiously, she approached the house. "Hello?" She yelled as she stuck her head into the doorway. "Anyone here?" The wind made enough noise to muffle her voice. Knowing it was wrong to enter without being asked, she called out again, louder this time. "Hello, is anyone here?" Melissa asked. One foot, then two, she walked into the kitchen, noting the dishes piled in the sink.

She stood at the table looking at all the envelopes ready to be mailed; then she walked over to the opening in the floor. She dropped to her knees attempting to see what was down there. Curiosity drew her. "Hello?"

Not knowing the carpenter had yet to screw the stairs permanently in place, Melissa started down. Her hand steadied her as she stepped onto the dirt floor. At the moment Melissa left the stairs, they shifted slightly. The movement was enough to allow the trap door to slam shut.

Caught in sudden darkness, Melissa screamed, "Hey, anyone!" The smell of old wood and chilled dirt lay pungently on the air. The cold dampness crept upon her, and she wrapped her arms around herself.

"Help me. Someone help!"

Scream after scream left her throat.

Midnight's ears caught her plea, and he pulled against his tether. The reins held. He stepped back and forth, frantic to reach her. His ears pricked sharply forward. His nostrils fully flared. Midnight whinnied until his sides shook.

Ray's anger carried him up the entry stairs through the front lobby of the casino to the elevator. He repeatedly punched the up arrow. Finally, the doors to the elevator slowly opened. He jumped inside and rode it up until it glided to a stop.

Ray raced down the carpeted hall, came to stop just outside room 1210, and he slid his key card into the slot. He heard the door unlock, and he pushed it open. His eyes narrowed as he walked boldly into the room. It held that silence of an empty room. He knew. They're gone. The money's gone. His money was gone. Ray made a fist. Anger built in him and he wanted to put a hole in the fancy wallpapered casino or someone's face.

He raced down to the lobby and to the information desk where he asked about Allison and Roland. They had checked out leaving him with the room. The clerk looked at Ray with expectation. Ray knew he'd never find them; they were gone. *So, I'm supposed to pay for this room?* He smiled his best smile at the clerk and backed away. He almost trotted out the front door to locate the blue sedan. It was gone.

Chapter Thirty-Six

4:46 P.M. July 17

Lieutenant Gilbert filled the doorway of Art's office his hands gripping the jamb. The lines in his face appeared deeper, dark brown circles hung under his eyes and showed he hadn't slept for a long time.

Art's stomach turned.

By the look on Gilbert's face, the news wasn't good. He took a deep breath wishing there wasn't so much bad news and waved indicating that Gilbert should sit.

Gilbert sighed. "They found Steven," he said as he came fully into the office and eased his body heavily into a chair.

Art sat forward. "Where?"

Gilbert's lips pouted, he looked at the floor then up at Art. "In a house in Plymouth." Gilbert shifted his feet. "He'd been set up, no doubt. They dressed him up, put a flower in his lapel, and marked him as a leader." Gil looked at the ceiling and said, "They cleaned him up, so even we didn't know him. You know, when he took the aka *Raven*, he lost all contact with hygiene. We always teased him that he had more lice on him than ten school kids. County called us on this about an hour ago said they found him near an open safe. Dental records and fingerprints identified him. Whoever left him there put a fake ID on him." Gilbert took a deep breath and let it out. "Damn safe was empty except for some manila envelopes proving

Steven guilty of dealing on a grand scale and indicating that there should have been a sizeable sum of money there."

Art turned his head and looked through the slats of the blinds, out into the parking lot, and to the large oak that stood sentinel over his city car. His mind gathered thoughts as he brought his attention back to Gilbert. "How'd he die?" Art asked as he placed his elbows on his desk clasping his fingers together and resting his chin on them.

Gilbert yawned and wiped his eyes. "Shot through the heart," he said as he shook his head. "Someone took that money, should have been about two hundred thousand." He looked at Art, shrugged his shoulders and said, "The question is, who? And how do they fit in all this? And, are we going to get another chance at this drug cartel? I have to tell the girlfriend, not something I want to do." Gilbert shook his head in frustration.

Tracy's heels clicked across the floor as she rushed into Art's office breaking the men's focus. She stared holes into Art and said, "You need to take the call on line two."

Art sat back looking at Gilbert finally bringing his attention to Tracy. He saw something in Tracy's expression that disturbed him. He grabbed the phone, "Hello, this is Lieutenant Franklin."

The phone rested in his left hand and against his ear. Gil took the hint and moved out of the room, drifting towards the detective's area as Art listened.

"This is Charlie at the stable. I don't mean to alarm you none, but Miss Melissa told me she planned to have Midnight bedded down before the storm hit tonight. Well, sir, she's not back yet. And the storm's a comin'." Charlie paused.

Art tensed his jaw and shot a look at the clock. "Has she ever been this late before?"

206

"Naw sir, not that I can say. Why she purely loves that horse, and she's all the time rubbing on the saddle. She wouldn't want any rain falling on that horse or her tack. No sir, it just doesn't feel right to me. That's why I'm callin'. You bein' her daddy and all. Besides, she said she was babysitting this evening."

"Charlie, give me your phone number." Art picked up his pen and wrote as Charlie spoke, then said, "Thanks for the heads up on this. I'll call you back in a minute. I want to call a few people and see if I can find her."

"You don't suppose she's with that boyfriend of hers, do yah?"

"What?"

Art about came out of his pants. His body jerked up out of his seat. He had to lean over to keep the phone in his ear, his voice dead serious, "Charlie, what boyfriend?"

"Ray— don't know the last name. The one wants to get a horse," Charlie answered as though Art should know.

Art's red-blond mustache twitched. "This is news to me. You've seen this boy?"

"Sure. He was here yesterday hanging around, watching Miss Melissa and Midnight. I, think he's quite smitten if you ask me. They put Midnight out in the pasture and took off in his car."

Art's knuckles turned white. His voice was changing as anger and concern set in, making him nuts as he asked, "What kind of car?"

Charlie took a moment. The line was clear then he said, "I don't rightly know; blue. That's all I remember."

"Thanks, Charlie." Art's hand went to his forehead and rested there. "I'll get right back to you. If she shows up, call me right away."

Art pawed through his desk for the friends list Melissa gave him at the beginning of the school year. He wasn't careful or neat that all flew out the window with the news of a boyfriend. Art was now a hunting dog, his

207

nose to the ground. He would get to the bottom of this or know why. Finally, he found the list. He called every number and came up zero.

It seemed even Sandy didn't know anything about this boyfriend Charlie mentioned or was she protecting Melissa? Something stinks, he thought. He grabbed his jacket off the hook and let Tracy know he was leaving the office.

It's 5:05 p.m. On my wrist watch. Three more hours and it'll be dark. He looked up at thunderheads crowding the sky, their tops glowing white, their underbellies steel-grey. They were heavy with rain and could make the Mokelumne crest.

Traffic seemed heavy as he worked his way across town. He drove twenty minutes before turning into the stables. As he brought the car to the barn, he saw Melissa's bike. His bottom lip rolled up, brushing his mustache as he considered the possibilities. One, he'd like to panic like any parent with a missing child. He felt like he'd been kicked him in the gut. And two, being trained, he knew missing children usually turn up with some plausible explanation. Three, what in hell was this boyfriend crap?

Art found Charlie in coveralls, a well-worn flannel shirt, and old cowboy boots that turned up at the toes placing flakes of alfalfa in the stalls. "Charlie," he said offering his hand. "Thanks for the call. When did you see her last?"

Charlie moved the well-chewed cigar around in his mouth, rubbed his hands clean on his jeans, then shook Art's hand. When they released, he pointed and said in his Texan drawl, "She took Midnight off down that there road to the trailhead along the river. Oh, along about noon, I think. Could be off, I didn't look at my watch. I was doing chores."

Art followed his direction seeing a mass of tall trees at the end of the road some distance off. He turned to Charlie and asked, "Tell me about the boy. Ray. What does he look like?" he asked.

Charlie shrugged his shoulders then said. "Nice enough. He's about five foot ten. Maybe twenty-something, maybe younger, brown hair, clean-cut guy."

Art looked around the stable area, "He wasn't here today? Didn't go with her?"

Charlie shook his head, "Naw, she was alone," he answered.

Art nodded and said. "Thanks, Charlie." He walked to the end of the barn and looked out into the dimming light. He couldn't wait any longer. He took his cell, punched in the numbers, and spoke as crisply and succinctly as possible, "San Joaquin, Lodi 402." Art waited.

A woman's warm, business-like voice answered, "Lodi 402, San Joaquin, go ahead with your traffic."

"San Joaquin, 402 requests an 87 with your Patrol area 22 unit at Lucky Horseshoe Stables, on Highway Twelve east. That's 10683 East Highway Twelve, reference an overdue rider."

"San Joaquin copies. Standby for ETA on the unit."

The heavens rumbled, and Art looked up as he said to the dispatcher, "402 copies." He brought the phone down from his mouth and felt loss settle in and the helpless feeling that comes when you can't seem to make it all better. That's what a parent is supposed to accomplish. Right now, he didn't know how to do that. Control over his life; that was what he was losing. He would be dependent on the help of others to find Melissa. It didn't sit well with him.

In a moment, dispatch told him that the patrol deputy was on the way. He turned, walked the length of the stables back to his car as the sheriff pulled off the road, came down the long driveway, and stopped within two feet of Art.

Deputy Jon Clemons, his tan uniform pressed into smart creases, stepped from the unit, reached out his hand. "Lieutenant Franklin, how can I help?"

Art smiled and said, "My daughter, Melissa, rode off down that trail," Art pointed, "about noon. She and the horse haven't returned."

Jon looked into Art's eyes with the practiced stare of a professional.

He nodded as Art continued, "She's fifteen," Art placed his hand breast high. "Five-Five and a half, one hundred five pounds, freckles. Green eyes, bright red hair to here." His hand moved to just above his belt. "Can't tell you what she's wearing," Art waved his hand toward the stable. "Charlie, the stableman, could." A look of worry settled on his face, and he looked at his toes for a moment. *This man can help, give him everything he needs.* "I think you met Melissa once a couple of years ago." Art looked into the Deputy's eyes and said, "Jon, Midnight's a large black horse, a cross between Quarter and Standard breed, with one white stocking on his hind leg."

"I believe I did meet her at the Grape Festival," Jon said.

"That's right." Art looked up at the sky, his face a mask of worry. "The storm's coming in." He hesitated a moment. "I called all her friends. No one has seen her. She was to babysit this evening, and she hasn't shown up over there either." Art looked at Jon. "I know you want me to stay put, but, Jon, I'd like to ride along."

Jon shook his head and said, "She might show up any minute, and you and I would be out there somewhere. Art, I know this area. You sit tight right here where I know how to find you. You be here for her if she comes in on her own."

"There's one more thing." Art eyes shifted off to the left, and he brought them back slowly and said, "There may be a boyfriend involved. Charlie can tell you more about him."

Together they walked to Charlie and Jon spoke with him gathering information. When he finished, he shook Charlie's hand nodded to Art, and they walked back to his unit. Jon nodded his head with understanding, "Sit tight and I'll be in touch."

Art keyed his cell phone. He watched the sheriff car move down the drive, past the tall grasses growing golden in the summer days. It turned following the path the horse would have taken when he carried Melissa.

The car was nearing the tree line as Art spoke, "Walt, I'm at the stables. San Joaquin's searching, I'm cooling my heels." He listened. "Yeah, I knew Tracy would tell you. Well, I now know firsthand what it feels like being a parent waiting on law enforcement."

"What can I do?"

"Just keep a cap on things there for me. I'll stay in touch, but I'm going to monitor the sheriff's channel as they search."

"We'll standby."

"Thanks, Walt."

Thunder clapped, rolling long and low. It rocked the air.

Art walked to his car and adjusted the radio and listened as Jon coordinated the search for Melissa and Midnight. Men were going from house to house now asking questions of the neighbors.

The collecting of information was the slow part of any investigation. Art knew how it worked all too well. He paced back and forth in the barn staying out of the rain that had been falling for the last few minutes, listening to nothing but static from the radio channel.

"Dear Lord, give me something."

Melissa shook from the cold. Slowly, she worked her way back up the shaky stairs. Her hand found the trap door, but it wouldn't go up when she pushed. She'd turned, placing her back to the floor above, then used her legs to shove upwards. The stairs trembled as the door held firm.

Remembering her Dad's words, she said them to herself. To conquer fear, get busy.

"How?"

Carefully, she felt her way down the stairs, determined to find a way out. With no light to aid her, the surroundings seemed both close and vast at the same time. To cross the floor filled her with dread. Would there be a floor under her next step?

Jon keened his ear, his hands gripped the steering wheel, his foot pressed the brake pedal. What had he heard at the end of the last roll of thunder? His sorted all the normal sounds; falling rain, wind moving through the trees, the sounds of life. Large trucks moved along the roadway, the sound of their wheels displacing water echoed.

Jon moved the Crown Victoria slowly forward. Thunder rolled, sending the rain harder.

There it was again!

Ahead, the land cut with tracks going into the trees. Jon turned on the path, and as he did, he heard a horse whinny. Jon drove the length of the dirt path, through the copse and into a clearing. He shut the unit off.

He's big and black, and there's the white foot. Midnight turned to the Sheriff's Deputy. His nostrils flared his eyes brilliant with excitement.

"Easy, big fella." Jon stepped from the vehicle and closed the distance between himself and the horse, placing his hand on the nervous animal's neck to soothe him. Then Jon moved away from Midnight and keyed up his mike, "San Joaquin, 3L20."

Dispatch answered, "3L20 go ahead."

"Request backup." He gave the location as he looked the horse over.

He turned his attention to the building seeing the back door open against the storm. That's not right. He left Midnight and walked to the house placing his back against the outside wall and calling through the doorway, "Hello, in the house?"

A woman's blood-curdling scream answered his call.

Jon's response was immediate. He keyed up and said, "3L20."

Dispatched answered, "Go ahead, 3L20."

"Possible female victim. Expedite that response."

Dispatch answered, "3L20 expediting."

Chapter Thirty-Seven

R ight after calling for backup, Jon hurried back to his unit, turned it to face the highway, then flicked the switch on the console. The lights on top of his car commenced to strobe, a beacon for his backup. As soon as he had set the signal, he raced back to the house. On the alert, gun drawn, he circled the building, glancing into each window as he moved around the house.

"Melissa Franklin. This is the San Joaquin County Sheriff's Department." He waited a moment and called out again. The wind buffeted his voice, and he knew he was not effective.

It does appear someone has been living here. Every room's been tossed. Jon didn't see any reason for the scream he'd heard. Just as he rounded the house to close the circle, his backup arrived.

Deputy Hal Dudley left his car door open and ran to join Jon. "What do we know?" he asked drawing his weapon.

Jon hollered against the wind, "Missing female, Lieutenant Franklin's daughter, 15 years old." He swung his arm extending his finger, "She came in on that horse. I heard a scream and responded. I've been around the outside parameter. It looks like someone was living here recently. Appears empty now."

Dudley nodded to him as they readied themselves, made eye contact and mentally agreed to enter.

"Hello, in the house. San Joaquin County Sheriff's Department. Come out of the house now," Jon yelled.

The howling wind whistled through the rafters. Jon looked at Dudley, indicating the inside of the house. They nodded to each other, wrapped themselves around the jamb and entered the kitchen.

Slowly, they circled the house, ending up back in the kitchen. They lowered their weapons and began studying each room's contents. Dried crusted food on the dishes piled in the sink. The milk in the refrigerator was still good. Jon set it back down and shut the door. They noticed the faded peeling walls, the dirty handprints at the light switches. The furniture looked unplanned. The living room held a card table filled with neatly stacked papers. "A mailing by the looks of everything," Jon said.

"You sure you heard a female scream?" Hal Dudley asked as they moved throughout the rooms.

"Positive, I heard a scream."

"Could have been the wind?" As he said that the wind whistled through the house. "Like that."

"No. It was the kind of scream that set your hair on end. No wind makes that kind of sound. It was human."

Dudley placed his hands on his hips and spread his feet apart, "Well, there's no one here. This place is empty. It's hard to say when anyone was here last. We ran some kids out last Halloween."

"I'd say a couple of days ago," Jon held up a two-day-old newspaper he'd picked up off the card table.

"What does that prove?"

"Look, I heard a scream," Jon said. He walked from the living room back down the hall and into Ray's room. For some reason, he leaned to study the pictures thumb-tacked to the wall. "Turn the light on, would you, Hal?"

"What'd you find?"

Light flooded the messy room and cleared the faces in the photos. Jon stood dumbfounded. There were several pictures posted. Four of them were of Art and Melissa in their back yard in their robes. It didn't make sense. The whole room was a stinking mess. Body odors mingled with the aged house and the stuff on the floor of this bedroom. Carefully aligned and thumb tacked to the wall were these pictures. "Someone must have used a ruler to set these pictures on the wall."

He scratched his head. "I've got Art cooling his heels at the stable. Melissa's not here, but this place has something to do with them. I think we need him here."

"Let's make one more walk-through to be sure; maybe we can find something of hers. You know, to place her here." They walked into every room, ending up in the living room. "Hal, check this out. The rug looks funny. Help me," Jon said.

Hal pulled one end of the rug, but it was fastened down. He picked up a corner. "A trap door?" Hal knelt and pulled at the door. "It's stuck." He got down on both knees and dug his fingers around the edge, pulling hard until the trap door gave.

The cool of the darkness rushed up into his face.

"Melissa Franklin?"

"Let's get some light down there," Jon said.

Hal used his flashlight, darting the beam around here and there. "No one is down there. These stairs are new."

"I'm calling Art."

"Art, come east and turn in where you see the unit's lights flashing. Can you bring a horse trailer?"

"I think so. Melissa; how is she?"

"We've got the horse, Art. Melissa's whereabouts is still an unknown."

"I'm on my way."

216

Art traveled briskly through the barn. "Charlie, they've found the horse. Can you trailer him back to the stables?"

"Sure thing," Charlie put the pitchfork down against the wall. "I'll hitch 'er up and be ready when you are." Charlie bit down on his unlit cigar, turned toward his truck pulling his keys from his pocket.

Art said, "I'm going ahead of you. It's east of here, riverside. Charlie, drive down until you see the Sheriff's car. The lights will be flashing. I've got to go. They haven't found Melissa, but there's something they want me to see." Art tried to maintain a sense of professionalism and dignity, but both had taken wings. His usual neat appearance lacked combed hair. He'd messed his hair by constant head rubbing. His heart pounded at Mach speed, and his face was red. Art was out of his comfort zone.

"Okay, Ah'll be along shortly," Charlie called back lifting the tongue to the hitch.

"Thanks, Charlie." He headed for his vehicle at the end of the barn. Art ducked his head and ran. His shoulders were well soaked when he sat. He backed the car around and headed out the gate toward the highway. The roadbed, shiny and reflective, smelled heavy in the damp air. Art kept the windows down just in case Melissa might call out to him.

He spotted the leaves changing in waves of red, blue, and white before he saw the cut in the trees. Art watched for a break in oncoming traffic before turning onto the dirt pathway. Melissa had been here and left Midnight. Why? It doesn't make sense. She loves that animal and wouldn't abandon him for any reason. As certain as he was about her, nagging doubts crept in with another question. One he did not have an answer. Would she leave the horse for a boyfriend?

217

Finally, he had a clearing. Art turned onto the dirt path following over ruts turning to mud. He drove past Jon's unit coming to stop by Hal's vehicle. Stepping out, he glanced at Midnight, noticing the animal's movements clearly indicated stress. "You, too? You saw her last. Wish you could tell me where she went."

The rain pelted him as he trotted across the expanse to the porch. "What we got?" he called out to Jon standing in the rain on the porch.

"Come inside. There are some interesting pictures of you and Melissa. They're on the wall in one of the bedrooms."

Wet footprints followed as they walked through the house. "Pictures of us?" He turned to looked at Jon. "In this place?" Art said as he followed Jon. "Boy, it's really beginning to coming down. Melissa's not here, but you thought you heard her scream?"

Jon nodded, "Yes, I heard a female scream, I'm not sure, but I think I heard the scream twice."

"But the place is empty. Where could she be?"

"Good question," Hal answered.

Ray was almost back to the house as Jon found Midnight and rubbed his neck. He'd noticed the sheriff's car coming along the farm road and knew he had to hurry. Knowing he couldn't get caught right now, he ditched his Ford in the copse near the old farmhouse and ran toward the river. He dropped down the bank and worked his way through the roots until he could enter the tunnel to the house. If he could get into the house and take his belongings, then get back out before the cop located the house, he'd be all right. A scream stopped him. *Someone was in the cellar!* Cautious now, he began tiptoeing toward the opening to the cellar. His hand pushed against the

218

tarp that walled the new opening to the river. He shoved the shelves, and they moved easily.

"Anyone, can you hear me?"

Ray froze in place, that voice..."Melissa?"
"Ray?"
A smile crept across his lips. How could this get any better? *Now I've got me a bargaining chip.*

Chapter Thirty-Eight

7:30 P.M.

The men left the kitchen of the old farmhouse, then walked into the living room and down a hall and into a small bedroom. Art scanned the card table over as they passed by. *Some sort of mailing. Ready to go out. Should check that out.*

"They're just in here," Jon said walking into the room and pointing.

"There's no furniture to speak of in this house, just what you need," Art said. He came to a stop by a pile of clothing. He placed his foot carefully not to disturb any evidence. Other items lay scattered everywhere, and a jacket lay in the corner.

I need a closer look at that jacket. He thought as he turned his attention to the pictures. Contrasting sharply against the mess were eight neatly thumb-tacked pictures.

"Someone took pains," Art leaned closer to look at the pictures. He squinted. "These are of us in our bathrobes, having breakfast in the backyard." His finger pointed, "That's recent. We just ate out there last Saturday morning." His eyes roamed around. *There was that flash of light. I caught it for an instant.* Art tried to assimilate this new information, but nothing made any sense. His fear for Melissa heightened.

FOR ELEVEN MILLION REASONS

Art studied the other photos feeling a sense of shock. They clearly were of Melissa's bedroom. None had her in them. *So, did she take them? Did she give them to this person who displayed them on the wall? What's going on here? Have we been targeted? Is it me, or her? If it's me what do I know, or have, that this person wants?*

Where's Melissa?

Art reached up and held the back of his neck where the tension tightened every muscle and left him rigid as a board. His neck felt stiff as though someone was pulling him down. *Aspirin would be good about now. If it's her, what could anyone want with my sweet girl?* "You said you heard a scream?" Art's eyes narrowed as he rubbed his neck and brought his eyes to Jon's.

"Affirmative; female," Jon offered as Art looked around.

"There's a picture of interest in the next room, taken in Tahoe by the looks of the background."

"All right, let's see." Art said as he followed Jon into a room as tossed as the last. "Not the neatest people, are they?"

"No, you wonder how people can live like this." Jon moved to the dresser where a gold-framed picture laid. Carefully he held the frame at the corner, lifting it for Art to see. "What's this?" Jon said. A second photo taped to the back of the frame caught Jon's eye. It showed three young people.

The hair rose on the back of Art's neck. He looked at the three zeroing in on the man in the tux with the blond wig. He took the framed photo from Jon. Turned the photo to the pair where the man's face loomed larger, then back over. *That wig is just too much of a coincidence.* The second man also dressed in a tux stood on the other side of a young woman in a soft peach dress. "What'd she do, marry them both?"

Jon's finger pointed to the woman's hand.
221

M.L.WEATHERINGTON

"My, my, how do kids afford rocks like that?" Art said. The young woman's left hand dazzled almost as much as her smile. "She can't be more than twenty-three or four. I don't know her, do you?"

Jon shook his head, "No, they haven't hit our radar as far as I know."

Hal Dudley's voice echoed up from the cellar, "Hey, come here."

Art and Jon left the bedroom and walked to the opening in the living room floor.

Jon leaned down looking into the cellar and following the light beam. "You found something?" Jon called.

"There's a blue ribbon. Looks new, doesn't fit the scene, and there's a tunnel leading out of here."

"Does Melissa wear hair ribbons?" Jon asked.

"She does. When she's gone riding. What about the tunnel? Could she have left that way?"

"Hal, could she have gotten out that way?" Jon asked.

"Yes, it goes to the river. I just walked it." Hal's echoing answer continued, "That's where I found the ribbon."

"Thanks, Hal."

"We'll get on this, Art. What about the ribbon? Could it have been blue?"

"She wears a lot of blue and Charlie said she wore blue today. He might ID the ribbon." Art's heart lightened, "I think we treat this as a crime scene. I want Walt and the crew here to go over the place."

"I understand that Art, and I appreciate that you feel your guys would work harder to find her. But, this is our jurisdiction. Need I remind you it's not a crime to have a ribbon in the cellar, nor is it to pin photos on the wall,

222

even of you? You know that better than me. Art, I can't make something happen here, even for you. Show me a crime that I can go along with you on and I'll be happy to turn this one loose. Right now, all I've got is the horse, which puts her here at one point." Jon pointed to Midnight for emphasis. "What happened next? Did she leave here on her own?"

"Let's show Charlie the ribbon if he ID's it; we treat this as a crime scene. Would that fill your bill?" Art said. He knew it was weak, and he was acting like a parent, not a professional.

Pointing, Jon said, "If Charlie can tell me she wore that particular ribbon today, then maybe I can call in and see if I can turn this over to you."

"Charlie's coming with the trailer. As soon as he gets here, we'll show him the ribbon. Jon, I want one more look at those pictures and the room."

The hunting jacket in the corner of the room interested Art. It had since he first spotted it a short time earlier. Art carefully lifted it. As he did, the sound of metal bouncing on the wood floor caught his attention. He set the jacket aside, moved jeans and T-shirts until he spotted the shine of gold. His right hand went to his left breast pocket and removed his pen. Art bent over reaching for the ring with the pen extended. Finally, he could raise the pen enough for the emerald ring to slide to his thumb's tip. Greeley's description snapped into his mind. *It's more ornate than this, 24 karats with an emerald set in the center.* Art's stomach fluttered.

This was the ring!

Wilma's hypnotized description of the jacket convinced him he was in the right place at the right time.

Art looked at Jon and said, "It's 7:35 in the evening Jon, this is hard evidence, the kind that District Attorney Zak Wright will salivate over. Jon, this is material in an

223

ongoing murder case my department is investigating now. I want this place sealed off this minute. I'm now calling Walt. You call your sergeant, let's get this ball rolling."

Jon made his call, and Art, feeling both elation and despair, waited for Walt to answer. When he did, Art almost took his head off. He rattled off, "Walt, start the paperwork to kick Gainey free. Then find Judge Daniel James. I want a signed search warrant for this whole place. Jon, what's the address here?"

"Not sure, wait a minute." He stepped outside and returned on the run,"7985 East Highway Twelve."

"I heard him, Art," Walt said.

Art said almost over the top of Walt, "After you do that, get a crew over here. I want this place gone through with a fine-toothed comb. You won't believe what I have in my hand right this minute. I'm holding the emerald ring. Get Greeley and bring him here when you come. Get this place processed before morning. Melissa's involved in some way and I want to know what, when, where, and how, and I wanted to know yesterday. I want a rogue's gallery made up that's got to be done now. I'll show you the people I want to be identified when you get here. Have Charlie, the stable hand, look at them and Wilma Concord. I want Murphy to visit her, got that? Hurry, Walt, Melissa's life might depend on how we proceed."

Walt scribbled it all down. "I'm on my way. I'll call the lab and have them standby. What age group shall I assemble?"

"Early twenties, men, and women. Dark brown hair for the girl, browns for the men. Tell the lab they're going to have to lift three images and to make them single head shots."

"Got it. Art? Nothing on Melissa?"

"Negative," Art answered, his heart sank just saying the word.

Chapter Thirty-Nine

Ray edged his way along Wilma's block, curious to know which house was hers, afraid he might have to knock on doors if he couldn't locate her house. His tools were at the hideout. He only had his knife to work with, and he couldn't remember what Allison had said about the old girl's house. He knew it had to be across from the dead guy's, but which one?

There was no way he could let her live. She knew too much. Ray's temples pounded. *The house the old hag lives in has to be one of these two. They're right across the street from Nelson's house. One was shut up tight, the other, wide open to the world. A piece of cake. It had to be this one. It just looked like an old lady would live here.* He could see the rocker back sticking up above a bunch of flower pots.

Darkness draped the city. The street lights, most of them nestled among mature trees, gave little illumination. Wilma Concord's home, deep in shadow, sat back from the street. The two front windows lit by lamps were open with lacy white curtains caught on a breeze. Ray stared at the house and thought, that'll be easy.

He stood next to the elm tree in the parkway watching her house and checking all around the neighborhood before moving closer. He paused again checking everywhere eventually slipping past the corner of her house where he stopped. Ray peered through the side

225

window as the old woman moved. It had to be her. She's ancient. He watched as she locked the front door, then closed both front windows, locking them. The table lamps went off, but not before he'd seen two rooms filled to the brim with overstuffed furniture, side tables, and knickknacks. One wall, acting as a divider between the living room and what he guessed would be the dining area, housed books floor to ceiling.

Confident this was the woman he wanted, he pulled the knife from his pocket, releasing the blade. He bent over, feeling along the wood siding of the house for the loose part of the telephone line. Finding it, he severed the phone wire. It now hung limply by the side of the house as Ray walked toward the back. He tried the door and found it locked. He walked around the house, checking out hiding places as well as entries and exits. He wanted to know as much as possible about this property before he committed himself to going in after her.

Arriving back at the rear door, Ray placed his hand on it and pushed. It held. He shoved again. It held. A solid kick freed it from the lock, and Ray walked in boldly, as though he owned the place.

The dimly lit kitchen showed him the way into the dining area. He stood in the doorway listening to her breathing. A smile parted his lips, and his eyes sparkled. She could hide if she wanted, but he'd find her. Everything was going his way.

Ray ran his hand over the dining room wall for the switch plate, but he couldn't find one. He gave up on lighting the room and moved into the dim room, letting his eyes adjust. Little by little, he made out the position of the couch and coffee table. He moved to the edge of the living room area from the dining room.

He heard her to the right of him as she shuffled her feet. Ray stepped around the bookcase, the knife held in front of him. "Why can't you keep your fucking mouth shut?" he said.

He lunged at her and met her tailor sheers that she held with both hands pointed at him. His knife just missed Wilma's shoulder as the shears sunk into his left side rendering a searing pain.

He backed away and stared at the scissors falling away from him. She had managed to cut him, but not deeply. It enraged him, filling him with a fury that carried him swiftly across the distance between them. He meant to jam his knife into her stomach, ripping straight up to her throat.

Four prongs jabbed him in the chest sending waves of pain shuttering through him adding to the pain from the slice on his side. He fought to catch his breath. This old hen was pissing him off. He sucked in a lung full of air and roared, "You bitch!" He lunged at her, "You're dead." His blade pointed right at her neck.

As he moved forward, she jabbed him again right where he zips his pants. He couldn't get his breath, and he fell to the floor as the door bell rang.

"Help me!" she screamed.

"I'm here, Wilma," Officer Murphy answered.

Wave after wave of pain had Ray's full attention until he focused on the fact that someone was ripping the screen door off and about to come through that front door. Ray raised himself and limped to the back door and was out as Murphy flipped the inside switch instantly sending light from the two lamps over the area.

Murphy saw Wilma, "What's happened here?"

Wilma didn't answer but looked at him pleadingly, her lips quivering as the cane lowered.

Murphy stepping across the room saw Wilma's eyes flicker as she fell limply to the floor. He lifted her like a prized doll and laid her gently on the couch.

He called for an ambulance, got her some water, and held her hand. She regained consciousness and looked into his warm brown eyes.

Wilma sat up, "Did you get him?"

Murphy knelt beside the couch. "Who?" he said as he spoke lovingly to Wilma. She reminded him so much of his grandmother that died five years ago.

"That maniac that killed Sam, he was just here." She adjusted herself on the couch. "How'd you know to come?" Wilma asked. Color flooded back into her face with each breath.

Murphy smiled, "I was asked to get you to ID, someone. Big boss wants it done before morning. I've got pictures in the car."

Wilma waved her hand. "Get them. We want to get the creep before he comes at me again, don't we?"

Murphy stood. "You sure you're okay enough for me to leave you?" She shot him a scornful look. "Alright, I'll check the outside out in case he's still here."

"I'm feeling fine now," Wilma said as she moved around on the couch setting her feet on the floor. She took an envelope from the table and fanned her face. "My, my, that about wore me out. You should have seen me, John. I whacked him a good one with my four-prong cane, right where it counts," she said swinging her arm for emphasis. "I knew it just had to have a better use than just me following it around."

"I wondered," he said smiling at her a long moment. "Give me a second and I'll bring the pictures. Murphy removed his weapon and began the search around the outside parameter careful where he stepped. The place was clear, so he ran back to the police car, picked up a rogue's gallery, and hurried back to Wilma. "Boss wants to know if you can recognize anyone in these pictures." He opened the book showing several loose pictures of cops in civilian clothing among photos of Ray, Roland, and Allison.

228

FOR ELEVEN MILLION REASONS

Wilma took the pictures and adjusted her bi-focal. She sifted through all the pictures, setting two of them aside. After looking all of them over once again, she went back to the two. "Well, for starters, this little lady is a college student. She came to see me about Sam, said she wanted to do a piece about winning the lottery." She paused a long moment then said, "And this is the one who just high-tailed it out of here."

"Names?" Murphy asked looking at her expectantly.

"No," Wilma studied the pictures and shook her head. "Can't remember. She told me her name, but I don't recall. She seemed sweet, however. The asshole..." Wilma pointed to Ray's picture. "And I've never been formally introduced, sorry." Wilma's voice dripped with venom.

John couldn't hide his amusement. "I don't know about you, Willy. I give you a tour of the police station, and a ride in my unit, and you turn into Rambo."

The ambulance came quietly into the neighborhood, parking in front of Wilma's house, lights flashing as personnel entered and took over. They wanted to take her to the hospital to be checked out. She refused, insisting that she was just fine. They listened to her heart and lungs, took her blood pressure and pronounced her okay. Finally, they packed up and left them alone.

"Go collect some of your clothes. We're leaving here. I've got three more hours of my shift, but I'm going to call in and take the rest of the night off, you're going into witness protection," he said, more an announcement than a choice.

"Am I now?" She said as she smiled conspiratorially, a bright pink rushing her cheeks.

"Yeah. I call it Murphy's Mansion. It's not much, a two-bedroom bachelor's pad."

"Can I take Slipper's too?"

Murphy slipped his hand around Slippers, "Yes."

Chapter Forty

8:45 A.M. July 18

A rt looked in the mirror, rubbed shaving cream over his chin and listened as the blade scraped the stubble away. Slowly he lifted the towel and wiped his face. No better, he thought.

The image in the mirror didn't help his ego. He was tired. He'd been up all night and not any closer to knowing Melissa's whereabouts. Fighting with her and getting the cold shoulder was tough. It didn't hold a candle to this feeling of emptiness. Somehow this wasn't quite a loss because he felt she would come home. Then as soon as he felt that, he questioned, will she come home?

Limbo. He was out on a limb. For him, this was just an awful place to be. He pulled on clean clothes as he thought. There's no apparent end to being trapped. If this is how I feel, how is she feeling? He looked in the mirror again. The shave didn't help. The fresh clothes didn't help. Everything he tried failed to hide his worry. His shoulders were up; he couldn't keep them down, the pressure on his neck tightened. Slowly he buttoned the top button and slipped his tie in place. He was supposed to be in control. He was trained. Come on. No one trains for losing a child.

I'm the leader, and right now, I couldn't lead anyone or anything out of a wet paper bag. I'm done. The only thing that would change things would be for Melissa to

walk in here right now. I'm a realist. It isn't likely to happen. God, my eyes burn.
Art leaned forward his hands resting on the edge of the sink. *Lord, help me. Bring her back to me, please. I'll try not to mess things up.* He looked heavenward. *No promises, Lord. You know me better than I know me. Just let me get my arms around her, I'll never let her go. Did she go off with this Ray person? He's dangerous. How can he be her boyfriend? Why didn't she tell me? If I could get my hands on her right now, I could kill her myself.*

The bathroom was serviceable, clean, and that just about covered the aesthetics of the space. Art wanted to wreck something. With all his heart, he wanted to put his fist through a wall, anything. It just couldn't be city property. He blinked the tears back, caught the time again.

Ten minutes and he had to be up and running. Art shut the light out in his office bathroom, shut the door, picked up his jacket, took a deep breath, and headed for the meeting room.

He gathered inner strength, at once he placed his hand on the solid wood and pushed the swinging door. People hushed as he walked into the briefing. It was a large room suitable for holding fifty people. Small tables and chairs sat in the center of the area focused toward the wall of boards and photo screens. The room painted in beiges and accented with oak furniture, white utility tables, and video equipment, was clean and functional.

The haunting aroma of bacon hanging in the air stirred his tummy into a growl. Art wondered, *Is Melissa hungry?*

He cleared his throat, "Good morning, gentlemen and gentle ladies. I don't need to tell any of you that you worked your butts off last night. I do need to thank you."

His eyes shifted to the floor, and he studied a square with a crack for several seconds. Then he looked up and said, "If you haven't heard, Melissa's still missing. On another note, we're kicking Gainey loose for the Nelson homicide. He's not our scumbag. We do have a strong lead, and the house you just worked is involved." Art looked from one worn face to the next and asked, "Did you have breakfast? If not, let's do that before we begin with the briefing."

Several moved toward the side of the room where a table held the bacon, sausage, country potatoes, and eggs in steaming trays. Orange juice, coffee, and tea were on another table. Alice, from the Country Pantry Restaurant, had brought two toasters and busied herself making English muffins and toast.

Professor Greeley cut through a group of detectives and eased up to Art. "Yah planning' to eat, young man?" he asked as he put his arm around Art's shoulders. "Remember that day in Sacramento? You said, 'I'm going to have that ring in my hand.'"

Art looked at Greeley through eyes with dark circles and heavy bags. "Yes, that's what I said," Art began filling a paper plate with scrambled eggs and two links of sausage. He took a paper glass of orange juice, looked at it a moment and downed it in one gulp.

Greeley filled a plate and followed Art to a corner of the room and said, "I wanted to tell you, son, Cora's diamond pin and Sam's leather-holstered pistol were in that farmhouse." He picked up a strip of bacon and smelled, then said, "Smoked the right way. I can tell it's deep southern style." He savored the bacon. "Anyway, we spent some time there."

Art ate quietly and listened to Greeley talk about going through the farmhouse. He inspected one of the sausages and bit off the tip. He ate the sausage along with the eggs without enjoying the food. After about twenty minutes, Art dumped his paper plate and said, "Let's get started."

Feet shuffled as people refilled their coffee cups and took their seats. Alice began cleaning breakfast away. As she took the last of the toasters out of the room and closed the door, Art spoke. "Would the farmhouse crew give us a list of their findings?"

A large folding board was slid into place, and a woman uncapped a black marking pen. She made a list as items were called out.

"We found a marriage license. Dated, June 29th, 1995. The two names are, Allison Lynn Fortney, Twenty-three, and Roland Allan Conley, Twenty-five. Under the witness, a third name turned up, Raymond Michael McNamare, Twenty-five."

Art's ears perked up at the mention of the name Raymond.

"We have DMV on Mr. McNamare and a general ID from Mrs. Concord that he's your person of interest in the Nelson case. There were no DMV records on either Fortney or Conley. However, late last night these two were found to be driving a stolen sedan, a chase ensued, and the sedan ended up slammed into an oak tree. The man was ejected and died at the scene; the woman, Allison Lynn Fortney, was taken into custody. An amount just short of two hundred thousand was found in a satchel in her possession. We are checking the connection, if any, with Gilbert's case."

Ray. That's the name Charlie gave me. He listened as the list on the board grew. He asked, "Do we have anyone on the DMV information?"

The detective sharing the information stopped and turned to Art and answered. "Yes, we have two detectives at the McNamare residence right now."

Art nodded. "What's he driving?"

"Eighty-six Ford, four-door coupe, dark blue," a detective said.

233

Blue that's what Charlie thought. *A coincidence? I don't like coincidences.*

He looked up, "Let's go on. Did anything pop out from the Concord residence?"

"We're going to be processing for some time, but so far just her prints are coming up. We've got a cut phone cord, no prints at that point. Looks like the perp left his pocket knife at the scene, and it looks like that blade cut the phone wire. Lab's processing it now. Lots of prints on the wall by the back door, they're mostly smudged, and one blackberry leaf."

Blackberry leaf? That sure doesn't belong. "Where?" Art asked.

The detective read down the list and said, "Carpet in the living room, right near the perp's knife."

Art nodded. "Did Concord see the rogue's gallery?"

The detective reached for the Concord file, opened it, and read down through the information, then said, "She picked out Allison Lynn Fortney-Conley and Raymond Michael McNamare."

Art stifled a yawn and asked, "And Charlie? Did he see them?"

The detective set the Concord file down and picked up another. "Yes, he pointed out Raymond McNamare as the young man he saw with Melissa."

Art's blood froze.

There was a connection between Nelson's killer and Melissa. There was no coincidence. "What about my place?"

In another file came the information. The detective told him Melissa's prints and a few of his were in her room. "There was one print that couldn't be identified. Smudged. We felt it didn't belong, but we can't be sure."

Art squeezed his eyes together to clear them and asked, "Anything else?"

The room fell still. Art let several seconds pass. "Well, then, let me say well done, everyone. Get some shut eye. One more thing, we have two memorial services at the same time, for Nevar and Steven Bird. Tracy will put the information on the board. That's all."

He left the room walking to his office and on his way he bellowed over his shoulder, "Tracy?"

"Top drawer, like always," she answered, carrying a glass of water to his desk. "Here, before it gets too bad, take two."

He looked at her and smiled. "I don't need the aspirin. I wanted to thank you for setting this meeting up, remembering to order breakfast for everyone, and getting Alice over here on such short notice. Taking care of their needs was the farthest thing from my mind."

Tracy smiled and looked down and nodded, she opened the drawer, then said softly, "Thanks, now take these before it's any worse."

Chapter Forty-One

9:35 A.M. July 18, 1995

*S*hit, everything's gone wrong. Too many people can identify me. Allison and Roland for sure, the old hag for another, and Melissa. That cop last night may have got a look at me. I can't trust anyone. Ray stepped behind a mulberry tree his eye keenly on the cop who was sitting in the police car across the street from his car.

Ray backed away from his Ford. It angered him because it just wasn't fair. He was losing everything. He needed a way out of Lodi. If he couldn't use his car, what could he do? Slowly a smile crossed his face.

Ray walked purposely in the opposite direction, making a roundabout journey to the Franklin property. Once there, he used Melissa's key to the front door, banking on the cop being out on the hunt for his daughter. The door opened, and Ray walked in.

Where would the boat key be kept? Ray asked himself as he stood in the foyer. *Probably in a drawer. Maybe the office. The kitchen, that's where I'd put them.*

"This is Lieutenant Franklin's neighbor, Mrs. Wilson. Yes. Well, I don't mean to be nosy but, well, with his daughter missing and all, well, I just thought he might want to know some strange person just entered his house."

236

"Mrs. Wilson, please hold a moment," Tracy said. She left her desk walking purposefully to Art, who held his head in his hands.

"Someone just went into your house. A Mrs. Wilson, your neighbor, is on the phone. Do you want to talk with her?"

His hand lifted the receiver. With his eyes shut he said, "Agnes, how are you? What's this about someone in my house?" She told him. "Agnes, what did he look like?" Art's head came up as he listened to her description of the person in his house.

9:45 A.M.

He hung up and looked at Tracy, "I think the son-of-a-bitch who was at Concord's last night is inside my house right now." Art pushed his chair back, checked his weapons, reached over to take his jacket off the chair. "Get the word out, Tracy. This guy is dangerous. I want him alive. I think he's Nelson's killer, and he can lead us to Melissa."

9:46 A.M.

The Franklin phone rang insistently. "Shut up already," Ray screeched. He came to a stop in the middle of the kitchen. *Where would a cop keep his boat keys?* Ray hurried over to the back door. He ran his hand along the molding. He found a wad of keys, some obvious house keys, some probably to a shed. He fingered one that stood out. *This one looks different.*

He ran out the kitchen door, over the flagstone patio across the lawn, and down to the dock. Ray jumped into the boat. The key fit. The boat rocked back and forth as he readied to leave the dock. Ray reached over and pushed against a piling. The boat turned lazily out into the middle of the river.

9:51 A.M.

Mrs. Wilson kept her receiver to her ear as she continued listening to Franklin's unanswered phone. She turned toward the street and hung her phone up as two squad cars raced onto the driveway. They arrived a second or two before Art's city unit, all parked in the driveway. The officers ran with Art toward the house positioning themselves at the entrances, front and back.

9:53 A.M.

Art guarded himself at the front door and announced, "Lodi Police."

Agnes rushing across the yard toward Art called out, "He took your boat, Art." She pointed toward the dock.

Art followed her gesture to the empty boat slip. *Shit!* "Which way did he go?"

She pointed turning away from Art and said, "Upriver."

Art closed the distance between them, "Give me your boat keys."

She ran for her house.

9:54 A.M.

Art turned to the two officers and said, "You two take the river bank. I believe he's got Melissa and my fourteen-foot, red and white Starcraft. This perp is twenty-five, Caucasian, brown hair, one hundred thirty pounds. I'm certain he's the same one who broke into Wilma Concord's last night. Treat him as armed and dangerous.

He's our suspect in the Nelson homicide, and I want the S.O.B. alive."

Agnes huffed and puffed and said. "I don't know if it's got fuel."

He grabbed the keys from her and headed for Wilson's aluminum boat. "Get a helicopter up," Art yelled over his shoulder.

Both units swung around and headed for the road into Lodi Lake and the wilderness area.

9:54 A.M.

Ray realized the river snaked and twisted back and forth for hundreds of miles, a true wilderness. Roots made navigation tricky. Some just under the surface of the water were almost impossible to see. The sun was glinting off the water and added to the problem of finding his hideout. Maybe today's the day to open one of his bottles of wine. His hands shook, and a nice red would help the nerves about now.

He was looking for a spot along the river with tall trees, one redwood in particular that stood several feet taller than the rest and twisted at the top. All the trees looked tall from this vantage point. Ray knew he couldn't maneuver up to his makeshift dock, the water being too treacherous. The boat rocked in the water as Ray took bearings and he saw the tree. His hand held the throttle, then he gunned it, keeping to the very center of the river heading for the tree.

Ray didn't know how much time he had, but he figured there wasn't a lot. He had to make every minute count. He brought the boat to the bank among tall grasses that swallowed the boat. He tied the boat up and left it bouncing against the bank.

Once upon the trail, he looked for anything that felt familiar. Every bush, tree, grass seemed the same. He jogged in and out of shadows over a well-worn path that meandered along the river. Finally, he found the rock. He ducked into the growth and pulled some of the vines obscuring the opening.

The vegetation grew ten feet wide and as tall as the trees. Vines encircled hardwood trees climbing to the tops. Blackberry feelers crawled freely. The verdant vegetation grew thick right up to the river's edge. It felt cool and safe inside this hollowed-out area. Ray walked on through the tunnel of leaves out onto the landing, a smooth mesa of dirt about eight by ten that dropped off suddenly into the river. The dock he'd built was still partly covered with his blue tarp. Dappled sunlight played over its surface, and Ray smiled.

Chapter Forty-Two

10:02 A.M. July 18, 1995

Agnes' fishing boat hugged the river as Art scanned both banks for any sign of his vessel. A breeze twisted and fluttered the many leaves of the trees causing a stifling of sounds. Add the resonance of the trees to the roar of the river rush, and Art had his work cut out for him. The warmth soaked through his gray jacket, he pulled it off and dropped it in the boat. Absentmindedly he loosened his tie. Art listened, his keen senses alert for any sound that might lead him to Melissa because he believed he was going to find her.

Art gave the boat more throttle lifting the bow as the boat sailed up to the next bend in the river. He cut the motor and glided into the new vista. Art listened for his boat motor's deep rhythmic throb. His heart filled with hope as he floated around each new bend in the river. There he saw nothing but trees and water, the artist's paradise, his nightmare. He pushed on. A family of ducks swam swiftly among the reeds. His hand pushed the tiller to head on up the river. "God, please help me find her."

Instead, the Wilson boat coughed, sputtered and died. Art pulled on the rope, checked the choke, and tried to start it again. He had pushed it as far as the fumes would take it. He lifted the paddle and turned the boat toward the bank.

Stillness settled in around him, like magic he heard a sound he knew so well. He looked to the right as a flock of birds took flight from the reeds. They flew across his bow, and he watched them fly low over the water then out of sight. He'd invaded their world. He slipped the oar into the water pulling the boat further around toward the south bank. A hollow bump caught his attention again. Yes, he thought. I know that sound. The reeds moved aside as his passage cut a wedge wide enough for the boat to maneuver through. He followed the sound until he could see slices of red and white. It was his boat tied to a tree. Tears glistened in his eyes as the bow hammered against the bank with each new swell of water. He was thankful to see the Starcraft. He fought the urge to call out to Melissa, wanting so to connect with her. Surprise remained on his side as long as Ray didn't know he was coming, it was keenly important, because he wanted the S.O.B alive.

Art pulled Agnes's boat alongside his and tied it off. He stepped into his boat using it as a pathway to the bank. For a moment, he did a balancing act as he stood on the bow of his boat, his weight sinking the boat lower in the water. Art jumped to the shore. He stood still while listening for anything that sounded out of the ordinary. The bugs, quiet a second ago, began their wild song building louder and louder. The grass seemed matted here. Art studied the indentation and the direction the grass bent. He stepped carefully along a trail left recently, he hoped by Raymond Michael McNamare.

He shoved in the clip of his 9mm. He leaned down and rubbed his hand on his ankle and leg checking his backup piece strapped to his calf. He felt the hard metal shield clipped to his belt. Art moved over the dirt path. Several small mud puddles left over from the rain gave him optimism that Raymond McNamare left a usable print in one of them.

Art searched carefully for any clue. A twig broke or bent that would show him the direction to take. Inch by inch, he made his way toward a large rock. At that point, the trail went cold. Art backed up, found the last footprint, and knelt down. It just stops as though the person had magically risen into the air. Art looked all around. The grass hadn't been disturbed. The heavy growth walled on both sides of the dirt trail rose ten feet for as far as he could see. There's no place to leave the path or to climb.

Art stood. Those vines, he walked over to them. Blackberry. The list had one blackberry leaf found on the Concord living room carpet near the perp's knife. His hand brushed the vines. Some of the long tentacles moved easily, exposing an opening into the thicket. Art pulled them back and scanned the area. He stepped carefully into the dimness of a lush tunnel. He heard a demanding voice.

"Stop wiggling!"

A threat? Art gripped his weapon. He focused beyond the leaves and what he saw chilled his blood. Melissa stood gagged and completely wrapped like a mummy in duct tape next to a crumpled blue tarp. Ray pulled Melissa back against his body, using her as a shield. They stood near the edge of the river, facing him. Coldness rushed through Art. He so wanted to find Melissa, but not like this.

Art's eyes fixed on the churning river. His stomach flipped, and he tasted acid. Melissa wouldn't survive the undertow, not with her arms and legs bound. Somehow, he had to keep her out of that river.

Ray kept the knife at her throat as Art watched him searching the vines for any movement. Art saw him narrow his eyes when he looked at the vines. *He must see white from my shirt.* Ray looked frantically around and gripped Melissa tighter when she started shuffling her feet and moving, and Art tried to see through the vines too.

There was no point in staying in this cavern. He stepped out onto the mesa just ten feet from where they stood. Melissa's eyes tried to give him a message, he noticed, but he was too busy locking eyes with Ray.

Tears of frustration glistened. She screamed out a muffled, "Dad." Tears rolled down her face. It broke his heart. He couldn't go to her, couldn't gather her up, and hug her, hug the pain away.

Art pointed the pistol into the air. He did his best to ignore her, forcing himself to center in on Ray and the knife. He could hear his voice quiver as he said, "I'm the girl's father. Walk away from her now."

The knife tip pricked Melissa's neck as Ray sneered and stared with disgust at Art. With venom, he asked, "You want her back?"

Art had one mission, to talk Ray out of hurting Melissa any further. It took every skill he owned to stay calm, focused. "You don't want to do that. You have enough against you now. Don't add this, too." Art took a step forward and said, "Move away. You know you're trapped."

The sound of a helicopter caught Ray's attention. Looking into the canopy caused him to jerk Melissa's bound body.

Art explained, "It's the police helicopter. It's just for you, Ray."

Reality set in, and Ray's shoulders dropped, he was trapped as surely as if he were the one bound in duct tape.

Art brought the muzzle down until it pointed right at Ray's head.

Ray's eyes went wide.

"Officers will be here soon, Ray. There's nowhere for you to go. It's over." Art's feet moved to the side; his knees bent to steady him, he brought his arms out and locked them holding the gun pointed right at Ray's head, "Move away from her."

Ray jerked his head in every direction. As he did, he pushed the knife into Melissa's neck, breaking the skin.

Melissa's eyes widened.

"Drop the gun now!" Ray said.

Art saw the blade slide toward her jugular. He brought the gun down, his other hand splayed out like a child pleading as he leaned over and placed it on the ground. "Okay, take it easy, my gun is down. You can back away from her now. There's no need to do this, Ray. We can work this out."

"Kick the gun into the river," Ray said as he looked from the gun to the father.

Art's shoe tip thudded against the firearm. It slid like a putted golf ball, down a slippery slope, and plunked into the water trap.

He watched the thoughts rushing across Ray's face, understood he was feeling trapped. *Good. He knows I'm blocking any chance of freedom, what's he going do now? All he has to do is make one misstep, and they're in the river.* Art took another step forward and said, "You're not taking her anywhere, it's over."

Ray backed up a step, "Then she dies here, too." In an instant, Ray jerked Melissa's bound body toward the river, placing his back to Art and, with a great heave, shoved her over the edge. She dropped like a bag of garbage, the splash wetting the mesa they stood on.

Art, consumed equally with rage and terror, lunged toward the bank, his voice hoarse with emotion. "Melissa!"

Ray spun around, barring Art's way. Their bodies collided, they tumbled over the blue tarp and the wooden dock. Ray missed Art's body mass and thrust the blade into Art's left upper arm.

Art yelled in pain, then clubbed Ray's temple. He wanted to reach Melissa.

My Beretta. Art drew his leg up, sliding his hand toward his calf.

Ray regained his balance and inched his arm around bringing the knife point toward Art's chest.

Art watched the knifepoint centering over his chest. He gave up on his piece, grabbing Ray's wrist as the knife blade took a position over his chest. Art ignored the agony from the wound in his arm. It hung lethargic.

It was clear from Ray's actions that he intended to bury the blade to the hilt. Ray raised his body, and Art felt his movement and just before he could bring his body into force, Art rolled their bodies to the right, relocating Ray's foot into the thin air. It threw Ray off balance, and he landed on top of Art.

He grabbed Art's hair and pounded Art's head until it dazed and angered him.

The clear cut right and wrong of police work suddenly changed to gray for Art. Who would blame him if he finished this coward right here, right now? "You son-of-a-bitch," Art's raspy voice yelled. He reached his calf feeling for his pistol.

Ray countered Art's movement. He dropped the knife as Art had freed his ankle piece, their hands met. Ray's hand wrapped around Art's; his face grimaced as he powered his arm to move the gun away from him.

Art hated Ray. He caught the look in Ray's eyes and knew the feeling was mutual. He was a younger man, a stronger man, and a man with two good arms. Art was losing. He screamed a roar that had the birds leaving the canopy in droves, the flapping of their wings a roar themselves. Art's and Ray's feet scraped on the blue plastic as they scrambled to outdo each other.

That roar gave Art the primal strength he needed to power the muzzle around; his finger squeezed the trigger. The bullet struck Ray between the eyes.

Ray stared at Art in disbelief, then he dropped.

Officer Owen ran through the brush. Gordon came right behind. "Thank God, you yelled," Owen said as he reached down and felt Ray's carotid artery, "He's gone."

Art caught his breath and said, "Melissa."

The officers looked around. "She's not here."

Art's hand rose, his finger extended to point, "The river." Art rolled over, his chin on the ground as he pushed at the lifeless carcass and dragged his body from under Ray's to get closer to her resting place. He wanted to drop his hand in the cold water and feel like he was soothing Melissa now that she was gone. It was all he could do as the knowledge of her death settled in breaking his heart.

Officer Owen stepped to the edge and looked over. He went down on his knees, and Officer Gordon joined him.

Melissa, her eyes bright, lay cradled by submerged roots. Cold dark-green water lapped precariously close to her nose. They slipped their hands around some of the duct tape, pulled her up, and placed her on the tarp.

Art sobbed out "Melissa!" He couldn't hold the tears or believe his eyes. The three of them worked at the wet mess to cut her free. Art's attempts seemed futile, and he depended on them. His breaths came hard and labored, the pain from his arm excruciating. Their bodies were making it hard for him to see Melissa. Finally, he sat back and let them work.

As soon as she could, she slipped into Art's waiting arm. Art didn't try to stop his tears; he didn't care what these boys in blue thought of him. He ignored the pain in his arm as she sobbed.

"Come here baby, come here." His good arm tightened around her. He pulled her to him as they rocked back and forth. His eyes brimmed with tears as he stared out over the water.

Through lips cracked and bleeding, Melissa smiled at him. They looked into each other's eyes for a long moment. Then she tucked her face into his neck, and he allowed his cheek to rest on the top of her head as he felt her body rest against his.

"Oh, Dad," she said as she hugged him." I thought I'd never see you again."

Some days later Art opened his personal and private score-keeping file he'd titled; The Franklin logs. Here he noted the homicides that fell under his lead and the length of time it took to solve them. His finger found the entry; Samuel T. Nelson, June 28, 1995. He wrote July 18, 1995. He noted twenty-one-days. After that, Art placed the pen in its holder and slowly closed the file.

THE END

Also from **Pynhavyn Press** you might enjoy these books:

Funeral Singer by Lillian Wolfe

Singing at weddings, parties, holiday events, and street fairs with her band are all just another gig for Gillian Foster, a dog groomer, and for-hire musician/singer. Following an accidental fall and head injury, she begins to have unusual dreams. When she is asked to sing at a funeral, she accepts the paying job and discovers that her music connects her to the deceased. But this new talent also leads her to more trouble than she could ever have imagined as one of her "clients" demands her assistance in locating the person who killed her.

Funeral Singer: A Song for Marielle is paranormal suspense with a touch of romance in the first book of a series of spirit mysteries. Book Two in the series, *A Song for Menafee*, will be out in the summer of 2016.

http://lillianwolfe.me/loft/
Facebook Author Page: https://www.facebook.com/LilliansLoft/
email: lily@lillianwolfe.me

Bitter Vintage by Riona Kelly

When the heir to Claremont Vineyards in Northern California is killed in an accident, his sister Martinique returns home for the funeral, but she finds her father reclusive and odd, her estranged half-sister in residence, and a mysterious person skulking around the property. Learning more about her brother's death, she grows suspicious of the accident, convinced there is more to the story and is determined to learn the truth. *Bitter Vintage* brings the suspense of treachery, greed and ambition along with romance and betrayal as the story unfolds against the California vineyards of the Napa-Sonoma region and the migrant workers' struggle for fair wages in 1964.

rionakelly@pynhavyn.com
http://pynhavyn.com/writers/riona-kelly/

Coming soon, the second in The Franklin Logs Series.

SIDESWIPED

Chapter One

3:35 P.M. Thursday, August 31, 1995

A husky male voice answered, "Nine-one-one, what is your emergency?" He listened as a voice broke, grabbed air and rushed forth.

"She's just in the crosswalk, lying there. She's not moving. I can't see her face. It's covered with hair, lots of hair, and blood. There's blood everywhere. You've got to come." The woman stopped talking; dispatch heard what sounded like her hand moving over her phone, then breathlessly, "I think she's dead!"

Dispatch modulated his voice. In monotone he asked, "Ma'am? What's your location?"

Her voice shook with each word, "Grape Avenue, across from the High School."

"Stay there please, I'm sending an officer now."

"Yes, okay."

3:35 P.M. across town.

Sweating over steaks is one thing, sweating over seeing a psychiatrist another. *My palms are wet. How can I clasp hands and feel confident?* Arthur Franklin asked himself.

Walk out of here. That's the best next move. His legs tensed to lift him as the door opened and Amanda Burtoni sailed through and into his heart. He was a lost pup as they strolled into her inner office.

"The knife wound," she said as she put her cell phone on the table, "how is it coming along?"

Art rubbed the back of his bad hand and looked the room over. It seemed the same. He remembered every detail from that day they came here for the Nelson case. The white tulips with their long, lime-green stems sat in the tall, clear, aqua-tinted vase on the coffee table. Art eased into one of the side chairs next to the couch, his knee close to hers. He rubbed his hand slowly over the texture of the beige fabric. *Maybe this will dry my palm.* It felt velvety soft. The walls were peach. The room looked like Amanda, business-like and yet feminine.

She sat on the couch almost across from him and crossed her ankles. He admired her expensive leather pumps. Today she wore gray; her blouse, a shiny silk, had a bow under her chin and a string of pearls hanging midway down her chest. She had those teeth, beaver teeth, but perfect and her makeup was flawless. She was a beautiful woman.

Art brought his hand up to the place where the knife had cut his upper left arm so deeply. He rubbed the area. "They tell me with time and therapy I will get most of the movement back. Until then it's pretty useless," he said adjusting the arm sling.

"Are you back at work?" she asked.

He looked at her. She sat with a pleasant smile on her face and brought her blue eyes up to meet his. Her blonde hair shone from the overhead light. She moved her arm, and a pleasant scent wafted his direction.

Art caught the deep fragrance of lovely petals and the heavy undertones he couldn't quite identify. It fit her so well.

251

He fought to bring his attention back to her question. "I'm on disability, can't go into the office right now." He sighed and shrugged his shoulders. "Walt brings me files to look over. I'm Walt's handyman these days." He frowned and said, "It's a far cry from being a homicide lieutenant." He looked down at the floor. "At least, I keep up on what's going down."

He couldn't help enjoying the perfume. It drew him to her. He felt desperate to find the right words to say to ask her to go out with him for a night on the town. Fear kept him, a grown man of forty-five and father of one teenage daughter, hostage. Art smiled and looked down. What woman would want a gimp, a loser? You're not a loser his inner-self screamed. He heard and brought his head up.

She looked into his eyes. "You've lost a few pounds since July." Her eyes made her statement a fact. "I like you in civvies, a blue checked shirt, and tan Dockers. Very nice, goes well with your green arm sling." She smiled, a caring softness flooding her eyes. "I was surprised when you called for this private, off-the- record meeting."

"Amanda, I'm sorry for taking up your time. I guess I shouldn't have called you," Art said as he shifted restlessly. He remembered sitting at his home office desk this morning and thinking how he was a waste of space these days. Both he and Melissa were suffering the after effects of Raymond Michael McNamare. Something happened this morning. He'd drifted out of depression for just a little while, and during that time, he'd called Amanda and made this appointment.

She turned more toward him, uncrossed her ankles. "Why don't you start where you were prompted to call me today? What made you do that?" she asked.

His good hand rubbed his weak one while he studied the floor. "I don't know. I was thinking how stuck I felt, and I thought of you and what you do. I thought you might get me, um. . . unstuck."

"Got a pry bar with you?" She allowed an astute smile to cross her face.

"You need to be somewhere?" Art asked noticing her glance at the French finish clock sitting on the side table.

She smiled. "Just wondering when you are going to get to it, whatever 'it' is."

"Oh, Amanda, I think..." he said and sighed. He looked off to the side of the window then brought his eyes back to her knees. He studied the shine of her hose. His eyes came up when her hand pulled at the hem of her skirt. He knew he was making her uncomfortable.

"Amanda. I need some help, your kind of help. I feel frustrated. I want to break things. I feel that way a lot and I know it's not good. For Melissa or me." Art slowly brought his eyes from the glow of her pearls up to the gentleness of her eyes as he said that, checking to see if she heard what he was really saying, then looked away.

She nodded, her gaze drifted to the floor as she said, "For all the wrong reasons, I had hoped you were here to ask me out." Her eyes came up and stayed on his.

He sat forward. "I want to. Not sure how. Amanda, I'm not sure of anything lately." A sheepish smile covered his face and reddened his cheeks darkening the freckles. "Things have shifted, changed for me. You sure you want to hitch up with me?" He shrugged. "I'm not such a great basket to put your eggs into lately."

She smiled. "We could make it something non-threatening. We could meet somewhere, spend some time together then go our separate ways. No stress, no expectations. Just see how things go."

"I wanted to ask you if you were busy this weekend. I thought we might go wine tasting. That is if you don't have anything to do," he said. "You do like wine?"

"Art, I'd love to. I can take the whole weekend."

They had a date before he knew it, and both of them sat there looking a bit surprised yet pleased. The meeting seemed to be over, and they both rose, standing and facing each other.

"So, it's this weekend, for wine tasting, you and me?"

"Oh, Art," she fished in her pocket and brought out a card. "I have a friend that would be perfect for you to see concerning being stuck. I am glad you decided to come in to talk to me. You understand, I can't see you professionally and socially. It's unethical," she said with a warm smile and sparkling laugh as she extended the card. He took it and headed for the door and as he did his pager went off.

"That's timing for you," she said.

He looked at the pager's screen. The message read; "Homicide."

"Got to go, Amanda." He slipped the card into his pocket and smiled, pleased that Walt needed him.

"A homicide?"

Art didn't answer her. He needed to call Walt for an address. His brows furrowed over his eyes, the lips tightened as his mind sank into deep thought. He'd slid into cop mode.

Author Page

Never stop dreaming is Mary's motto. She's had a lifelong desire to write entertaining stories. Now there's time to do just that, and this debut novel is the first of several inspired endeavors she has undertaken. She's studied creative writing with the Long Ridge Writers group. Mary's traveled to England, Ireland, Scotland, Wales, Canada, Mexico and throughout the United States of America. She survived the rapids of the Truckee River, backcountry hiking to waterfalls, and fishing Diamond Lake, Oregon. She's a gardener, a quilter, an artist, and an avid reader. She likes history, mysteries, thrillers, autobiographies, and religious works. She enjoys movies and old sitcoms. She is noted by family and friends as a spellbinding storyteller. She's picked up many tales from her ten years of traveling in a fifth-wheel R.V. Residing now in Northern California with her two pups, Mary finds inspiration from her garden and the world around her. It is there that she allows herself to dream.

Make believe with her.

Contacts

Blog: MLWeatheringtonauthor.com
E-mail: Weatheringtonmary@gmail.com